BEWARE

—— OF THE ——

BANKER

A Maine crime fiction story
Inspired by the true tale of Bonnie and Clyde, the most
notorious bank robbers in United States history

BARRY SOMES

NEWMAN SPRINGS PUBLISHING
320 Broad Street
Red Bank, NJ 07701

First originally published by Newman Springs Publishing 2019

This book is a work of fiction. Names and events are fictitious. Any resemblance to actual people, businesses or events are entirely coincidental and unintended. There are, however, some exceptions. This story was inspired by actual events.

ISBN 978-1-64531-235-2 (Paperback)
ISBN 978-1-64531-236-9 (Digital)

Printed in the United States of America

To my wife, Sally, and daughters Hannah and
Sarah. Not sure how I got so lucky!

"Hi, my name is Clyde. Someday I'm going to be famous, and you can say you read about me! This is my story—a story of how I met an inspiring leader with the vision to put this all together and introduce me to a beautiful gal named Bonnie. A story of how I went from a little known trash collector to the national news! How I followed in the footsteps of the great Clyde Barrow. Yes, the story of how I did indeed become famous!"

"Hi, my name is Bonnie. And someday I'm going to be famous, too, and you can say you read about *me*. This is my story—a story of how I met and eventually fell in love with a banker who helped fulfill a lifelong dream. A story of how I went from an unknown waitress to the national news! How I followed in the footsteps of the great Bonnie Parker! Yes, this is the story of how I did indeed become famous!"

ACADIA BLANCHARD

When you were told she was the most beautiful girl in the world, I'm sure you were skeptical. But by the time she was eighteen or nineteen, she *was* beautiful. Absolutely, positively, stunningly beautiful. Long jet-black hair, high cheekbones atop deep dimples that seemed to frame her full pink delicate lips, her complexion almost always showed a slight blush. To look straight into her deep, dark eyes would put you in a trance—like falling into a black hole. The experience could change your life forever. The Bible tells us black is the color of mystery. They said she could look right into your soul. She stood about 5'10". Her long legs moved with confidence, giving her the looks of a supermodel. You would never forget her if you ever met her. Some guessed she was from Eastern Europe. But no, she was born and raised right here in Maine. So keep an open mind and if you ever have the opportunity to meet her, there's no doubt that you will agree that she's like no one you've ever met before. But her true beauty was not on the surface but from deep inside.

Apnem mus ar saru garu

Her mother grew up in Oxford, Maine, and despite being only thirty miles west of Portland (Maine's largest city), it's a very economically depressed area. As a junior in high school, she went on an overnight school trip to Maine's Acadia National Park. As part of the trip, they got up early and rode the bus to the summit of Cadillac Mountain to watch the sunrise. Seeing the fiery red ball seem to pop up out of the ocean was the most spectacular thing she had ever seen. She was not permitted to return to school for her senior year as she was pregnant and estimated that the father could have been any of over twenty different guys. In fact, it was even possible Cady could have been conceived on that class trip to Acadia! Her mother decided to name her after that beautiful park and gave her the name Acadia. At an early age, Cady became her nickname, and it stuck.

Bar Harbor, the town that borders the park, was originally known as Eden—the most beautiful spot on earth. So it would only make sense that as Cady grew up, she would become the most beautiful girl in the world. One observer remarked that if *Sports Illustrated* ever put her on the cover of their annual "Swimsuit" issue, they wouldn't have to publish any more pages!

Being very young and not married, her mother found Cady to be nothing more than a nuisance. To make matters worse, Cady was claustrophobic and very shy, often avoided people and crowds of any kind. She was subject to wild mood swings which put even more demands on her mother. She would often lose her temper. She could turn violent without any warning and could even endanger herself. Although the diagnosis may have been wrong, in school, Cady was classified as a special-needs student and was assigned an ed tech—an adult who would accompany her all day in school. She was very lucky to be paired up with a wonderful woman named Eileen, a loving person who had over a dozen grandchildren. Eileen became her really only trusted friend and stayed with her until she graduated. Cady's mother found that she could get state aid as a result of Cady's symptoms and milked the system for all it was worth. She found a neighborhood variety store that would let her trade her food stamps for cigarettes and Allen's Coffee Brandy. Cady qualified for meal assistance at the school so had breakfast and lunch there, often eating accompanied only by Eileen. There was a room off the gym where special-needs students could go whenever they needed private time away from the other students. Cady and Eileen spent a lot of each school day there. Cady was extremely intelligent and could recall, with almost 100 percent clarity just about anything that had happened in her life.

The girls at the high school tended to stay away from her. Stuck up, too good for them, maybe even too pretty. The boys at the high school also stayed away from her despite how attractive she was. They knew she was different, seemed to have some sort of a force shield around her. Not really sure how she'd react around them. She intimidated them. She really didn't even want any friends. She preferred to be left alone. She enjoyed long walks in the woods, alone with mother nature. She never had a boyfriend. Never was in love. But that was about to change.

Throughout her life, Cady was passed around from her grandmother to a neighbor to her aunt whenever her mother wanted to invite a boyfriend to sleep over—which was often. As Cady became a teenager and started to develop her hauntingly beautiful good looks, her mom's boyfriends started to pay more attention to Cady than to her. This caused a deep form of jealousy and a further division between the two to the point that Cady was almost completely ignored. Her mother never observed or celebrated her birthday. She was never taken to a doctor. Oxford was a small town, and everyone knew of her mother's reputation. There was hardly a man at the factory where she worked that she hadn't slept with. To make matters worse, Acadia did not get her good looks from her mother. Her mother was overweight, had a smoker's cough, deep, dark circles under her eyes, and scraggly hair. The two of them lived in a trailer park just off the Skeetfield Road in Oxford.

The story of Bonnie and Clyde appealed to Cady. After she first heard it when she was a teenager, she could see herself as Bonnie. Next to Jesse James, Bonnie and Clyde were the most famous bank robbers in US history. Cady wanted to enjoy a thrilling life playing the role of a famous bank robber, be the star of the show and be able to order people to follow her instructions. A chance for her to be somebody—somebody people would fear! She practiced being Bonnie and often dreamed about the day she'd make national news as a famous bank robber.

BLAKE

Blake had a history of stealing things. Often impulsively, he shop-lifted—even if it was just for a bottle of beer. At Greely High School in Cumberland a few miles north of Portland, just before graduation, he forgot his lunch box, and his mother drove it over to the school. He went to the office to pick it up and noticed an envelope on the counter stuffed full of cash—donations for a teacher who was retir-ing. The secretary handed him his lunch box, and he set it atop the envelope, then thanked her, and slid the lunch box off the counter along with the envelope full of cash. He decided to hide the envelope for a few days, so he taped it inside his locker near the top where you couldn't see it and would only know it was there if you reached up and felt around for it. He had the same locker all four years, num-ber 627, in the math wing. You know what? After the graduation ceremony, he went back to get the envelope from the locker, but the doors to the wing were locked. He came back a couple days later and still wasn't able to get it. He never did get back, so chances are good the money is still taped to the top of that locker!

He is now employed by Coastal Waste Systems as a trash collec-tor. He stood about six feet, slight build, and always looked like he needed a haircut. Hardly ever seen without wearing a worn-out pair of jeans. As for his IQ, most likely in the single digits.

TONY

Tony was a late thirties guy, single, never married, who lived by himself in a duplex apartment on Stevens Avenue in Portland. Stevens Avenue is the only place in the United States where someone can go all the way from nursery school to college all on the same street. The woman who shared Tony's duplex was one of only a handful of people to actually have done that and now she was even living on the same street. Tony worked as the branch manager of a bank on Route 1 in Falmouth just outside of Portland. One little known fact about Tony; he was a graduate of the University of Maine where the athletic teams are known as the Black Bears, and they have a black bear mascot. Tony had the Black Bear tattooed on his butt. A favorite pick-up line he often used was, "Do you want to see my *bare* butt?" Probably explains why he didn't have much luck with women!

When they opened a casino just a half-hour drive from Portland, Tony would go up there every Friday night after work with a pledge not to lose more than $50. He became addicted to the slot machines and often felt his luck was changing so despite his pledge to stop at $50, he would often continue and lose $100—sometimes more. At some point, he decided to switch to a casino in Connecticut where he heard you could win much, much more. Those higher paying machines did pay out more but required more money on each spin. So you could lose more money faster. As he became a recognized regular, the casino "rewarded" him with free drinks and eventually even a complimentary hotel room to spend the night. The hookers noticed too and being a single guy, he seldom slept in his hotel room alone. The casino realized that hookers attracted high rollers so allowed them to "work the floor;" security even protected them.

Being single, Tony found these Asian girls irresistible and surprisingly affordable (little did he know they were also subsidized by the casino). He was going through a lot of money but truly believed that it was only a matter of time before he hit the big one which would put him back in a healthy financial condition. He lost all his savings, cashed in his 401k, and maxed out his credit cards. He was seriously addicted to casino gambling. As his financial condition deteriorated, he spent more and more time trying to find a way he could steal money from the bank where he worked without getting caught. He knew he was clever enough, and desperate enough, to find a way.

CT, Director, Boston Office, FBI

When CT's dad grew up, he lived in a small town just outside of Bangor, Maine, near an Indian reservation. When he was only ten years old, he was invited to join a friend and his grandfather on a deer-hunting trip. The boy's grandfather was a full-blooded Indian and had learned hunting skills that had been passed down for several generations. CT's dad was fascinated by what he observed and became a good hunter himself. In fact, he worked hard to perfect those skills and became somewhat of a legendary hunter in his own right. He was taught to use all five senses when hunting. He learned first to observe which way the wind was blowing and to hunt into the wind so the deer wouldn't smell a human advancing toward them. He learned how to study the ground for tracks. He could tell by studying the tracks not only what animals were nearby but also what direction they were traveling in and how fast they were going. Even how much they weighed. Bird calls could also reveal the presence of deer. Broken twigs on small trees or shrubs indicated the presence of deer and direction of travel. He studied piles of poop on the ground and could tell what their diet consisted of and where in the area they were eating which would be the best place to hunt. Keen eyesight and listening skills also were sharpened to hone in on his prey. He knew how to walk through the woods swiftly and so quietly that the birds did not even announce his coming. To hunt with him was truly an impressive experience.

So it was no surprise that CT would learn these skills and become a skilled hunter in his own right. He grew to love the woods so much that he became a game warden and literally lived in the outdoors. Although it was a law enforcement job, he often turned the other way when spotting illegal hunters whom he knew had to hunt just to provide food for their families. But other people who were jacking deer illegally or drinking in the woods would get the message that they were never to be seen again in CT's territory. He could be a tough son-of-a-bitch that you didn't want to deal with if you were hunting illegally or showing disrespect for nature. Being in the woods with no witnesses around gave him a certain amount of license when administering punishment. He also was able to successfully track down and stop many smuggling operations of goods coming across from the Canadian border. But surprisingly, he also enjoyed a great sense of humor, probably what helped him cope with the stress (and danger) of the job. He was a tall man with big broad shoulders and muscular hands. He always had an expression that was studious, always involved, and always alert. Sometimes you would be speaking with him and he'd stop you and ask, "Did you hear that?" And of course you didn't, but he would look off in another direction to identify what it was he heard. He also had a fairly gruesome scar almost the entire length of his left arm. Best not to ask what happened.

The first day of fifth grade was a life-changing event for CT. A dark-haired girl in a pale yellow dress sat just a few seats from him. She was new to the town. He could not take his eyes off her and after school, asked if he could walk home with her. She shyly agreed, and they have not been separated since. These childhood sweethearts eventually married and had four children. Her name was Jane.

CT showed a lot of promise in the warden service and the department decided to send him to the FBI training school for three months to improve his skills. Instead of hunting animals, CT learned how to hunt humans—criminals. Surprisingly there were a lot of similarities to his job as a game warden and his instructors were impressed with his natural instincts. He graduated from Quantico at the head of his class. So much so that he was offered a job with the FBI in their criminal investigation unit in the Boston office. He accepted the position and tackled projects of unsolved crimes with some success.

He earned several promotions and with each one, added more and more skilled staff members to join his team. He favored army rangers and those with special forces experience. He scanned files of FBI cases that had been solved against all odds and determined if it was just luck or truly the work of a talented individual and if so, would offer them a job in the Boston office. That's how he came across Katie. She had served in the army and was now based in the Houston FBI office, working as a behavioral investigator, compiling personality profiles of criminal minds—examining their psychopathic purpose. This was a position that few held in the FBI as it was considered just part of a detective's job, but she had perfected it to a science. She was trained to look for clues that most detectives would overlook. She maintained a vast database that often helped solve crimes. She was offered a job with CT in Boston and was impressed with his determination to not stop until every major crime was solved.

You know the expression the FBI always gets their man! It wasn't long before he had as much respect for her as she did for him. She worked hard to study unsolved crimes for clues and similarities to other crimes that may be the pieces to the puzzle they needed to make an arrest. She was tough and loved challenges with many of the same instincts CT had. Any spare time she had was spent in the gym. Not only keeping in fantastic shape, but she also found, while working out, she could clear her mind and concentrate on projects she was working on. Eventually CT was promoted to head the Boston FBI headquarters.

Oxford High School, Six Years Ago

The only thing Acadia liked about school was that it gave her a chance to get away from her mother and the small trailer they lived in that reeked of cigarette smoke. For her mother, school was a great way to get her daughter out of the house for the day. Acadia was classified as a special-needs student and granted 504 status. Eileen would often suggest rather than go to class that they would just work together in a quiet place. Eileen had a collection of short stories about famous people followed by a dozen or so multiple choice questions to see how much of the material was retained. There were stories about Hellen Keller, Eleanor Roosevelt, Joan of Arc, Madam Curie, various Olympic champions—Eileen tended to choose stories about famous women. Cady rarely showed much interest and seldom answered the questions correctly. That is until Eileen shared the story of Bonnie and Clyde! Cady was fascinated with Bonnie and how she avoided arrest for many years and was one of America's most iconic outlaws. She pictured herself as an exciting and glamorous bank robber. A person who wore a mask, and everyone did what she demanded. She had finally found a role model! She wanted more than anything to be a modern-day Bonnie! She asked Eileen to read the story of Bonnie and Clyde over and over again. What oh what had Eileen done?

At home, Cady would look in the mirror and pose like Bonnie. She would even put on a mask and pretend she was pointing a gun at herself in the mirror. She would try to look mean and order everyone to put their hands up. Watch out for Bonnie!

ELIPHALET GREELY JR.,
1784–1858

There is no doubt that there isn't a student at Greely Middle School or high school who has a clue who Eliphalet Greely was. Most likely, none of the teachers either. But he was perhaps the most respected person who ever lived in the town of Cumberland, Maine. Mr. Greely was born shortly after the Revolutionary War in 1784 and died shortly before the Civil War in 1858. It was an amazing time to be an American with all the changes the country was going through. Eliphalet's father owned several cargo ships and as a teenager, Eliphalet signed on as an apprentice. He joined several other notable Cumberland families in the sea trade such as the Blanchards, Sturdivants, Lorings, and Yorks. At the age of twenty-two, he took command as the captain of his own ship. He was a hard worker and made sure everyone was treated fairly. He earned significant wealth and when he gave up his life at sea, he worked for Casco Bank in Portland (they had a branch for many years in the area where Starbucks is now on Route 1 in Falmouth). At the bank, he demonstrated his financial skill, integrity, and good judgement and eventually became the bank's president.

His reputation was noticed by the governor, and he was appointed as the state bank commissioner. He later represented Portland in the state legislature which led to being elected mayor of Portland. As mayor, he made the public schools his highest priority. He considered himself the steward of the community and watched public spending scrupulously (something Cumberland could use today). He made sure there was no waste of taxpayer money and no backroom deals. He was a major force in establishing the Atlantic & St. Lawrence Railroad which was considered one of the greatest achievements ever undertaken in the history of the state of Maine. When he died, his will expressed his desire for a school to be built in his hometown of Cumberland. He left plans for the building and sufficient funds to build it. He personally designed the school which still stands today almost exactly as it looked when it was built in 1868. His architectural plans included the cupola which is atop the roof which many would agree is the iconic symbol of the town of Cumberland. The school was named after him—Greely Institute.

There have been rumors over the years that the school is visited from time to time by the ghost of Eliphalet Greely.

*There's a long told story about students who have been trapped on the second floor overnight, unable to unlock the door.

*There are rumors that there are secret doors and passageways designed in the building.

*In fact, the windows to the basement have been permanently covered up so that you can't peer in from outside. They are not just boarded up but actually covered over with bricks. Somebody doesn't want you to know what's going on down there! So what are they hiding and why?

*Some students have claimed to have seen Mr. Greely climbing the stairway, describing him as an old man wearing a dark suit.

*Others have caught a quick glimpse of him sitting at a teacher's desk in a second floor classroom.

All have the same description—a thin older man wearing a dark suit.

*One of the best stories came from a custodian who was sweeping the ground floor about midnight and heard a man's voice coming from a classroom upstairs. He assumed it was a teacher preparing a lesson and walked up the stairs to see how much later he planned to stay. He could hear the voice become stronger as he climbed the stairs. He knocked on the classroom door then opened it only to find a dark classroom. The voice stopped as soon as he looked in. The only exit would have been through the door he just opened, but no one passed by him. He turned the lights on and found no one in the room. But this is all a story for another day, perhaps for another book.

If there is such a thing as Mr. Greely's ghost, you can rest assured that it is a friendly and kind ghost. Mr. Greely was a charismatic leader and widely respected. When he walked down Main Street, people went out of their way just to shake his hand. He cared a lot about the people in town and wanted to see the children get the best education possible. He did not have any children of his own.

Blake, by the way, is a graduate of Greely High School.

A Hot, Humid Evening in August

The windows in Tony's apartment had been closed all day and after returning from work, the heat was unbearable. Had to be the hottest day of the summer. He'd been in an air-conditioned office and really hadn't noticed how bad it was. So he quickly decided to drop by the Leaping Fish Tavern in Portland's Old Port for a cold beer (or two) and a plate of Irish nachos for dinner. He stopped by there just about every Tuesday evening to take advantage of their two-dollar-Tuesday deal. A friend had once shown him a small parking lot nearby at the end of Church Street which was always empty in the evening. Sure enough, there was only one car in the lot when he got there, and it was just a short walk to the tavern on Fore Street. His favorite place, he was a regular, and the staff knew him by name. He went there once or twice a week, probably for three or four years now. He also loved parking on Church Street as whenever he spoke with his mom, he assured her he'd been to church recently. It was just off Middle Street by the police station. His mother was so proud of him. Such a nice guy!

The tavern was owned by three guys who enjoyed sport fishing on the ocean and often, they would talk about opening a bar in the Old Port. They decided it would have a fishing and hunting theme. They agreed the logo would be a bluefish jumping out of a pint glass, and they would call the bar the Leaping Fish Tavern. So when space became available, they opened June of '87. It became an instant hit despite the competition.

Tony took his favorite seat by the window and before he even sat down, Libby brought him a frosted-cold glass filled with a pint of his favorite local craft beer. As he took a drink, he looked out the window—a busy day in the Old Port, but he was too preoccupied to notice the passersby. Financially he was ruined. He was desperate. Depressed. His addiction to casino gambling was ruining him. But at the same time was fully convinced that he was due to win big at the slots. And then he could pay off all his debts. He even borrowed $2,000 from a loan shark at the casino with $200-a-week interest until paid in full. Can you imagine—10 percent interest per week? That's how desperate he was.

A young man had joined him at his table. He turned around to see Blake sitting next to him. He was somewhat startled.

"Blake, buddy, how you doing, how long you been there?" he asked, trying not to look surprised. Despite the fact that Blake was probably ten years younger, they got along great and seemed to have a lot in common. Both single, both lonely, both struggling for a better life. Blake came in a couple times a month and always sat with Tony, perhaps for over a year now.

"Couldn't be better, my man, couldn't be better. Living the dream!"

"Bullshit. Have a good day at work?"

"Oh sure, at one of my first stops, I found an aluminum baseball bat poking out of the trash bag. Pulled it out and found three others, all in good shape. So tucked them in the cab of the truck, and then I noticed a green compost truck was behind us. They tend to follow our same routes, so we know them pretty well. The driver shook her finger at me in jest, then got out to pick up the compost bucket and looked at me and said, 'Hey, you're busted!' She was just kidding as she knows we can keep anything we find along the route. Sort of an employee benefit. But the bats are in great shape. I bet I can get $25 each for 'em."

"Wow, does that happen often?"

"I usually make about $50 a week selling things people are throwing out. Makes the job kind of fun."

"What's been your best find?"

"We have a house on our route, an old house with a barn that could collapse any day. Paint peeling, old shades pulled down on all the upstairs windows. An old truck with no tires sitting beside the driveway and some miscellaneous junk on the front yard. You can tell from the trash that they aren't exactly living the high life. I'm sure you've seen houses like this one. But one day, the trash bag was torn, and I noticed the edge of a laptop poking out, an Apple. I took it home and found most of the keys missing on the keyboard. I ordered a new keyboard from Amazon and replaced it, cleaned it up a bit, and it worked great. Put it on eBay and got $400! Bingo!"

"Any funny stories?"

"Yeah, I had a real bitch on one of my routes. A very wealthy woman with a movie-star type house. She didn't want anyone to know she created trash, so we couldn't stop in front of her house. In the corner of her lot, she hid the trash behind a hedge." Blake rolled his eyes, then continued. "So one day, we noticed a crew putting up a tent on her front lawn. A couple days later, we were running a little late and when we stopped at her house, we noticed she was hosting a party with all sorts of ladies, all wearing dresses and white gloves—all very fancy. I could see her get up with this horrified expression as if to say, 'No, no, please don't stop today.' So of course, we stopped anyway and before getting off the truck, I reached in my lunch box and pulled out a banana. I then walked over to her trash can, rattled the lid when I took it off so as to attract as much attention as possible, then reached in (with the banana hidden in my hand) and pulled the banana out, held it high in the air, and yelled to the driver, 'Look, Sam, look what I found in the trash!' then proceeded to eat the banana! I didn't look, but Sam said the ladies were shocked. Nearly busted a gut when I got back to the truck!"

"So you're an actor too?"

"Actually almost history as a garbage man. Was called into the office as soon as I finished the route. The boss had two comments. First he had heard from the woman and pointed out to me how competitive this business is and how this joke could jeopardize the contract we had. A very serious problem that I agreed would not happen again. Once that was understood, he looked at me and said,

'It must have been funnier than Hell!' He knew what a bitch she was as she called all the time to complain about us. One thing I find kind of sad though is that most of the women on our routes are widowed, living alone, and no matter what time of day we pick up their trash, they are dressed in ratty old bathrobes. Seems to be a uniform for old ladies."

"Remind me about that when I get to be an old lady," asked Tony. "But I'm sure not everyone on your route is an old lady!"

"Oh yeah. There was one house, number 28, that everyone knew. I only got that route once a month but couldn't wait till we got to number 28. Absolutely gorgeous. It was actually very rare when we saw her as her trash was usually out when we got there but when she did come out or was in the yard, time seemed to just stop. There was a stack of lobster traps by her garage, so we figured she must be married to a lobsterman which would explain why we never saw a guy around in the mornings."

"Sounds like it could be a porno movie, *The Garbage Man and the Housewife*."

"Oh man, almost happened once!" Blake was really excited. "We had this one house, middle-age couple. He was a mean son of a bitch, a big guy, always dressed in a stained white T-shirt with suspenders. One spring morning, we stopped at the driveway, and the trash can wasn't there nor was his truck. We waited for a few minutes, then she came out carrying a bag of trash and wearing a work-out suit. When she got to the truck, she dropped the bag and when she reached down to pick it up, the top opened to reveal a fantastic set of bare boobs. Her top hadn't been zipped up. The thing is, she stood up slowly, then arched her shoulders back—it was as if her boobs were talking to me! Slowly she zipped up the top and gave me a look I'll never forget. Then she walked back to her house, taking her sweet time. The driver had watched it out his side mirror—I asked him if we could come back after we finished our route!"

"I can't tell you how hard I tried to figure out a way to get back to her house after work but was afraid her husband would be there if I tried it. A couple weeks later when we stopped at her house, she blew me a kiss from the kitchen window—oh man, but it was not long after that my route got switched again. Never went back... She had a tattoo of a red rose on one of her boobs. Will never forget that sight."

Tony looked around the bar. Very few people tonight. A table of five guys eating burgers (wonder if they were eating fries as well?), a couple women dressed in office attire, two young couples throwing darts, and an older man sitting by himself in a corner.

"Blake, there I am in another forty years," said Tony, "still coming here for a beer every now and then." Blake looked around but couldn't see the man Tony was referring to. "He must have left, he was sitting over in the corner there just a minute ago."

Tony leaned over and asked, "Blake, have you ever had sex?"

"Me, yeah, of course, dozens of times, lots of times, of course."

"Blake? You can level with me."

"Oh man, to be honest, but don't tell anyone, no, I never have. Not even close. Never really even had a girlfriend." Blake looked sad. "How about you?"

"Well, of course. I'm a lot older than you, but most of my experiences have been with hookers—paid professionals."

Blake looked really awed. "What's that like? I mean, really, man, what are they really like?"

"Well, they're professionals. To them, it's not about making love, it's a business transaction. They have something to sell, they know you want to buy, and they want to get to the next customer as soon as possible. It's over and they're gone before you know it. But for a while, they can make you feel they're hopelessly in love with you. That's how they get repeat business. I did have a serious girlfriend once. But she was into a multilevel marketing program, a pyramid scheme, that drove me nuts."

"I really don't know what you're talking about."

"It's like a cult. Some people got her into this business by convincing her she could make a six-figure income within a year. She had to pay a fee to become an authorized sales rep and once authorized, she was to sell people vitamins. Some kind of miracle vitamin made of water from a lake filled with algae in the Swiss Alps. Scientists had documented that people who lived near the lake lived to be well over

100 years old and looked like people half their age. It sold for $100 a bottle."

"Sounds great, what's wrong with that?"

"Well, it was all bullshit. To make money, she had to recruit others to sell the stuff. When they paid the fee to become authorized, she got half of it plus a percentage of all the sales they made. Plus if the people she recruited got others to join, she got a percentage of their sales as well. This went on for five 'levels' which created the pyramid. If you recruited enough people and they recruited heavily as well, you could make some serious money. So it was more about recruiting others than actually selling the vitamins."

"So obviously if I wanted to keep her as a girlfriend, I had to sign up and whenever we went anywhere, she would constantly be approaching strangers, trying to get them to become sales reps. She could be very aggressive. I often found it embarrassing. She would also host meetings at her house and I was expected to be there and brag to everyone about the health effects I was enjoying since taking the vitamins and how I was planning to give up my job to do this full-time. Instead I gave up on her. Blake, you know how I work at a bank?"

"Yeah, out in Falmouth somewhere?"

"Right. Just between you and me, I plan to rob the bank soon."

"What? Did I hear you right?" asked Blake.

"I opened a phony business checking account at a credit union in Portland today where they don't know me. I opened it as a sole proprietor, not a corporation. That way, the feds don't know about it as I used my own social security number, didn't need a Federal ID. It's called a d-b-a. Tony d-b-a Diversified Document Processing Co."

"Sounds impressive, but what does that have to do with robbing your bank?"

"I have a customer coming in soon for a loan. He's not too bright and is desperate for the loan, so I am going to charge him a loan-origination fee. The bank charges origination fees for mortgages and equity loans, so this isn't unusual."

"So he makes out the check for the origination fee out to Diversified Document Processing Co.?" asked Blake.

"Yup. Good for you. He gets the loan, I get the fee. His check for the fee is made out to Diversified. I deposit it to the Diversified bank account, I withdraw it with a debit card and bingo, cash in my pocket."

"Why won't the bank find out?" asked Blake.

"Because the bank doesn't charge an origination fee for installment loans, so they won't be looking for it. I will give him the loan, deposit the funds to his account, then ask him to write a separate check to Diversified Document Processing for the fee. I've given it a lot of thought and think it's foolproof. I'll let you know how it works out."

"Boy, if my parole officer could hear us now!"

"Parole officer?"

"Long story."

"Hey, Blake, buddy, but have you ever thought of doing something like this?"

Blake thought for a moment and then shared his wish. "My dad has a half-million-dollar life-insurance policy with my mother as beneficiary. So if he dies, she gets a half-million. And when she dies, I get whatever is left as I am the only child. So if they both died together, I'd get it all instantly."

"I bet it's tax-free too."

"But if I murdered them, no matter how careful I was, and got caught, it's not going to do me any good. So just have to hope they meet a drunk driver some night!"

Just then, Jeff came in, saw Tony and asked if he could join them. Jeff lived in Falmouth and was a customer of Tony's. He introduced him to Blake, then Jeff sat down and ordered a local IPA like Tony.

"What do you do for work, Blake?" asked Jeff, trying to make conversation.

"I work for a waste-removal company, riding a garbage truck out in the Gray/Pownal area. Coastal Waste Systems."

Just then, Libby arrived with a pint for Jeff and Tony. Tony leaned over toward Blake and told him Jeff worked for MEDCU, the city of Portland's ambulance service.

"Wow, you must have some stories," exclaimed Blake.

"It's not as exciting as you'd think. You could probably think of my job as similar to yours like driving a garbage truck only with flashing red lights. Most of our stuff are homeless people and drug cases. We're just cleaning up the waste in the city."

"Oh, come on," said Blake. "There must be some excitement out there. For instance, what did you do today?"

"Kind of a quiet day, actually," answered Jeff. "Had an out-of-town call for an elderly woman who fell down her stairs. Sure she broke her hip. But as we were carrying her out of her house, I couldn't help but notice a framed photo on a table by the door of her with two grandchildren sitting on her lap. Don't think they'll be sitting on her lap anytime soon. She was in incredible pain. I thought how bad those two grandchildren would feel if they knew how much pain their grandmother was in. But hey," continued Jeff, "did you guys hear the story of the Mannequin Murderer?"

A no came from Tony, and Blake just shook his head no.

"A guy strangled a woman up on the Elmwood Road in Pownal, an older woman, then positioned her sitting on a lounge chair with a straw hat and a scarf around her neck to hide the choke marks. He put sunglasses on her and posed her holding a glass of iced tea."

"And she was dead?" asked Blake.

"Yeah, two boys found her late yesterday afternoon. They were riding their bikes after school from Pownal Elementary on their way to grab a couple of Pownal Porterhouses at a variety store about half a mile from school. Apparently they said hi to her and on the way back to the school, they noticed she hadn't moved, so they stopped to take a closer look. They could tell something wasn't right and notified the principal as soon as they got back to school. A sheriff patrolman said he had passed by her twice during the day and never suspected she was dead. So they've nicknamed the killer the Mannequin Murderer because he positioned her like a mannequin. Seems that killing her was only necessary so he could pose her on the side of the road for the benefit of passing cars."

With that, the men decided to call it a night. They stepped outside, and Tony told Blake he'd help him get laid.

"Are you shittin' me?" asked Blake.

"Hey, what are friends for?"

As Tony headed back to his car, he stopped for a second on Middle Street. Had he really just told Blake about his plan to embezzle from the bank? He glimpsed down Middle street, and the illuminated sign that read "Portland Police Headquarters" seemed to shine on his face. What a spot to be thinking about committing a crime! As he walked up Church Street, he realized Blake had given him another idea. Life insurance? Maybe he could take out a million-dollar policy on *his* mom. Hmm, something to think about! And he knew a good insurance agent who could assist him.

Oxford High School, Two Years Ago

It was graduation day from Oxford High School. When she woke up, she went into the living room and noticed a note taped to the television. It was from her mother saying that her boyfriend invited her to the White Mountains for the weekend, so she wouldn't be attending her graduation but assured her that her Aunt Beth would be by to pick her up and take her. Cady looked at the note and began to cry. The biggest day in her life, and her mom was going to miss it so she could sleep with some creepy guy. Cady sobbed. She was *so* upset with her mother, her own mother. She knew that she was a burden but couldn't believe she would not even attend her graduation. She felt sick and ran into her mother's bedroom and threw up on the bed then pulled the bedspread over the pile of puke and tucked it in nicely. She went into the bathroom and washed her face then brushed her teeth. She sipped on a cup of water and felt much better. She wrote a quick note to her mother: "Thank you for being the best mother I ever could have asked for. Sleep tight. Love, Acadia." She then placed the note on the pillow.

Cady was scared. It was the first time that she realized how school had been the only stabilizing force in her life. The harsh reality was now hitting her—hitting her hard. No more routine of going to school, no more Eileen to help her get through life. No plans for the future. No more house to live in.

Her Aunt Beth, bless her heart, would be over soon to pick her up and attend graduation with her. She often spent nights at Beth's house. Beth could be counted on for help whenever she needed it. Truly a saint!

Cady's mother told her that once she graduated from high school she would have to find a place to live and get a job to support herself. No more living at home. Finally she would no longer be Mom's "problem." Her mom asked Beth to help Cady find an apartment. Nice Mom!

Beth worked quickly and was able to find an inexpensive room for her to rent in New Gloucester, Maine, at 512 Morse Road, not far from a set of railroad tracks. Cady moved in right after graduation. She enjoyed listening to the passing trains and often wondered what the cars were carrying. Someday she wanted to research that. There was also a convenience store just down the street in Gray Center that was looking for help. Beth helped her apply and get the job. She would earn enough for rent and meals. Thank God for Beth! Beth even helped her find a decent used car so she could get to work.

It was an older home that had once been a bed-and-breakfast. The owner lived in the basement and there were four bedrooms on the second floor. The first floor was used as a guest reception area, community kitchen, and breakfast area. Viktoria bought the B and B a couple years ago and converted the four upstairs bedrooms to two two-room apartments. Each apartment had one bedroom, the other room converted to a small living room—great for single people. Beth met with Viktoria and told her about Cady's history and her special needs. Viktoria was very understanding (she had a daughter not too much older than Cady) and after meeting with Cady, offered her a lease. It was a perfect fit.

The other apartment was rented to a scientist. Tina worked just down the street at an old hospital that had been converted to office space. The company she worked for, Magnetic Solar Systems, was researching the possibility of producing a solar-powered desalinator that would use electromagnetic energy to separate salt from sea water, producing potable, drinking water. She was a very smart woman who was excited about her work. She had jet-black tight curly hair that always needed brushing. With her black-framed glasses, she actually looked kind of scary. But she too was aware of Cady's past and also looked out for her; often inviting her over for dinner, watch TV, or explore some things on Google. One day, Cady went over to have lunch with her and noticed a book on her coffee table titled *Satanic Rituals* (wow!). Tina had a girlfriend, Rebekkah, who dropped by often. Rebekkah worked in a medical lab taking blood samples all day. Can you imagine? She referred to herself as Dracula.

The house was surrounded by woods in a very quiet area. Cady had a view of the backyard from her bedroom window and could often see deer. Her living room window looked out over the front lawn toward the street. There was a hedge of arborvitae along the edge of the road. It was a back road, and cars seldom drove by but when they did, they were often traveling well over the speed limit. Viktoria had several bird feeders in the backyard, and Cady loved watching the birds. In fact, there was a patio out back with chairs and a table with an umbrella, and Cady would often go out early in the morning just to sit and listen to the birds. She also loved to take walks with Viktoria. Viktoria had a miniature schnauzer that would often join them. They would walk along the railroad tracks, follow a path through the woods to Webber cemetery, out to the street, and back along Morse Street. They would stop at the cafe at Pineland to enjoy a pastry and cup of tea together. The more Acadia told Viktoria about her life, the more Viktoria wished that someone had contacted child services at the Department of Human Services years ago. Yet she couldn't believe how Cady grew up to be such an intelligent, beautiful young lady. Guess Aunt Beth and Eileen get all the credit!

Because Cady did not have a normal childhood, she decorated her bedroom like it belonged to a young girl. She had Winnie-the-Pooh pillow cases and blankets, a Mickey-Mouse desk lamp, a *Frozen* rug, and Nemo curtains. The overall effect was very cute and created a certain comfort for her. Her living room was very sparsely furnished. Pretty much just an old couch, a second-hand desktop computer (which she used primarily for *Netflix*), a coffee table she found at a garage sale that had been made from a lobster trap, and one photo on the wall—a photo of Bonnie and Clyde that she printed from a website and had framed. Her bathroom had a Barbie theme with matching Barbie toothbrush and toothpaste. She even had a Barbie doll hanging from the ceiling on a twine swing she made.

She enjoyed the job at the variety store and after a couple months, a regular customer approached Cady and asked if she would consider working as a waitress in Portland. She was the manager of a restaurant in Portland near the AMTRAK Transportation Center and thought Cady would do very well there and with her looks, would attract customers. She told Cady she could easily double or even triple her income which appealed to her big time!

When she got home from work, she asked Viktoria for advice. Viktoria had helped Cady open a checking account and helped her reconcile her statements every month. She helped her set up a budget and showed her what would be possible with more income. Even though Cady was subject to severe mood swings, Viktoria encouraged her to give waitressing a try.

She worked the evening shift and at first, didn't like it. Several customers flirted with her and some made some nasty suggestions with unwanted sexual advances. Some were pretty rude, some offered her jobs. One man was a property manager in Portland and offered her a new Mercedes as a bonus if she would come and work for him. When she asked what she'd be doing, he didn't really have an answer. Hmmm? What was wrong with that picture? Whenever she was uncomfortable with a customer, she was told to turn the table over to an experienced waitress. So they tended to give her families and senior couples that came in to avoid any awkward situations and they also walked her out to her car at the end of every shift to make sure no one was waiting for her outside. This made her feel much more comfortable and as a benefit, she could eat there for free—anything on the menu!

They offered chicken nuggets shaped like little dinosaurs that kids loved, and she got a kick out of seeing their expressions when she served them. She did have one customer, a single man, about ten or twenty years older than her, who came in about the same time every Sunday and Wednesday evening. Always ordered the same thing: spaghetti and meatballs with garlic bread. It was good, but you could no doubt find better spaghetti in other places around town.

They became friends, and she always held a table open for him, the same table, whenever he came in. It was table number 4. He always seemed kind of depressed and lonely. She didn't know much about him, not even his name or what he did for a living. She found great satisfaction in cheering him up and having him leave with a smile. But then again, there weren't really many men who could resist her.

She had another favorite customer—an elderly woman who joked that she was about two hundred years old. Said she was born in Eastern Europe and at a young age came to America with her uncle aboard a cargo ship. Her father had to stay behind as he had an important job with the government. Her uncle homeschooled her and taught her many things about life and mother nature. She always wore sunglasses as she had a very rare eye condition. It was called Schmid-Fraccaro syndrome, giving her vertical-shaped pupils similar to cat's eyes. One of the benefits was the ability to see clearly in the dark. She hid her eyes with the sunglasses as they tended to gross people out. Cady liked Iona a lot and saw her like a mother figure. Iona could almost always tell what was on Cady's mind and offered wise advice. She was a very gifted woman. Iona told her that next summer, her granddaughter Anita will be visiting from Estonia. "You will like her. I think you two have a lot in common," Iona told her.

Acadia still works there today. She makes a darn good living most of which comes from some very generous tips. She is a very pretty girl and knows how to use her looks to her advantage. It didn't take her long to figure out how to separate men from their money. She enjoys working at Lenny's.

Friday Night at the Casino

Tony enjoyed his Friday nights at the casino. The ride down was filled with anticipation and plans on what to do if he hit the big one. The ride home, however, was often long and filled with desperate thoughts on how to get out of the mess he was in. Once there, he would go right to his favorite slot machine and play aggressively. Tonight he lost almost a hundred dollars in the first fifteen minutes. Not long after he started to play, two men came up behind him, one stood on his left and the other beside him on the right.

"Tony, it looks like you need to take a leak. Mind if we escort you to the men's room?" The man wore a really cheap suit and before he knew it, the other man, a big rugged guy with a shaved head, took Tony by the arm and practically lifted him out of his chair. He had a tattoo of Stonehenge that wrapped completely around his head. They walked quickly and did not say anything. They were the loan sharks Tony had borrowed $2,000 from.

Once inside the men's room, Tony looked in the mirror to see the two men. No sooner had he looked up when the big guy swung and hit Tony in the stomach and as Tony was falling to the floor, he hit him a second time, just grazing the side of his head; obviously he'd intended to break his nose but missed.

"Tony," the man in the cheap suit growled, "we lent you $2,000, and the deal was for you to pay us $200 a week in interest. So far, you haven't paid us shit. We ain't just a couple of librarians collecting on an overdue book. We'll give you until next Friday to pay us back in full plus interest. By the way, we know where your mother lives. Have a good week."

Tony groaned on the floor and gradually pulled himself up. Even though the second punch hit the side of his head, he was already starting to get a black eye. He went over to a stall and puked. Someone came in and could see Tony was hurt. He offered to help, but Tony said he'd be fine. After sitting on the toilet for what seemed like a couple hours, Tony decided it was best to head home.

On his way out, a man handed him a postcard. It listed seven signs of a person addicted to gambling. "If you or someone you know has a gambling problem, have them call 2-1-1. Help is available." Somehow it seemed ironic, but he was sure he was not the type who needed help. But if you looked at him tonight, you would certainly disagree.

On the way home, he kept thinking how close he came to winning big. The 7's almost came through for a big payoff. So close. Then he thought more about his scheme with Diversified Document Processing. He had a customer coming in for a loan and if he could convince him the loan origination fee was legit, Tony would have enough money to pay off the loan sharks—with interest! If the scheme did work, he might be on to something!

He also thought about Cady at Lenny's. She was more than just a pretty girl. There was something intriguing about her personality. He looked forward to seeing her Sunday night. He needed to see her. That would take some of the pain away.

SUNDAY NIGHT AT LENNY'S

Tony couldn't decide if he should go to Lenny's or not. He kept looking in the mirror and examining his black eye. It *was* black, purple, and swollen. It really was ugly. He didn't want Cady to see him this way. On the other hand, he needed some sympathy. He had been resting with an ice pack all day, but it didn't seem to help with the swelling or the pain. He decided to make his regular drive over to Lenny's. He usually went in the evening but today, he left in the late afternoon. It was very crowded with a line out to the door. He did not see Cady.

He observed another waitress, Sarah, show a single man to a table. Cady had been trained by Sarah. She recognized Tony and told him Cady was working in the kitchen but would let her know he was here. Then she showed him to his favorite table. She was an incredible waitress.

Just then, he saw Cady in the kitchen and when she noticed him, she waved for him to follow her. She noticed his eye right away and asked him what happened. She was really concerned.

"Oh, it's nothing. Fell in my yard yesterday, stupid mistake."

"Did you go to the hospital or have someone look at it?"

"No, really, it will be okay. But thanks for your concern."

"Well, I really am concerned. Spaghetti tonight? We're really busy, and they even have me helping out in the kitchen. But I really wish there was something I could do to help." She placed her hands on his shoulders and looked at him directly into his eyes. The soothing touch felt so good—he could feel the pain slowly drain out of him. He could feel his pulse slowing down, and he felt totally relaxed. She took her hands off, and he felt *so* good.

"Hope you feel better, I've got to get back to work." As she walked back to the kitchen, she looked back to take one last look at Tony. He had been watching her. *Hmm*, she thought to herself then turned back so he wouldn't see her smile.

Boy, she didn't have any idea what thoughts were going through his head.

The Following Monday Morning

Shannon entered the drive-through to pick up a quick cup of coffee at a nearby coffee shop before starting her day. The line was long and the service painfully slow, cars had already come in behind her, so there was no way out. She was trapped but eventually got her order and thought for sure she'd be late for work. So she was surprised to see she was the first one to arrive at the bank. She checked her hair in the visor mirror then took a nice sip of coffee just as Tony pulled in. She waited in her car while he went in, turned off the alarm, and checked the branch quickly to make sure no one was hiding inside for them. In a few minutes, he waved to Shannon and blinked the lights twice to indicate all was clear and okay to come in. Standard bank branch procedure practiced at banks all over the country.

Shannon had been with the bank for almost ten years but just transferred to the Falmouth branch four or five months ago. She lived north of Falmouth and commuted on I-295 which was a dangerous road to travel in the morning. Too much traffic, too much tailgating, too many accidents. Tony worried about her. She was in her midfifties and a very friendly, likeable person. She was popular with the customers and always made them feel special. After she waited on them, they always left feeling good. She always made it a point to ask them something personal and was always interested in their responses. Made customers feel like family. Great employee!

She freaked when she saw Tony's black eye and hesitated to ask what happened.

"I slipped on my cellar stairs. Actually pretty lucky I didn't get hurt any worse than this. Kind of nasty, but I'll be all right." Customers commented on his black eye all day.

A Diabolical Scheme!

Tony was sitting in his office when he noticed Cindy was waiting on Martin. Tony had known Martin before he was the branch manager in Falmouth through the chamber of commerce. Martin was an insurance agent and Tony guessed a darn good one. They were friends, and Tony knew Martin could keep a secret.

Tony got up and went out into the lobby, greeted Martin, and asked if he had a minute, then invited Martin into his office. He offered Martin a seat then closed his door.

"We're friends, so what I'm going to ask you has to be kept in strict confidence, okay?" Martin nodded in the affirmative.

"I have a friend who is an only child. His father has a half-million-dollar life-insurance policy with his mother as sole beneficiary. As he is the only child, he would get the entire proceeds if both of them died at the same time, say, in a car accident."

"That's true." Martin began fidgeting in his chair. "What are you getting at?"

"Right, he has no wish to see them go but still, he is very aware of the half-million policy. But here is my question. If I took out a million-dollar policy on myself and named a fictional person as beneficiary, could I fake my own death, have the check issued to the phony person, then deposit it to a joint account with me and the phony person?"

"Hmm, sounds like you've been thinking about this, that you're actually serious? First, with a million-dollar policy, you'd have to wait a couple years after you take it out, or it's going to be really suspicious, and there will be a lot of investigation. Your death would have to be very convincing. Naming a fictional person could also be a problem. I'll have to think about that one. I suppose you, as a banker, could open an account for the phony person and set up a PO box for a mailing address then deposit the check when it comes in. Then if you fake your death, I mean, you have to be dead like forever, and they will need a body, your body, to issue a death certificate."

"Someone dies every day in Maine from opioids. Many of them die in the Bayside area of Portland. I just have to walk through there regularly until I find somebody about my age and build. Then take out their teeth, put my wallet in their back pocket, put them in the front seat of my car, and shoot them in the back of the head, execution style. Now those who know me wouldn't be surprised as lately, I have been dealing with some very bad loan shark guys and haven't been real good about paying them back on time. Then I would soak the car in gasoline and touch a match to it. Car comes back registered to me, body burned beyond recognition, no teeth to identify body with. I take off for Vegas, you handle the claim and deposit check to my fictional bank account. It's beautiful!"

"You really have thought this out." Martin seemed to be having a hard time thinking Tony was serious. "It's a lot for me to process right now. Give me some time to work this out and see if I can help you. In the meantime, I heard nothing! Good to see you again."

SUMMER CONCERT SERIES, GREELY HIGH SCHOOL

Every other Sunday evening throughout the summer, there is a concert on the lawn in front of the old Greely Institute school building. It's a free event that brings out the locals—arriving with chairs, blankets, picnic baskets, and some bring their pets. The music is different every time, providing a little something for everyone. Typically the entertainers are local, but tonight features a guitar player from North Carolina. Turns out, he went to the University of Maine with one of the town recreation directors—the sponsor of the concerts.

While he was setting up, the audience was gathering with most going directly to their usual spots. Peter was speaking with Randy while his wife, Liz, was spreading out a blanket. Pam was there, proudly wearing her Bates sweatshirt with her husband, Bill. Don and Jackie were holding a space for four, waiting for Spencer and Connie to arrive. Don was the rec member who had arranged for Bruce to play tonight. Viktoria was there with her tenants Cady and Tina and Tina's friend Rebekkah. Sarah was walking by with her dog, Tigger, and her friend from France, Apolline, and they decided to watch for a little while. They were on their way to pick up a pizza at the store across the street. Hannah was there with some guests from college; Sydney, Olivia, and Carolyn. Hannah worked as the European representative for the OLS summer camp in Raymond, Maine, and was home for just a couple weeks. Off in the distance, you could catch a glimpse of an old man wearing a black suit, standing next to a tree, then he just sort of disappeared into the distance. And high atop the cupola on the school sat a big black crow, casting an eerie shadow across the ground below. The crow was often spotted flying over the school grounds keeping a watchful eye on the activity below. The students nicknamed him "Jimmy."

Bruce was introduced as the crowd began to quiet down. They had provided a stool for him to sit on. Though bald, he had a long ponytail and a somewhat crazed look on his face. But after all, he was an artist and believed music was the thread that held the world together. He worked as a music therapist—healing people with music. He was introduced as a southern bluegrass player, but his first song was a Gaelic ballad from a group called Steeleye Span. The crowd loved it, but Bill, a town councilor, looked at the people he had invited and said, "I know bluegrass music, and this just isn't bluegrass!"

When he finished, he received a strong applause. He laughed and said the whole night should probably feature more Steeleye Span music. "Just thought I'd try out some new material." Then he played bluegrass music almost nonstop for a little over an hour then thanked the crowd for their interest. He told them they were free to go, or they could stay for a new song he had just composed a couple weeks previous. He had only played it once in public—at a seedy kind of place called Stacy's Roadhouse back in Raleigh, North Carolina. The crowd that night at Stacy's consisted mostly of the girls from Joyner Hall at nearby Meredith College.

"I saw an ad for an estate sale at an old abandoned house over by St. John's Baptist Church, an old Victorian that had been empty for years and was rumored to be haunted. Since it was only five minutes away from where I live, I decided to check it out. Curious, you know. The bank holding the sale did little to clean the place up. Dust and cobwebs everywhere. There was a mahogany-paneled library and someone had purchased all the old books on the shelves. A woman was asking how much the China plates were in the dining room, and her teenage daughter was protesting—she would never eat off plates from a haunted house. But behind a chair, I discovered an old guitar that had been neglected for years. They said they'd take ten bucks for it, so I took it home, cleaned it up, polished it, and tried it out. But one string wouldn't work—no sound came from it when I strummed it. But whenever I tried it, I felt chilled like I was in a snowstorm. I mean a real nor'easter! A blizzard with strong winds that blew the snow sideways. A very strange snowstorm! Late that night, I dreamed that my father (who had passed away not too long ago) visited me. He didn't say anything but communicated with symbols. He put his hands over his heart and then pointed at me as if to say, "I love you."

"I played that guitar at the end of the show at Stacy's. I strummed the silent string and asked if anyone felt the snow swirling around them. Six people did and stood up with outstretched arms to feel the snow. The next day, they emailed me with messages that loved ones had visited them in their dreams just like my Dad did. I found the music from that guitar brings a moment of enchantment, of solitude and inner peace. It is a very special guitar—I brought it with me tonight if you'd like to hear it.

"So it appears the string does not produce any sound that humans can hear but does reach out to the spirit world. Just like a dog whistle that only dogs can hear, this produces a sound that only spirits can hear. So I've written a song I call 'Strange Snow' which I will perform for you now. If you feel the snow, stand up and stretch out your arms in the blizzard. You may even spin around with the wind gusts."

So he began to sing, "Even though I've taken my last breath, I'm not ready to accept my death." It was a song about the spirit world, a world with people who have died but still want to communicate with us. When he got to the part in the song where he played the silent string, about 10 percent of the audience stood up with outstretched arms and spun around and around slowly. This group included a young woman in the audience named Acadia.

After the show, Acadia rushed up to Bruce and asked if she could buy a CD of the song. He told her he had just written it and honestly hadn't thought of producing a CD but would look into it. When he got home, he convinced his agent to produce a CD at a local recording studio. It was distributed to some local radio stations and within weeks, it became a nationwide top-ten seller! "Strange Snow" was sweeping the country and was going to make Bruce a very, very wealthy man in a very short time.

That night, Cady went to bed early; excited to see if "Strange Snow" worked and if a spirit would visit her in sleep. Maybe her father would reach out to her! At the concert, she had experienced exactly what Bruce had described. She felt a sense of being surrounded by heavy snow swirling around her—swirling around her, snowing sideways in the strong winds. With the sensation of snow whipping around her like a tornado, it certainly was "strange snow."

Thursday Morning
at the Bank

The armored-car service made a cash delivery to the branch every Thursday morning. Fridays were always busy. Many customers came in to cash their paychecks, and they also needed to fill the ATM for the weekend. They dispensed a lot of cash through the ATM. As head teller, it was Shannon's responsibility to monitor the cash levels in the branch and place an order every Tuesday for the Thursday delivery. The cash came from the bank's main office. Today they were expecting $62,330. The $330 was largely coin, the rest cash. Very rarely did they need to place an additional order during the week, but sometimes local businesses deposited more cash than anticipated on Mondays (due to weekend sales) that had to be transferred back to the main office. This was almost always the case after a three-day weekend. The branch had maximum limits as to how much cash they could have at any one time, so it had to be monitored closely. Reports were sent in to the main office at the close of business every day with the total amount of cash on hand.

Cindy came in shortly after Shannon, the other full-time line teller. She suffered from some kind of severe mental illness and had a very stubborn streak. She had a negative aura around her that customers could sense. She really wasn't a very nice person. Always had a negative comment about every customer she had as soon as they left. Tony was always hoping for some way to transfer her to another branch.

There was also a part-time teller named Claire who was a sweetheart, but she wouldn't be coming in today. She didn't drive so came with her roommate, Lucy. They were both a lot of fun. Lucy would often visit with Tony for a few minutes before she left for her job at a local hospital. Claire could be kind of crude sometimes and Tony wondered if perhaps she went too far with some of her customers, but they kept coming back for more. One afternoon, Claire used the restroom then decided to walk around the branch, tidying things up. That is, until someone noticed her panties were down around her ankles! Oh well, that gives you an idea of Claire. Lucy was gay and enjoyed sitting in Tony's office and checking out the girls with him as they entered the branch. One hot summer day, a woman came in wearing jeans and a bikini top. Lucy looked at Tony and gushed, "I saw her first!" That gives you an idea of Lucy's sense of humor. As mentioned, they were both a ton of fun and helped take away the stuffiness of a bank branch.

After greeting the staff and unlocking the front door, Tony looked at his desk to see what he had to get ready for. Four loan applications pending. One for a used car, one for a couple who wanted to replace and upgrade all their kitchen appliances, a landscaper who wanted to buy a second-hand plow truck for the winter, and a woman who wanted to consolidate her credit card loans. There was no way the loan consolidation application would be approved; the bank didn't want to take over her problems. The used car was being purchased from a reputable Jeep dealer in Westbrook, Maine, so would probably go through; and the couple for the appliances had A-1 credit and a very disciplined budget. Wish all customers had their finances in order like them. As for the landscaper, Tony had an idea—a devious idea. Time for Diversified Document Processing!

When the armored car arrived, Tony went out to greet them. There was a driver who stayed in the cab and a guard, Ralph, who unloaded the truck and brought the money into the branch on a dolly. He was proud to point out how he carried a gun, that he was licensed to do so and would not hesitate to use it. As Ralph was wheeling the money to the front door, Tony suggested that it might be easier for him just to put it in the trunk of his car.

"In your dreams!" said Ralph. "But I think you would have preferred last night's load if you had a choice."

"Why so?"

"Every Wednesday night, we take a truck to the fed in Boston and come back with ten to twelve million."

"Cash?"

"Yes, sir, all cash. That's the truck you want!"

"Now you've got me thinking," said Tony.

Ralph went into the branch and was greeted by the tellers. Shannon buzzed him in, and they went into the vault with the cash delivery. The delivery slip was signed, and the truck drove off. Tony stood by his window, watching the truck pull out into traffic on its way to the next delivery. Ten to twelve million? OMG, can you imagine!

LATER THAT AFTERNOON

Necco was early for his appointment with Tony. He looked nervous and was wearing a sport coat and necktie that he probably had since middle school. He started a landscaping business a couple years ago and was always looking at ideas to expand his business. Although he called it landscaping, essentially he just mowed lawns. It was a seasonal business, so he supplemented it by working as a line cook at a restaurant during the winter months. Mowing lawns in the Falmouth area, however, could be pretty lucrative. He had customers sign a contract for the season, guaranteeing him payments whether it rained or a drought kept the grass from growing. He also offered lawn-fertilizing services and tree pruning. In the fall, he raked leaves and in the spring, offered specials to prep lawns. But he wanted to make his business year-round and was coming in for a loan so he could buy a second-hand plow truck.

Tony had loan authority up to $50,000—about the highest a branch manager could have. This means he could make a loan decision by himself on any application seeking up to $50,000. If he had a request for more than that, he had to pass it on to a senior lender with more authority. Loan requests for over a million had to go to a loan committee made up of the senior lenders plus the bank's president. Necco's request was for $17,500 for a second-hand plow truck.

Necco banked with Tony and always greeted him when he came in to make his deposits. He read a lot of landscaping magazines and always had some trivial fact to share. Today he asked Tony if he knew why the winner of the master's golf tournament was given a green jacket. Why not navy blue or some other color? "It's a specific green color chosen to match the color of the eighteenth green at Augusta."

"You've been watching too much *Caddyshack*," said Tony. "Tell me more about your plans for this truck."

"It's only four years old and in great shape. I had a mechanic look at it, and he couldn't find any mechanical things to worry about and said the plow had hardly ever been used!"

"So why are they selling it?" asked Tony.

"It's a retired guy who bought it for his yard and now has decided to move to Santa Barbara, California, permanently. Can't take it with him."

"So what exactly are your plans for it?"

"Obviously I plan to offer driveway plowing to my customers and also try to get some commercial accounts with bigger parking lots. I can also offer to clean up yards in the winter time when ice storms drop limbs and also clear up any trees that fall. Since it's a good truck, I can also use it during the summer to carry my mowing equipment and either replace the smaller truck I use now or keep it as a spare or if I hire an assistant, they can use it."

"And they're asking $17,500?"

"No, actually more, but it's getting closer and closer to his date to move, so he's willing to come down quite a bit down for the original asking price. It's really a good deal, honest!"

"Well, Necco, I've got to be honest with you. I don't think too many banks would make this loan for you. I do understand that when you're in business for yourself, there is uneven cash flow that can cause you to be late from time to time in paying your bills. So that has been reflected in your credit score which isn't exactly giving you a passing grade. What I'm trying to say is this would be considered a high-risk loan."

At this, you could see Necco's expression change to one of disappointment.

"The bank does have a new program for high-risk loans, however, that you may wish to consider. The way it works is that we grant you the loan but charge you a 25-percent fee that goes into a high-risk pool."

"So you can give me the loan?"

"So here's the deal. I'll lend you the $17,500, plus another $2,500 for working capital as the season is just about over and this will help you until the snow starts. That would make a $20,000-loan plus with the 25-percent fee, you would end up with a total loan of $25,000. You would have to pay it back over five years with interest. If that sounds good to you, I can have the papers ready in about twenty minutes."

"Okay, let's do it."

"So I will give you a check for $25,000, and then you will make out a check to Diversified Document Processing Co for $5,000, the fee for making the high-risk loan. Necco," asked Tony, "is that your real name?"

"Sure is. It's my legal name. Necco is the company that makes the little candy hearts for Valentine's Day. My mother wanted to give me a name full of love. So there it is—my name is Necco."

So Tony prepared the documents, Necco signed the loan agreement, Necco got a check for $25,000, then wrote a check for $5,000 for the fee. Tony sent the documents to the loan clerks in the main office with the installment note for $25,000 and a copy of the check payable for $25,000 to Necco. Tony put the $5,000 check to Diversified Document Processing into his briefcase and would deposit that into his account at the credit union in Portland on his way home.

Tony had just stolen $5,000 from the bank and no worries at all about getting caught. Necco didn't question it; he really wanted the loan and knew he wasn't qualified for a loan of that size. If he went out of business, the loan to the bank would show as one of his debts, but the $5,000-check wouldn't even be looked at. It would have just been seen as one of the expenses in running his business. And if he was successful, he would pay off the loan over the next five years. And Necco is not the type to call the bank to question the fee. Foolproof!

This also gives Tony the money necessary to pay off the $2,000-loan plus interest from the loan sharks. Plus, no more black eyes!

THE NEXT DAY

Tony couldn't wait to get out of work today. It was Friday and every Friday after work, he drove to Connecticut to gamble, spend the night, then drive home Saturday morning. With money in the bank, he was looking forward to a big night. He was truly addicted, and the casino knew it. He was losing more and more money. The casino staff knew him by name now and made him feel like he was part of the family. They welcomed him with open arms and did everything they could to keep him coming back. The casino had a word for people like Tony. They referred to him as a "whale." Casinos loved whales. They are the ones who get the VIP treatment.

On the drive down, Tony was thinking about what he would do if he hit the big one. He was certainly due. How much would go to paying back his debts? How much he'd save. If he won big, would he travel? And if so, to where?

Most of the money bet at casinos goes to slot machines, most by people addicted to gambling. Casinos are well aware of this and do all they can to drain as much money as possible from these people with a variety of tricks. Once a person becomes addicted, they can't stop themselves, they have no control over their thought process. It's worse than a nicotine addiction. The National Council on Problem Gambling reports that one in five gambling addicts will attempt suicide.

Tony had just parked his car when a black Cadillac pulled up alongside. Two men got out—the loan sharks—and started walking toward Tony. Their deliberate steps showed they meant business. One stood on one side of his car, the other on the other side. One pulled his jacket aside to reveal a pistol hanging from his belt. Tony flashed a wad of hundred-dollar bills. He got out of his car and handed the money over. It was quickly counted, and the man said, "Well, guess you learned your lesson."

Tony hoped he would never see these guys again. He could breathe a lot easier knowing he had them off his back. Although he looked cool, he was trembling inside. He walked to the casino entrance and didn't look back. He couldn't wait to get inside where he would feel safe.

Tony always played the same machine—even considered it *his*. He reasoned that by playing the same machine every week, his odds of winning the big jackpot were far better than if he tried different machines. The one he played was known as the Rich Devil. When he arrived at the casino, he went right to the slots area. The casino was just starting to get busy but even still, there were very few people at the table games; most were playing the slots. Someone was sitting at Tony's machine, so he flagged down one of the hosts who gave him a free-dinner coupon and told him he'd save the machine for him as soon as it became available. So Tony went down to enjoy dinner on the house. When he came back, there was no one at the machine, and it had an "Out of Order" sign on it. Soon the host came over and removed the sign and asked Tony if he could get him a drink or anything to make him more comfortable. Tony was anxious to get going so passed on any more freebies and inserted his loyalty card into the machine, a card that rewards him but is also used by the casino to track his activity.

The outcomes of every bet on the slot machine are now controlled by sophisticated computer programs. The physical reels spin but are not stopped at random, the computer tells them when to stop. They are also programmed to generate near misses which are a tease to keep the gambler waging, to think that his luck is changing. Casinos don't list the odds, but the odds of hitting the big jackpot are approximately 1 in 140 million, about the same as Powerball. A near miss will show the jackpot symbol above or below the pay line so it looks like the gambler almost won when in fact it is just a cruel trick. This is referred to in the industry as a "subliminal miss."

Some machines allow for bets to be placed on five lines. So if you put in $1 for each line, $5 total, you may win $2 on one of the lines. Psychologically you feel that you're winning, perhaps your luck is changing, when in fact you actually lost $3. It's a deceptive trick to keep you staying longer. It's a trick that works. No wonder the slots are called "electronic heroin."

And yes, Tony was an addict. Lost virtually all his savings. Maxed out a bunch of credit cards. Was subject to depression and severe mood swings. And always scheming on ways to steal money from the bank just to pay his debts. Which he just did at his bank yesterday afternoon with Necco. Tony was not a thief—just desperate to fuel his addiction.

About 10:00 p.m., he felt two hands on his shoulders. Smooth, gentle hands, massaging his shoulders from behind. It felt so good. And he could smell a unique perfume—a very expensive perfume. "Nice to see you, Tony," a young woman whispered in his ear. "Looks like you're having a good night."

It was Jade. "Afraid to say my luck hasn't been all that good tonight. Maybe seeing you is all I need to change things."

"Wanna date tonight? I can make you forget about all this."

"I'm in room 232 tonight, the usual room. Come by around one, two o'clock?" asked Tony.

She then nibbled his right ear and gave it a slow lick with her tongue. Talk about driving him crazy. She rubbed her hands on his cheeks and said, "Can't wait, honey, I'm all yours! You can do anything you want to me, *anything*."

6:50 P.M., SUNDAY EVENING

Cady was having an "off" day and really didn't want to be with people. Tough for a waitress. She knew though, that her favorite customer would be in soon, and maybe she could give him most of her attention and avoid other customers. He always came in around seven so should be in any minute now. She saved his favorite table and even drew a smiley face on his napkin.

It was now seven and no sign of him. It was a slow night, and she only had one table to wait on—a father and son. Dad was treating him to a burger as his soccer team had just won their game. The kid had just knocked over his water glass and was laughing at the waterfall it had created over the edge of the table. Nice kid!

She was bending over, trying to mop up the mess, when she heard his voice. There was something about him that she found comforting, and she needed it. Although the sign asked people to wait for the hostess to seat them, Tony just walked right over and sat down at his usual spot.

He didn't seem to be much happier (bad weekend at the casino). She took his order, same as always, and placed it with the cook. She then poured a glass of water and filled it first with ice, the way he liked it.

"What's the matter?" he asked. He could tell something was upsetting her.

"I don't know, just kind of tired I guess."

"Sorry. I'm not too anxious to go back to work tomorrow morning, would like to have another day off," said Tony.

"I guess I don't know where you work or even what your name is, even though you've been a regular since I've been here."

"I work in a bank branch in Falmouth. Thought you knew my name but anyway, it's Tony. I'm the branch manager. Been in banking for several years."

"You know I'm Cady, just like on my nametag. Tell me something interesting about yourself, something must be fun and daring!"

At that, Tony choked on his water. He asked if he could confide in her, and she nodded. Then he told her he just robbed the bank he works for.

"But how could you do that if you work there?" she asked, somewhat confused.

"That's how I got away with it. An inside job if you will. I figured out a foolproof method to embezzle some cash."

She was really getting interested. Her dream was to get involved in crime. "Can I ask how much you stole?"

He leaned over closer to her and could see her big eyes, she was really in awe. "Five thousand bucks," he replied.

"Wow," she blurted out, then realized she was supposed to be quiet and apologized.

"It's okay," he said, "but you've got to keep it a secret."

"Sure will. What do you plan to do with it?"

"Might take a trip to Vegas. A friend of mine owns a travel agency, and I think she can get me a good deal. Jane's the greatest if you ever need travel plans. Quest Travel in Windham. I also had some debts I had to pay off, so about half of it is already gone."

"Wow," she said, "I've never been to Las Vegas!" Then she realized that it sounded like she was asking to join him and was embarrassed at her enthusiasm. He too took it that way.

"Ever travel much?" asked Tony.

"Not really. In school, they took us to a museum in Augusta and once a trip to Boston, but that's really about it," she replied.

"If you could go anywhere, where would you go?"

"Canada," she replied. "I hear there are more haunted houses in Canada than any other place in the world. Something to do with the arctic weather I guess."

"Do you believe in ghosts?"

"Not so much in ghosts, but I do believe in the spirit world. I believe we're surrounded by spirits, many of them are trying to communicate with us. To me, it's comforting," she said. "My dad died when I was very young. I never really knew him, don't really even have any memories of him. He was never buried, not sure what happened to his ashes. But sometimes, I walk into cemeteries by myself and hope that I can communicate with him somehow. My life would have been a lot different with a dad. I believe many spirits are from people who can't accept the fact that they're dead. They just float around in an in-between world, trying hard to get their lives back."

"My dad died just a few years ago and I'd give anything to be able to communicate with his spirit. Your mom never remarried?" asked Tony.

"No, she's had a ton of boyfriends, but they don't last long. She blames me—no one wants to go out with a woman who has a child. She has always held that against me."

"You mentioned Canada. You should visit Quebec City. It's a city in Canada not too far from here. Very European. Great atmosphere, beautiful old buildings, great restaurants, lots of festivals." Tony was going to go on but stopped. "Cady, you seemed interested in what I just told you, about stealing from the bank. Have you ever stolen anything or done anything against the law?"

"No," she said, "but in high school, I learned about Bonnie and Clyde and have always admired Bonnie and have dreamed that one day, I would find a Clyde and go on a life of adventure. Bonnie had such an exciting life!"

"Yeah, I guess. But it didn't last long before they were ambushed by the police and shot to death."

"Well, she went out doing what she liked the most and became famous in the process."

At that, Tony decided it was time to go. He paid the bill then walked back to Cady and whispered, "If you're serious, I might be able to find a Clyde for you." As he walked out, he realized that his relationship with Cady just became much closer.

DEPUTY DON

Blake was heading home after a night with a couple friends at a strip club in Portland. Despite only buying two beers, he had gone through over $50. But he wasn't complaining. He was thinking about one of the dancers, Marilyn, when he noticed blue lights in his rearview mirror.

He was almost home but could see the car was after him. "Oh shit," he said out loud. What could he have possibly done wrong?

So he pulled over and took out his license and registration. That morning, an old man had put a trash bag out full of porno DVDs with his trash, and Blake had the bag on his passenger seat. He discreetly moved the bag to the floor and did his best to tuck it under the passenger seat. It seemed like several minutes before the cop got out of his cruiser. It was a deputy sheriff carrying a flashlight. He shined the light directly into Blake's eyes and asked him for his license and registration. Then he went back to his cruiser.

The road was dark and with very little traffic, the blue lights were all that were lighting up the area on 115. The only thing you could hear was the engine from the cruiser. The deputy returned and asked Blake to step outside his pickup truck. As Blake got out, the deputy introduced himself as Deputy Don. He then asked Blake if he knew why he was pulled over.

No, in fact Blake had no idea. Deputy Don asked if he had been drinking. "No, sir, not a drop. Just on my way home from work."

Deputy Don asked him to lean back and first touch his right hand to his nose, then his left hand. Convinced that Blake was sober, Deputy Don flashed his light in the bed of the truck. Nothing more than a pair of jumper cables and a rake.

"Listen, kid," Deputy Don said in a sharp voice. "I noticed you've spent some time visiting our house (the county jail) and have a lengthy driving record. I stopped you tonight because your registration expired three days ago. I'm going to give you a warning, giving you forty-eight hours from now to renew your registration. Listen, kid, we'd better not run into each other again! God bless you."

"Yes, sir," Blake answered and got back into his truck. He took the card that the deputy gave him, *What an asshole*, he thought, and put it on the passenger seat. He then realized how lucky he was Deputy Don hadn't seen or asked about the trash bag under the seat!

LATER THAT NIGHT

Cady always enjoyed a nice, warm bath after work. She smelled like food and after all the close contact with customers, it felt good to soak it off and relax before going to bed. She usually got home around midnight. She would light a couple candles and pour a very hot bath, add some soap bubbles, and slowly ease herself into the tub. Rather than relaxing tonight, however, she was very excited that finally, her dream of becoming Bonnie might become a reality. She trusted Tony; he had been a steady customer. He was older than her and in some respects, she saw him as a father figure. He always seemed somewhat depressed and lonely, but he never tried to flirt with her. Perhaps this was the reason she trusted him. To learn that he had just stolen $5,000 from the bank he worked for excited her like you wouldn't believe. A real bank robber! It looked like Tony would be her Clyde!

After her bath, she always dried off in her living room. She turned on the lights and enjoyed standing next to the front window. Tonight she imagined that Tony was standing out on the front lawn, watching her. She closed her eyes and slowly dropped the towel, finished drying off, then took her time to rub moisturizer over her shoulders, then slowly over her voluptuous breasts, making sure to expose her naked body. She fantasized that it was Tony's hands, gently massaging her. She knew she had a killer body. The moisturizer was vanilla scented. She loved the smell and inhaled deeply, pausing slightly before letting it out slowly.

She always listened to hear if a car slowed down—she enjoyed the tease but felt safe inside her second-floor apartment. If a car did slow down or stop to watch, she would arch her back and pose seductively. It was a game she enjoyed playing. It gave her a strange sense of power that she found thrilling but at the same time, it was after midnight, and very few cars drove by. The chances of someone driving by and seeing her were pretty slim. When she turned off the lights, she would go back to the window to see if anyone was parked outside, watching her. Once a car did skid to a stop and actually backed up for a longer look!

She stood in front of the mirror and pointed her finger at her reflection. "My name is Bonnie Parker. This is a hold up!" She wondered what the feeling would be like when she started her life of crime as Bonnie. The adrenaline rush of robbing a bank must be awesome!

THE NEXT MORNING

A quiet morning at the bank. A couple of hockey moms came in to see if the bank would renew their ad to support the hockey boosters. The bank had a marketing department that handled things like this, so Tony took the materials and promised them that he would forward it on to the people who make the decision and would add his recommendation that they renew. He was quite confident that the bank would, and the ladies left happy.

Claire came into his office to show him a check a woman was trying to cash. It really was suspicious—an obvious black and white photocopy. Tony asked to speak with her and it didn't take long before the customer could tell it wasn't going to work and left quickly. Tony wondered if he should notify the police but decided against it. He looked out the window and saw she left on foot. Most likely to try the bank next-door. Tony asked Claire to give a call to alert them.

Shannon took a phone call for Tony while he was looking at the bad check. "Tony, Leon just called from the money center. Wants you to call him back about a jumbo CD coming due in a couple weeks."

Martin was at the teller line and waved to Tony. Although he had no direct experience, Martin had a reputation as being about the best insurance agent in the area. Tony wondered if he had given any thought to Tony's idea of taking out a million-dollar life-insurance policy on himself.

Just then, Dave knocked on Tony's door. Just a formality as the door was almost never closed. Dave was about Tony's age and managed a high-rise apartment house for seniors in Portland. He explained that he desperately needed a temporary receptionist as the one he had was taken by ambulance to the hospital where she's being treated for an internal bleeding problem. Hopefully she'd be back soon but until then, he needed someone to take over temporarily. Wanted to know if Tony could think of anyone.

"What does the job entail?" asked Tony.

"Greeting visitors and having them sign in and out, taking phone messages, greeting the residents as they come and go, and sorting the mail when it comes in. Not exactly brain surgery."

"Can't think of anyone off the top of my head but will give it some thought," replied Tony. Tony liked Dave, he had a great sense of humor. So he was sincere when he said he would try to find someone.

After Dave left, Tony noticed the armored car was in the lot and Ralph was bringing in a cash delivery on a dolly. Looked like mostly coin.

Tony caught Ralph as he was leaving. "Ralph, got something for you to think about."

"What's that?"

"You were talking about your Wednesday night run from Boston. I was having a few beers with a friend, and he got very interested in robbing the truck on its way back."

"What?" exclaimed Ralph. "It's an armored car, impenctrable. No way could it be done."

"If he had an inside connection, it could be done."

"Are you suggesting I help someone rob my truck?"

"Think about it. You'd pretend to panic, open the truck for the guy, then report it to the police. You'd get a share of the bounty. Think what it would be like to have a couple million in cash under your mattress at your age!"

"Well, you got the wrong guy. I should turn you in to the police for even suggesting something like that!"

"Okay, I'll pass that along. The guy is good though, an experienced thief."

It was now the end of the day and the tellers were balancing their books when Shannon yelled over to Tony, "Hey did you ever call Leon?"

"Oh shit," said Tony. "Forgot all about it."

He quickly got on the phone to Leon in the money center. "Leon, it's Tony in the Falmouth office returning your call, just got your message."

"I sent you an email too," Leon answered. "Mrs. Rosewater has a jumbo CD maturing in two weeks, and I need to know if she plans to renew it or make any changes. As I said, all the details are in the email."

"She has several, do you know which one this is?"

"Yes, $200,000, two-year term. Let me know."

"Thanks, Leon, I'll get in touch with her tomorrow if I can," replied Tony.

TUESDAY NIGHT IN THE OLD PORT

Tony went out for a beer after work. The sidewalks were crowded, and he stopped to offer a suggestion to a young couple from Vermont on a good place to eat. They wanted seafood but not lobster. Tony gave them some ideas. Really hard to go wrong in the Old Port. They commented on the sculpture of the lion in the street directly in front of the Leaping Fish Tavern. Tony told them it had once been a water well for horses to get a drink as they passed through Portland pulling carriages. Been there a long time! The couple took a photo of it then thanked Tony for his suggestion. Then he went inside and found Blake was already there, and a cold beer was waiting on the table where Tony would sit. He always sat by the window, looking out over the cobblestone street and the old water fountain.

"Libby saw you coming," said Blake.

"Man she's the best." Tony looked over at the bar and gave a thumbs up to Libby to acknowledge it was appreciated.

"I hear she's an awesome drummer too!" said Blake.

"Wouldn't be surprised," replied Tony. "What's the news, Blake?"

"Oh, great news today. My boss got approval to replace my truck with a brand-new one."

"Your trash truck?" asked Tony.

"Oh yeah. They ordered a new Mack heavy-duty, high-capacity rear loader. With a cab over configuration, making for lots of room inside and a 605-horsepower engine for extra muscle."

"Cool."

"That means we can compact the trash faster and go up the hills faster. But you want to know the coolest feature?"

"Can't imagine."

"It will have a multispeaker stereo with CD player!"

"But you ride on the back, don't you?"

"Well," explained Blake, "not all the time. I ride in the cab while we drive to the start of our route. It will be so cool!"

"Oh man, you know what else? It's gonna be equipped with bitchin' yellow LED strobe lights," exclaimed Blake.

"I guess I never thought much about trash trucks. Really thought they were all pretty much the same," commented Tony with only minor interest. He was very preoccupied.

"Blake, buddy." Tony looked at him but seemed somewhat nervous. "I've been thinking. Would you ever have the guts to rob a bank?"

"Wow, where'd that come from?" asked Blake. "Too much security and alarms and all that shit, no thanks."

"Not if you robbed my branch. I could set it all up in advance so you wouldn't get caught."

"You familiar with the story of Bonnie and Clyde?" asked Tony.

"Famous bank robbers, weren't they?" answered Blake.

"Right! Well, I'm looking for a Bonnie and Clyde to rob my bank!"

"So you're thinking of me to be your Clyde?"

"Well, think about it. I could make it fun for you," said Tony.

"Do you have someone in mind to be Bonnie?" asked Blake.

"Oh yes," replied Tony. "*Oh yes!*"

Just then, four women asked if they could join Tony and Blake at their table. They were much younger than Tony, probably even younger than Blake, but definitely out for a good time. They sat down before either of them could answer.

After a few minutes, Tony excused himself and left. Blake looked at him, kind of disappointed, but gave him the thumbs up. The girls didn't seem to be upset that he was leaving which actually upset Tony; he didn't think he looked that much older! No doubt they were just looking for a sucker to buy them drinks.

Tony ran into Hadwen and Tiny Tim on his way out. He almost went back in as they were great to hang out with. Hadwen was always in a good mood, and it didn't take much to get him laughing. It was easy to see why they called him Happy Hadwen. Tiny Tim was just the opposite of what you may think; he was a big guy who worked as a bouncer at a rowdy nearby Old Port night club. Tough work, but he was a tough guy, a rugged guy. About 275 lbs., 6'4", arms like Popeye. Not someone you'd want to mess with. They chatted for a minute on the sidewalk, urging Tony to come back and join them, but Tony really needed to call it quits for the night.

On the way back to Church Street to get his car, Tony was thinking about his day. He had asked an armored car driver if he'd help him rob his truck of millions of dollars, old lady Rosewater had a $200,000 certificate maturing and wouldn't Tony like to renew that through his fake business, and he just asked his buddy if he'd consider robbing his bank! And as he was thinking more about his day, he thought about his friend looking for a receptionist and got another idea. One of the duties was to sort the mail. Mail coming into a senior home would be very desirable for Tony!

Church Street was off Middle, just a few feet from the police station. Just as Tony was approaching Church Street, two police officers left the station and as they walked by Tony, they both greeted him. Man oh man, if they only knew what Tony was up to. And it almost scared Tony to think about all he was planning. The FBI had an office across the street at 100 Middle, and a young agent named Colson was looking out the third-floor window down at the sidewalk. He noticed the two uniforms and Tony then went back to work. Wouldn't he like to know what was on Tony's mind!

Colson was a drug specialist from Miami and was on a short-term assignment in Portland, trying to trace the source of heroin shipments coming into the port. Originally he focused on the containers coming in from Iceland and worked closely with Interpol. When that didn't pan out, he studied the marine traffic website and noticed a fishing trawler based in New Bedford, Massachusetts, was making a stop in Boston then coming to Portland before returning to New Bedford. The route raised his eyebrow, but a thorough search of the ship did not turn up anything. Now he has noticed the heroin seemed to hit the market on Tuesdays and he found a cruise ship was calling on Portland every Monday all summer on a route from New York City to Montreal. He was now concentrating on crew members and was ready to raid the ship on its next port visit with agents from Homeland Security and ICE.

Tony walked up Church Street to get his car and looked back to make sure the cops weren't following him. Well, at least Tony could tell his mother he'd been to church again this week. He started up his car, turned on the radio, then took a right on Middle to High Street, then left on Park to head toward Stevens. Soon he was about to pass Lenny's where his favorite waitress worked, and he decided to stop in to see her.

It was close to eight thirty, much later than when he routinely dropped by and not on one of his regular nights. It was fairly crowded, and she was surprised to see him. She was just ringing up a customer at the register and seemed to turn red.

"Tony, surprised to see you tonight. But glad you came. Looks like your table is taken tonight though."

"It's okay, just want to run something by you. Can I just get a glass of ice water?"

She found him a quiet table and brought him the ice water. "What's up?" she asked.

"I may have your first assignment as Bonnie if you're really interested in getting your feet wet."

"Ooooh," she purred like a kitten. "Tell me more."

"You work nights, right?"

"Yes," she answered, "generally five to shortly before midnight."

"There's a high-rise apartment complex nearby that needs a receptionist for about a week, a day job, very easy job duties."

She looked kind of disappointed. "A receptionist? I've never done anything like that."

"It's housing for seniors. You would work there as Bonnie. Part of the job is to sort the mail and Social Security checks will be in the mail soon. More and more seniors are using direct deposit, but my guess is there are still some that prefer the old-fashioned paper check.

Your job would be to take four or five of them which we can process through my bank."

"How do we do that?" she asked.

"Don't worry, I'll figure that out. But each check could be for $1,500 or more, and we would split whatever you get."

She leaned toward Tony, put her hands on his shoulders, and whispered in his ear. "I'm your gal."

Tony almost lost his breath. She was so beautiful, in every way, and to have her that close to him was almost too much for him to handle.

"Good, I'll get back to you as soon as I have more details. Good night, Bonnie!" He couldn't help but wink at her as he left. God was she good-looking. She noticed the wink and pulled her hair back over her shoulders. She took a deep breath and let it out slowly. She watched as Tony left the restaurant. She wondered just what that wink meant.

The Next Morning
at the Bank

Tony was restless all night. He woke up early and decided to head to work. He arrived at the bank and decided first to walk down the street to a place where he could get breakfast. One of his customers, Rob, was there and invited Tony to join him. Rob was a local tennis pro. Tony was impressed with his physical shape despite being about fifty. Rob ate a very healthy breakfast and then offered Tony a ride to the bank. With Rob in such good shape, Tony felt guilty about the thousands of calories he just ate and to accept a ride back to the bank made him feel even worse. But Rob was a great guy and had once helped Tony out of jam.

Cindy was at the door when he got there. She didn't say hi; he didn't even try to greet her. Then Shannon pulled in and got out of her car wearing a new outfit. She could be really stylish, and this was no exception. She was carrying a box of blueberry muffins she had just made. "Thought you all might enjoy these this morning!"

All Tony could think of after seeing Rob was, *Oh my god, a ton more calories*. But once inside, he helped himself to one of the muffins after he warmed it up in the microwave. Boy, was it good!

Tony was anxious to contact Dave and as luck would have it reached him on the first call. "Dave, this is Tony. Hey look, if you still need a temporary receptionist, I got just the person for you."

"Boy, you work fast. Yes, actually I'm kind of desperate so send him or her over as soon as possible."

"It's a her and believe me, there is no doubt she's a she. Probably midtwenties and gorgeous. I actually don't think a word has been invented yet to describe how beautiful she is.'

70

"Okay, I got it, she's a dog. But I'll take her, when do you think she can start?"

"I can have her there by nine tomorrow morning if that works for you."

"Hey, Tony, you're the best. Thanks for thinking of me," said Dave. "Oh, Tony, by the way, what's her name?"

"Bonnie," answered Tony.

Next Tony gave old lady Rosewater a call about her jumbo certificate but got her personal assistant. She was visiting with some friends at the country club and wouldn't be home until midafternoon. But a message would be left for her to return the call.

He sat at his desk for a moment quietly. He could still smell Jade's perfume on his shirt collar. He closed his eyes and took in a deep breath. Oh, *so* nice.

"Hey, Shannon, is Claire coming in today?" asked Tony.

"She's covering lunches today, so she'll be in from eleven to two. Actually should be in any minute now."

"Hey," exclaimed Tony, "these are absolutely awesome muffins!"

"A little different. Mostly blueberry, but I added some raspberries to make them moist then mixed them with some cinnamon," said Shannon, somewhat embarrassed as they were really easy things to make. "Also used coconut sugar."

"Don't be modest, these are just incredible!" emphasized Tony.

Just then, Claire came in with Lucy. There were some customers in the lobby and they already began to stand in line at Claire's teller station, hoping for some humor to get their day going. Lucy noticed Tony seemed a little preoccupied so went over to cheer him up.

"Oh, nothing really," said Tony, "just have a lot on my mind."

"Well, I hope it's all good," said Lucy, then she left to get to her job.

At the end of the day, Tony went directly to see Cady and give her the news.

"Guess what? You start tomorrow!" exclaimed Tony.

"I've got to give you some details before you go. Remember, this is your first criminal activity, and you've got to be very careful. Your name is Bonnie and keep very little about your personal life to yourself. You don't want to leave any kind of trail for them to find you. When you arrive every morning, park in the far corner of the lot so your car won't be noticeable. Wear a hat with a wide brim. There is a camera over the front door that records everyone entering the building. It is the only camera on the premises and it's a revolving-loop camera," explained Tony.

"What does that mean?" asked Cady, or rather, Bonnie.

"It means it records everything for twenty-four hours then starts again with the same film, so everything is erased every twenty-four hours if it's not needed."

"Wow, how do you know all this? Have you been staking it out?"

"You should be there by about quarter of nine and ask for Dave. Tomorrow is Thursday, and he just needs you through Monday. He has hired someone to begin full-time on Tuesday. This works out great as the Social Security checks come out on Thursday. Your biggest responsibility will be to have guests sign in when they arrive and sign out when they leave. You'll also be answering phone calls—most will be for Dave—and taking messages. And of course, sorting the mail when it comes in. Everyone has their own mailbox in a cluster built into the wall. Dave will show you everything you have to do when you get there. He's also going to pay you in cash so he doesn't have to fill out any employment records.

"The Social Security checks will arrive in the mail Thursday. The return address will be from the government. You only need to take four or five. Figure out a place to hide them before you start sorting. Perhaps you can stick them in an unassigned box until you have a chance to put them in your tote bag. Excited?"

"I've dreamed of this since high school!" There was no doubt she was excited. "Hey, do you know how Bonnie met Clyde in real life?"

"No, I don't remember," replied Tony.

"She was a waitress in a diner, and she met Clyde when he came in as a customer."

"Wow, I didn't know that. Well, good luck tomorrow, Bonnie!"

THAT SAME EVENING
AT BLAKE'S HOUSE

Blake pulled up his driveway after a long day. Before he turned the truck off, he checked the gas. Almost empty. It seemed like it was always on empty. He lived in an extended farmhouse with his parents. He lived in a separate apartment behind the main house. He never locked the door, so he just walked in, kicked his boots off, and pulled out a cold bottle of beer from his fridge. He twisted off the cap and took a big chug then felt something rubbing against his legs. It was his cat, Whiskers; his mother must have been cleaning his room today and let Whiskers in. He set the bottle down on the table and reached down to pat Whiskers. Just before he reached the cat, Whiskers jumped up on the table and knocked the beer bottle over which started to spill and then rolled off the table only to smash on the floor. This apparently scared the cat, and he jumped onto the curtain by the window only to shred it with his sharp claws. Blake tried to grab him, but he quickly hid under the bed.

Blake changed his T-shirt then walked down the hallway to see his mother. She said his dad would be late and she had made some tuna casserole which he could have whenever he was hungry. He put some in a bowl and microwaved it, then sat and ate it while talking to his mother. He told her about the new trash truck and as much as she tried, he could tell she really wasn't into trucks.

He then made himself a bowl of ice cream and covered it with chocolate sauce and took it back to his room. He popped in a video from his new collection and sat back to enjoy a movie. He couldn't help but think about his conversation with Tony. Robbing a bank?

Ordinarily that would scare him to death but robbing Tony's bank didn't seem real, more like two buddies having a good time. He trusted Tony and was sure if Tony was going to handle all the details, he'd be able to get away with it. He began to think of what could go wrong but was sure Tony had thought of everything. He also started to imagine how much money he would make—$10,000, $100,000?

And he began to get excited.

Then he clicked on the play button, and the movie began. It started with a close-up of Stormy. OMG!

And once again, he began to get excited.

Cady's Dream

Cady had a difficult time falling asleep. She was very restless in bed, thinking about how her lifelong dream was about to become a reality. She enjoyed watching crime shows on TV and knew she would be good at it. Yes, soon she would be as famous as Bonnie was. Would she need a handgun or maybe even a machine gun? Could she elude the police? For how long? She had just watched a program about a Maine man from Waterville who took orders for firewood last spring, totaling over $25,000, collected all the money upfront, and now that it's heating season and time for delivery, he's disappeared. But the police caught him easily as he left too many clues as to who he was. Really stupid, thinking he could get away with it. It was deliberate fraud, and it looked like he'd be facing a jail sentence. No, she'd be much more careful. She was confident she could cover her tracks and elude the cops.

She eventually fell off into a deep, deep sleep and began to dream. All she could remember of the dream when she woke up was that she was in an office and a man was sitting behind a big desk speaking to her. Could have been the principal at her old high school maybe? He was a very old man, and he was urging her to stay away from Tony. Said he cared about her and Tony was bad news. "Promise me you'll stay away from him," the old man said. "*Beware of the banker.*"

Cady really liked Tony and trusted him unconditionally. What a weird dream to have.

Thursday Morning
at the Bank

About twenty past nine, the phone rang, and Tony answered. It was Dave, almost breathless. "Oh my god, Tony," he said, "you weren't kidding!"

Tony had no problem knowing what he was referring to. "Think she'll work out?"

"She knocked on my door, came in, and must have noticed my jaw drop to the floor. I started stuttering and was ready to leave my wife!"

"Told ya!"

"I'm in love!"

"Hope she works out."

"I owe you big time, Tony, and I mean big time!"

Tony hung up and looked out into the lobby to see Mrs. Rosewater standing there. She gave him a cute little wave, and he got up to greet her. "Come in, come in. Can I get you a cup of tea?"

"That is so nice of you, but I'll pass, am on my way to get my hair done and thought I'd just drop in to see you if you weren't busy."

"I called to remind you that you have a jumbo certificate of deposit expiring next week. Have you decided what you'd like to do with it? Do you want to renew it?"

"Yes," Mrs. Rosewater answered. "I'd like to roll it over."

"For two years like you usually do?"

"Oh yes. I have no immediate need for the money and don't anticipate any reason to need it any time soon."

"We have a slightly different procedure this time. The bank will deposit your funds from the matured jumbo CD into your checking account, then you have to write a check payable to Diversified Document Processing Company for the new one. I will then give you a certificate with all the details."

"You always take such good care of me, Tony. I don't know what I'd do without you."

"Get home before the storm hits," urged Tony.

Mrs. Rosewater really was a sweet little old lady. Her husband invested heavily in commercial real estate when it hit rock bottom during World War II. Left her a fortune. Despite that, she lived in a fairly modest house on Winn Road. She employed a full-time housekeeper who filled all kind of roles; but most importantly, they had become good friends. She was a great companion. Mrs. Rosewater did not have any family nearby, so it was nice to have someone to depend on.

Tony saw her to the door and watched as she drove off. A very pretty and shiny robin's-egg-blue Jaguar sedan which he was sure had all the creature comforts possible. Things were happening fast. Bonnie would have the Social Security checks the day after tomorrow. He was going to cash them in his branch and would have to do that soon before they were reported missing. He would like to have Blake rob the branch the same day he processed the stolen Social Security checks to add to the confusion. Probably best to look at a week from Thursday, a day when the branch had its highest cash levels. Although things were happening quickly, Tony was being very careful and was thinking through everything. On his way home, he'll deposit the $200,000-check from Mrs. Rosewater into his Diversified account. This was too easy!

A tropical storm was to hit the southern Maine coast by midafternoon today. It had started out as a hurricane coming up from Florida but had just been downgraded. Despite that, the rains would be very heavy, accompanied with strong winds. Lots of power outages predicted. There was hardly any traffic on Route 1, and several stores announced they'd be closing at noon. It was already 10:30, and the bank hadn't had any customers yet.

This was the first of the month and the day Bonnie was to intercept a half-dozen or so Social Security checks. He planned to have dinner at her restaurant to see how she did. It was funny how excited she was about being involved in a crime.

Tomorrow night after work, he planned to make his usual trip to the casino and drive back Saturday morning. On Sunday, he planned to meet with Blake, now known as Clyde, to discuss the details on the upcoming bank robbery. Next Thursday sounded like the perfect day, and Clyde was the perfect idiot to pull this off. He had created a modern-day Bonnie and Clyde! Brilliant!

Just then, the door opened and it was Ralph with the weekly cash delivery. Tony had completely forgotten about it, but Shannon was ready for him. Man, he was soaked. After he finished with Shannon and the cash was delivered to the vault, Ralph stepped into Tony's office and closed the door behind him. Because of the weather conditions, Tony had raised the temperature on the thermostat so that the branch would be nice and cozy for anyone coming in out of the rain. Ralph commented on how good it felt.

"Can I get you a towel?" asked Tony.

"Yeah, if you have one. But just quickly, you said you had a friend interested in robbing my truck. I've been thinking a lot about that. The only way it could be done is if I was in on it, so I would have to have a generous share of the proceeds. Still thinking about it but need to know how many people I'd have to share it with."

Tony thought for a minute. He hadn't expected this. Not at all. This took him by complete surprise. Then he answered, "There'd be three of us."

"What?" asked Ralph. "Did you say *us?*"

"Yes."

"I didn't know you'd be in on it, guess I should have figured that out." Ralph paused then said, "Well, that makes a big difference. Let me think about it some more and I'll get back to you."

Tony got a towel from the cleaning supplies. Ralph tried to dry his head as best as he could then left.

"Bye-bye, Ralphie," flirted Claire.

Tony watched the armored car leave his parking lot then sat back and couldn't believe that Ralph was actually considering working with them on an inside job to steal over ten million dollars!

The ringing phone brought Tony back to reality. Claire picked it up on the first ring then yelled over to Tony, "Can you take a call from Dave?"

Tony picked it up and just heard Dave making groaning noises. "Tony, I am *so* in love with this girl. She is a real sweetheart!"

"So she's been working out okay?"

"You wouldn't believe what she's wearing today. Oh my god!"

Tony thought for a moment and realized he'd never seen her in anything but her black waitress uniform which really wasn't very flattering. "You keeping her busy?"

"Oh yeah, I think she's sorting the mail now. Just wanted to call you and thank you once again. Tony, I owe you big time."

Tony said there was no need for thanks then hung up. Imagine, he had her sorting the mail. Hope she doesn't lose any!

You could tell by listening to the rain on the roof that the storm was really intensifying. You could hardly see out the windows. People were cautioned to stay at home. Tony got an email from the main office that the bank and all the branches would be closing at 1:00 p.m. The worst of the storm was to hit the area in the late afternoon.

There had been reports that there had been so many accidents on the interstate that traffic was pretty much at a standstill. Tony decided to take Allen Avenue to Portland. When it was time to leave, Tony let the girls go first then locked the branch door and ran to his car. Despite wearing a trench coat and hat, by the time he got there, he was completely soaked. When he opened his car door, a gust of wind blew it right out of his hands and he thought it was going to break off. Nasty storm!

His windshield wipers couldn't keep up, there were deep puddles on the road and even some flooding. It took him almost three times as long to get home, but he finally got there. He got home about 2:30 p.m. but decided he was in for the night. He really wanted to see how Bonnie did, but there was just no way. He did not have a phone number for her, so he'd have to catch up with her tomorrow.

Tony found a blanket and decided to take a nap on the couch, perhaps watch something on ESPN. He grabbed the remote and stretched out, but the TV wouldn't come on. Of course, he realized, there was no power. No problem enjoying a quick beer though.

He began to think about Ralph's surprise message that he may be interested in helping with the armored-car robbery. The only way they could do it would be with an insider and he was sure he could do it in such a way that Ralph wouldn't get caught. They would probably have to run the truck off the road some place, some remote place, and surround them with guns. Order Ralph to open the back door then force him on the ground where the driver could see him while we unloaded the cash from the back then take off. Something like that. He also thought about Clyde robbing his branch bank. Thought he was competent enough to pull it off, although there was lots of detail and even if he did get caught, Tony didn't think he'd rat on him.

He slowly drifted off to sleep. The rain was blowing against the windows hard, the wind blowing and despite it only being three thirty, it was already dark outside.

FRIDAY

Tony woke to bright sunlight in his eyes. He looked at his iPhone and it was almost 7:30 a.m. His television was on and he was still on his couch, still dressed. He had slept almost sixteen hours! He had to be at work by eight so he rushed—no time for a shower; he could grab something and eat it in the car. He stepped outside and it was unusually calm. There were puddles, tree limbs, and leaves everywhere but a blue sky and almost a surreal warmth. The weatherman on his car radio said the center of the storm was now over Nova Scotia and heading east. There may be occasional gusts of wind but for the most part, we could expect warm, sunny weather today. There were reports of widespread power outages throughout southern Maine. Wow, what a difference from yesterday.

Despite looking like hell, Tony made it to work by eight. Three cars were lined up at the ATM—no doubt people who had paychecks directly deposited and were there to get cash for the weekend. The tellers arrived almost simultaneously and were eager to share stories of the storm. Power had been restored to Route 1.

Tony's first customer needed a document notarized, a service the bank provided its customers for free. The next customer was an elderly woman who could not reconcile her checking account and was convinced the bank had made a $100 error in its favor. After about fifteen minutes, he found that she had written a $100 check to her granddaughter and did not record it. That solved the mystery and the woman was satisfied that everything was now in order. She said her daughter surprised her by bringing over a pizza for them to share. She reimbursed her $100. A one-hundred-dollar pizza? Gotta love those Foresiders! Going through her checking activity, Tony was

81

surprised to see how many five-dollar-checks she had written to charities, mostly to benefit children or animals. Must have been fifteen or twenty of them. Cute.

It was Friday and Tony was anxious to make his trip to the casino as soon as he got out of work. He planned first to drop by the credit union and take out a thousand dollars from his Diversified Document Processing account then drop by to touch base with Bonnie and see how things worked out, stop by his apartment for a quick shower and pack his things, then off for the night to the casino. In between customers he did a quick computer search of apartments for rent in Las Vegas. His plan was simple: rob the armored car, move to Vegas! Looking forward to a night with Jade as well. Life was beginning to look good for Tony!

CUMBERLAND CENTER, FRIDAY MORNING

A pickup truck pulled into the Greely High School parking lot and stopped close to the old institute building. The sign on the truck said "M & M Roofing." They had been hired to replace the shingles on the old institute building and wanted to do it before the cold weather settled in. Mally and Mark hopped out of the truck and stood back to size up the job again. Most of their work was in the Biddeford/Saco/Old Orchard Beach, Maine area, but one of them had a tie to a school-board member which helped them get the contract. They hadn't been back to look at it since submitting an estimate last August before school started.

Mally was dressed in fairly traditional work clothes, but Mark had on a pair of tartan plaid pants that really looked like pajama bottoms. They both agreed that the project should be completed in a couple weeks if the weather cooperated. They went over to meet someone at the facilities building to let them know they'd be starting Monday and to see if there was any particular space where they could drop off some equipment. Anywhere on the side of the building but just not in front of the gas piping. It was all pretty loose, so they went back to their truck and unloaded their ladders and a couple packages of shingles. They had ordered a dumpster for the old shingles and noted it had not been delivered yet. They made a quick cell call and learned it would be delivered Saturday morning. So far, so good. They got back in the truck to head off to another job when Mark asked Mally to stop the truck so he could get out. "What's wrong?" asked Mally.

"You farted! I need fresh air! Oh man, it stinks in here!"

MEANWHILE, BACK
AT THE BANK

Lucy arrived early to give Claire a ride home. While waiting for Claire, she took a seat in Tony's office. She was always lots of fun to talk to, and Tony really enjoyed her company. He told her they may have a new teller training her next week and he urged her to make it a point to check her out.

"That nice, huh?" asked Lucy.

"We're talking US grade A," Tony replied. "She'll take your breath away."

Just then, a customer came in carrying a puppy, a black lab that could literally fit in the palm of your hand, eight weeks old. Everybody stopped whatever they were doing to hold and pat the new puppy. Claire and Lucy said goodbye and left after checking out the dog.

When asked what the dog's name was, the owner replied, "McBarker." She had him wrapped up in a white blanket that was actually a diaper; probably a good idea with a nervous little puppy.

That was no doubt the highlight of the day—didn't take much to add a little excitement to the office!

The bank was closed Saturdays, so they'd be closing up for the weekend. Tony had approved over $100,000 in new car loans this week, so he wanted to make sure all the documents got into the installment-loan department. A good week all in all.

They locked up the building and stood outside for a few minutes, discussing everyone's weekend plans. They all knew about Tony's gambling addiction so didn't press him much for details on his weekend. None of the others really had any plans except to clean up limbs around their houses.

As Tony started to pull out of the bank's driveway, a Falmouth police car drove by, and the officer waved. Tony waved back and felt like saying, "See you Thursday!" He had done so much planning for the robbery that he was really excited to see it unfold. He compared it to writing poetry as all the details were falling into place so beautifully. You'll see too that everything was well thought out. Every possible detail was considered.

He usually filled his gas tank in Portsmouth where the prices were much cheaper and would stop for a take-out dinner to eat in the car. He checked and had enough gas to get to Portsmouth, so he continued on to make a quick withdrawal at his credit union on Forest Avenue then swung through Deering Oaks to the restaurant where Bonnie works.

She was there, cute as ever, very anxious to talk to him. Difficult as the restaurant was very busy. No chance for privacy. She couldn't take a break. He ordered a chocolate shake and took a seat. She wrote him a note that said she had taken only five checks, but they totaled $7210.00! Tony told her once they were cashed, she could have it all. Every time she walked by, she leaned over and whispered more of the story. Apparently due to the storm, the mail was delivered late and the residents were gathering in the lobby waiting for their mail. Dave said he would help her sort the mail when it came in (no surprise, am sure he would have liked to have helped her all day long), so there was added pressure not to get caught. But this made it all the more thrilling for her. There were a few mailboxes that were assigned to apartments that were empty so she sorted some of the Social Security checks into those boxes, and Dave didn't suspect a thing. She also took four other checks and held them until Friday to make it look like they were still dribbling in.

Residents often hung out in the lobby and a few would come over and introduce themselves to Bonnie. One woman that Dave overheard asked her if she had a boyfriend.

"No," Bonnie replied and kind of blushed.

"Oh, such a pretty girl. You should meet my grandson, Leo. You'd get along great with him. He likes to climb mountains. He even climbs with tampons!"

"Oh," Bonnie replied. "What does he do with those?"

"He ties them to his boots."

Bonnie smiled. Thinks she means *crampons*. Sweet little old lady. "Well, if he's your grandson, I'm sure he's a nice guy."

But at the end of the day, Thursday, a couple residents asked if all the mail had been sorted and said they were looking for something but just assumed the bad weather had effected the postal delivery. On Friday she sorted the four extra checks she had held aside on Thursday and the news spread quickly so people were optimistic their missing checks would arrive soon. Dave didn't give any indication that he was aware that she had taken some of the checks.

Tony asked her if she would like to work in his branch next week from Tuesday to Friday as a teller trainee. That way she could actually cash the checks she took like she was doing it for a customer. As she cashed the checks, she would conceal the money in a tote bag. Really not too hard to do. When the people reported that they did not receive their Social Security check, it usually takes the government a month to six weeks to process the details. Even though the checks would be cashed right away, they would not return the checks to the bank as stolen for at least a month. More than sufficient time for Bonnie to be long gone.

Bonnie was very excited about working with Tony as her long-time dream of a career in crime finally seemed to be coming together. Soon she would be famous! Tony told her he'd stop by Sunday night, and he'd give her more details on where his bank branch was and the hours. He then gave her a twenty-dollar bill for the shake and told her to keep the change. Then he took off to the casino for the night.

Bonnie gave him a hug before he left. *Bonnie and Clyde*, she thought. Tony smiled. Her hug was unexpected. He was actually a little flustered. *Oh yes!*

Sunday Afternoon, the Dry Run

Tony and Blake met at a coffee shop in Falmouth then walked over to the bank. There was a camera monitoring the parking lot mounted over the front door, so they walked toward the side of the building, and Tony had him look through the window to see the layout of the office. "Okay, Blake. The bank closes at 4:00 p.m. so plan to be here at five of. Leave the car running and park it so it is heading out and as close to the front door as possible. Wear a hat and sunglasses, plus latex gloves. Don't want to leave fingerprints anywhere. If you can find a reversible jacket that would be great. Wear it with the most colorful side showing when you rob the bank then change it later to the more plain color. Usually they come in a plaid side and a tan side. Make a lot of noise when you enter, you want all the attention on you. Tell everyone to get on the floor except the middle teller. Approach her and ask for all her tens and twenties. Won't be much, but this is a practice run."

"Practice run?" Blake asked. "Why only tens and twenties? I thought you wanted me to rob this bank!"

"Yes, but I've got more plans I'm working on, depending on how you do with this one," answered Tony. "Now listen to me. Every teller has something called a bomb pack in their cash drawer. It looks like a band of twenties with a real twenty on the top and on the bottom, but it will feel more like a TV remote. Once the pack leaves the teller's drawer, a two-minute timer begins and when the two minutes are up, it explodes. It contains red dye and tear gas. The idea is that it will explode in the bag you've put the money in, soaking the cash with red dye so it's useless and the tear gas will force you to pull over and get out of your car. What I want you do to is toss it on the floor inside the bank before you leave. What a mess that will make! It will also add to a lot more panic and confusion."

"Once you have the money and have dropped the bomb pack, tell them to count to one hundred before they get up, and no one will get hurt. Then leave, get in the car (which I hope you left running), and drive at very conservative speed to the library. Oh, almost forgot, just before you enter the bank, I want you to call the police. I will give you a cheap TracFone to use—the beauty is they can trace the number but can't tell who it is registered to. Call and report a bad head-on accident on the other side of town, the dispatcher will notify the police and send them—that will give you some extra time till they figure it's a hoax."

They both got into Tony's car and headed down the street to a car dealer. "Okay, what you're going to do is show up here about 3:30, no later than that, and ask to test-drive a car. Not just any car, see that bright-yellow used Monte Carlo over there?"

"You want me to take it out for a test-drive, cool!"

"Tell 'em you've been looking at it and would like to try it out. Tell him if you like it, you'll be able to buy it today. Get the salesman excited that he's going to make an easy sale. He'll ask you for the keys to your car to hold while you're test-driving. Tell him your girlfriend dropped you off and won't be back for an hour to pick you up. You hoped to hand her the keys to the new car when she got back. In that case, they will probably agree to just taking a photo of your driver's license."

"I've got several with fake names."

"Find the one with the least clear photo. Wear your hat and sunglasses and the rubber gloves. If they ask about the gloves, tell 'em you burned your hands on your wood stove and need to keep them covered. The sympathy will help. But it's very important you don't leave any fingerprints in the car. Don't even sneeze 'cause they'll try to collect a DNA sample."

Then Blake asked, "But why go to all the trouble to borrow a car?"

"It's bright yellow, if we have any witnesses to the robbery, they will report that your getaway car was yellow, very easy for the police to spot. The tellers will also report the car they saw you leave in. Everybody will be looking for the yellow car. You will ditch it quickly and transfer to your black pickup truck which no one is looking for."

"The library is a very short drive from the bank. Drive slowly. Try to park in the middle of the lot between two cars. Change your jacket and leave the car there. Let's drive over and I'll show you. Once you leave the car, walk slowly to Depot Road, cross the street, then take the path to the ice rink."

They parked at the library where Tony suggested (it was right by the flagpole). They walked across the street and stopped at the entrance to the path. Then Tony asked him to walk a little further.

"See this building?" asked Tony.

"The finance business?"

"Yes, if you see this, then you've walked too far and missed the path." Then Tony paused for a moment. "Actually if you stick with me, you'll have so much money you'll need their services for investment planning!"

Blake laughed. "Oh yeah, as if."

"Well, just keep it in mind. You'll need help when you're sitting on stacks of cash! Ask for CG when you're ready to work with them. She's a good customer of the bank's and I'm sure she will take good care of you. Best wealth advisor around!"

The path through the woods was short but would provide him the necessary cover in case the police started looking for him in the area. They came out to the parking lot and Tony showed where he should leave his truck before walking over to the car dealership. "Park by the skating center, right in the far corner by the gazebo. Once you get in your truck, head over to Stillwater Drive and then out to Route 1. Head north to Bucknam Road and drive home, always obeying the speed limit. You don't want to get stopped. Follow me?"

"So cool. So far, so good."

"When you rob the bank, don't give any indication you know me, none whatsoever. They can't have any indication this was an inside job. Can you get your truck here about 2:00 p.m.?" asked Tony.

"Sure, why?"

"I'm going to put a tote bag under the front seat with some cash in it. Can you hide it somewhere on the way home? A spot where no one is likely to find it?"

"I'll think of someplace," replied Blake. "I know the area pretty well."

With that, Tony invited Blake to have a beer with him in the Old Port and to discuss anything that may not be clear. When they got there Tony was disappointed to see that his favorite waitress, Libby, had the night off.

Blake looked surprised. "Didn't you know she plays in a band? We'll have to go watch her some night, she's awesome! She's going on the road later this week and is getting ready for a twelve-city East-Coast US tour!"

"No shit, I never would have known."

"Ever hear of the Pasami and Cheese? Libby's the drummer. They're going to be playing at the Garden in November—want to go?"

"Libby's really in Pasami and Cheese? Man, that's big time, I mean big time!"

Blake pointed toward the bathroom door. "See that poster for the Pasami and Cheese tour? Next time you take a leak, check it out and look at the drummer."

"Libby? Our Libby?"

"Yup," answered Blake, "she is indeed big time stuff."

"Is she the one who did that awesome spontaneous ten-minute drum solo where she played so fast you couldn't even see her hands?"

"Oh yeah, that was her! That solo certainly made her famous!"

"I never knew that was her. We've got to go to Boston and see her show! All the time I've been here and she's never said a word."

After a few minutes of letting that sink in, they settled right down to business. Blake asked how Tony came up with the idea of the yellow car and placing the phony police emergency call.

"Whenever there is a bank robbery in the area, the details are shared with bank branch managers. Being a manager, the details are important for me to see if I can learn something and prevent a robbery at my branch. But I also enjoy reading the details. Most of the robberies are spontaneous events that aren't thought out, brought on by the desperation of drug addicts. They are often caught fairly quickly. There hasn't been a well-planned professional bank robbery in this area for quite some time. You're about to impress them!"

"Oh, and from now on, you will be known as Clyde, as in Bonnie and Clyde, notorious bank robbers!"

"One question though, Tony," asked Clyde. "I'm familiar with the story of Bonnie and Clyde and all and think I could make a good Clyde. But what about Bonnie? Will there be a Bonnie?"

Tony choked on his beer. "Oh man, oh man, wait till you meet her. Yes, there is a Bonnie and she's damn good-looking. I hope to get you two together this Saturday afternoon. She is very excited about entering a life of crime—it's something she's dreamed of ever since high school. And we're going to make it possible."

"Well, I don't mind the good-looking part at all!"

"I didn't think you would. She lives in New Gloucester, sounds like not too far from your trash route."

"We cover Pownal and parts of Gray but not New Gloucester," replied Clyde.

"Oh, one more thing." Tony seemed not to be listening to Clyde. "It is typical for the police to announce the amount stolen from the bank as much more than was actually taken."

"Why do they do that?"

"The thinking is that if you stole, say $2,000 and the police report that $4,000 was stolen, you're apt to wonder where the other $2,000 is. If you have a partner, they're going to accuse you of hiding it and they hope you'll get into an argument and one will rat on the other. Or your partner will beat you up, trying to get you to confess, and you'll wind up in a hospital and possibly confess. So don't be surprised by the amount reported if any amount is stated. Just a psychological trick," said Tony.

Clyde leaned forward, "You're opening up a whole new world for me!"

"Oh yeah," said Tony, "and this is only the beginning."

They started to walk back to Tony's car, and Tony asked if Clyde could get him a fake driver's license.

"It would be my pleasure," answered Clyde.

Then Clyde said, "I gotta tell you what I did this morning, could be fired any time now."

"Oh no, what did you do?"

"Well, we have this really mean old lady on the route," explained Clyde. "People have to buy trash bags but recycling is free. So this lady often wraps up her trash in newspaper and hides it in a recycle bin. It's so bad that I dump her recycling in the back of the truck before I put it in our recycle compartment. Anything that shouldn't be there, I just toss on her driveway. She lives alone and hates me because I go through her recycling. She even tries to tie it harder so I can't get in."

Clyde pauses and then continues. "So this morning we don't see any trash in her driveway so we slow down in front of her house and the driver notices she's just coming out of her side door, so he stops the truck (I would have kept on going). So she's dragging this trash bag down the driveway and when she gets closer, she asks me if she's too late for the trash. I answer her back, 'No, just jump in!'"

"What did she say to that?" asked Tony.

"I really regretted it as soon as I said it then hoped she didn't hear me, but she did and gave me a really icy stare. I'm sure she called the company to complain—anything she can do to get back at me."

Monday Afternoon at the Leaping Fish Tavern

Two men, wearing dark suits and carrying briefcases, entered the tavern just after the lunch crowd thinned out. Libby spotted them and tried to figure out what they were there for. They didn't appear to be customers and were too dressed to be salesmen. They seemed to be taking it all in when one noticed Libby was looking at him. "Can we have a minute with the manager?" he asked.

Libby replied that she was in fact the manager and bartender.

"Can we sit down for a few minutes?"

Libby took them to the dining room and invited them to sit at a table in the corner by the dartboard. "How can I help you?" she asked, somewhat nervously.

"We're from the Portland Police Department. I'm Detective Willett and this is Detective Hodges."

Libby took a deep breath, not having any idea what could be up. "Okay," she answered, "is there something wrong?"

"We received a phone call this morning from a woman who overheard a conversation while she was here last night. Were you working last night?"

"No, yesterday was a day off." Libby couldn't imagine what the woman heard.

"She heard two men plotting to rob a bank in some detail. Any thoughts on who it could have been?"

Libby thought for a moment. "Sorry, but I really can't help you."

"She said they sat next to the window, and I see you only have two window tables. One was about forty, the other midtwenties to early thirties."

"Okay, I know exactly who she is referring to. Bank robbers?" Libby smiled. "I don't think so."

"Why not?"

"If it's who I think it is, they've been coming in for over a year now, just about every Tuesday night and from time to time, on other nights. We have a special on Tuesdays, we call it two-dollar Tuesdays. Nice guys, buy a couple beers and some finger food, then take off. There are some other people who join them from time to time. They always order the same thing. They talk about work a lot. They also come in from time to time on Sundays, so it was probably them."

"Do they appear to be the bank-robber type?"

Libby laughed. "No, not at all. The older guy, don't know what his name is, works for a local bank. He was probably sharing stories of bank robberies he knows about from being in the bank business. He's really too much of a wimp to pull off a robbery!"

"Know their names?"

"No, they always pay cash so never even see it on a credit card. But I'm sure the woman just heard the older guy telling bank stories."

"Well, look. Here's my card. Please pay a little more attention to them and if you begin to suspect anything, please give me a call. Sounds like a false alarm. Thanks for your time. We would like to come back and speak with the person who waited on them last night. Let us know when a good time to drop by would be." At that, the two detectives left. Libby looked out the window and saw them shake their heads as if to indicate there was nothing there.

Tuesday Morning
at the Bank

Tony got there early, Shannon and Cindy were scheduled to open with Claire coming in at ten. But the most exciting news was the introduction of Bonnie who would also be coming in at ten for her first day on the job. It would be interesting to see how the customers react to her and how the branch staff treat her. Of course, if she didn't fit in, she'd be welcome to hang out in Tony's office!

Both girls arrived at just about the same time and Shannon commented on Tony's new shirt (he didn't think it would be that obvious). Tony just had one appointment today; that was all he knew of. It was a man who habitually overdrew his checking account and was hit with a $35-service-charge for each check that overdrew his account. He was furious with the bank for a recent $70 service charge and wanted Tony to reverse it. Poor guy had racked up over a thousand dollars in overdraft fees this year and just to look at him, you could tell he couldn't afford that loss. Tony really hoped the man would close his account and take it elsewhere. Otherwise Tony was working on third-quarter reports of how his branch performed and an explanation as to why the branch didn't meet its goals.

He reminded Shannon and Cindy that Bonnie would be coming in at 10:00 a.m. today and would be observing Shannon for the day. Claire would also be coming in from ten to two today.

At 9:40 a.m., Cindy poked her head into Tony's office and said there was a young girl in the lobby asking to see him. "I assume she's the new teller, the one you described as irresistibly attractive?" Then Cindy turned around and smiled to Bonnie, "You can go right in."

Cindy then walked over to Shannon and whispered, "Are all men creeps?"

Tony stood up. "Good morning, good morning, gee, you look great!"

Bonnie was wearing a very tight navy blue dress that was much too short and a necklace made of delicate shells. "But first, let me introduce you to the staff."

She followed him back out into the lobby. "You've already met Cindy, our full-time staff teller," to which Cindy smiled. "And this is Shannon, our head teller. You'll be observing Shannon today."

"Welcome, Bonnie," greeted Shannon. "We'll do everything we can to make you feel at home and help you learn the ropes. What a pretty dress. I had one once just like it when I was younger." Then she kind of giggled, wondering if that was the right thing to say.

"We have one more teller coming in, Claire, who works part-time but should be in any minute," said Tony. "But for now, I need you to fill out an application form, then you can begin."

They went back into Tony's office and she took a seat by his desk. He looked at her for a second and sort of asked himself how he was able to pull this off. He handed her an application form and said he'd be glad to help her if she had any questions. Right away, she asked, "Name and address?"

"Bonnie is your name, make up an address."

She wrote down Bonnie Parker then sat back and thought for a minute. She reached into her purse and pulled out a refrigerator magnet. She had just been to a sandwich shop in Freeport and took one of their magnets; so she copied down their address and phone number. "Looks good to me," said Tony. "Freeport girl, huh?"

Just then, they could hear a commotion in the lobby—Lucy and Claire had just arrived. Lucy walked into Tony's office and looked at Bonnie.

"Hi, I'm Lucy. You must be the new teller. I'm Claire's room-mate. Claire doesn't drive, so I give her a ride every day. Well not every day, just the days she works. Nice to meet you." She was really tongue-tied and held out her hand to shake Bonnie's. Bonnie then stood up to shake hands and told Tony she'd go out and see if she could get started with Shannon.

"Oh my god," whispered Lucy. "Oh my god. She's beautiful! I'm all flushed, almost shaking. Where oh where did you find her? I shook her hand, and it was so soft and warm. I didn't want to let go. I am *so* in love!"

"Sad thing is that she's only here until Friday. Think she'll be good for business?"

"I tell ya," said Lucy, "if I cashed a check with her, I'd go right back to the end of the line and put it back in just to be waited by her again."

Eventually Lucy caught her breath and realized she was going to be late for work if she didn't leave soon. But first, she went back out to welcome Bonnie once again and wish her luck. She then said goodbye to Claire who just gave her a dirty look.

Tony went out to say good morning to Claire and noticed they were all eating warm coffee rolls that Shannon made at home for Bonnie's first day. She had just heated them up in the microwave and they smelled wonderful. She had one on a paper plate for Tony and he was only too happy to take it.

A few minutes later, Claire came into Tony's office. "I know what you're up to, and I don't think it's legal," she said.

"What?" asked Tony jokingly.

"You know what I mean. This girl is no bank teller. She should be on a fashion runway in New York City or Paris, not behind a counter in Falmouth. I'm sure that with you being single, there's a deal here. I'll give you a job if you give me something? Right? She's just a kid, you can't take advantage of her like that!"

"Oh, come on, Claire, you know me better than that. Slow down."

"I do know you better than that, that's why I'm letting you know—I'll be watching you. I'm going out for a cigarette, back in a minute."

Tony was kind of surprised at Claire's reaction but not really. Claire was truly a sweetheart and meant the world to him. She was just trying to keep him out of trouble. But boy, oh boy, she had no idea of the trouble he was planning!

Shannon invited Bonnie to join her for lunch, so they headed off to the shopping center for a salad. They seemed to be getting along quite well. Tony watched them walk out to Shannon's car. He couldn't help but wonder why this girl's lifelong dream was to become Bonnie and Clyde.

He turned on his computer but really wasn't looking at it. But then the silence was broken by a man raising his voice in the lobby. Tony went out to see what was going on and found old man Hamilton yelling and screaming nonsense about the bank. Then he threatened that if the bank didn't refund $1,140 in overdraft charges, he was going to write the paper, call the consumer affairs' reporter at the local television, Better Business Bureau, call the senior center and the district attorney. He would do everything he could to ruin the reputation of this bank! He would even ask to hold a press conference!

He had a stack of bank statements with him and pointed out that every month he had Social Security and a pension payment directly deposited to his account, so he was always good for the checks he wrote. The bank should know this and honor his checks!

Tony tried to explain that if he waited for the deposits to be made, there would be money in his account to pay the bills. But Mr. Hamilton wouldn't listen. He was an older man, his wife passed away several years ago, he was mostly bald with little bits of white hair above his ears, fairly short, and wearing suspenders to hold up his loose pants.

Tony invited him to come in and sit down in his office, but Mr. Hamilton refused unless it was to refund the bank fees. Tony explained bank policy prohibited him from doing that and the yelling began again. Tony did feel bad for him but had heard all this many times before, and Mr. Hamilton continues to write checks before his deposits come in. Finally Tony suggested he close his account and open one at another bank. "Have you noticed Route 1 in Falmouth?" Tony asked. "All it is, is one bank after another."

Mr. Hamilton left the bank still very upset.

It wasn't long after when Shannon and Bonnie returned, having missed the whole episode.

The afternoon was mostly quiet, most male customers went right to Shannon and Bonnie's teller station. One customer, Maz, welcomed Bonnie and then, on his way out, flashed a thumb's up sign to Tony.

Just before closing, Tony heard a man come in and instantly, he said hi to Bonnie, even calling her by name. This startled Tony, so he had to go out to the lobby to see who it was. It turned out to be Dave. They chatted for a minute, then Dave came in and sat down in Tony's office.

"How'd you pull this one off?" he asked Tony.

"Oh, you referring to Bonnie?"

"Who else? Man, I miss her."

"So she worked out okay?" asked Tony.

"Yeah, she has a certain sweetness that the older ladies loved. Some have asked why she didn't stay. She was very patient listening to their life stories. She really was great and helped fill in when I needed temporary help. Thanks again for referring her to me, I owe you one."

"She's just here for this week then she will go on to another branch. Just training here."

"How can you get any work done? If it was my bank, I'd be doing all her training, one on one. And you're single!"

"Okay, okay, that's enough, Dave."

Just then, the phone rang, it was the bank's legal office. A Mr. Hamilton was threatening to sue the bank for stealing from him. Would Tony write up a report on what the background on this was? Dave waved to Tony as he left the bank and to leave the call to Tony to handle. Tony assured the bank's lawyer that there was nothing to this.

The end of the workday came; Tony locked the door, and the tellers began to prove up. This was a process of looking at how much cash they started with, adding in all the cash they took in during the day (from cash deposits), and subtracting all the cash they handed out during the day (by cashing checks). The end result must equal the amount of cash in their drawer. They need to physically count all the cash to make sure it is all there. It's usually a fairly simple process that doesn't take long unless a teller made a mistake during the day or miscounted the cash in the drawer.

Bonnie paid particular attention to Shannon and the way she totaled the cashed checks. She seemed to understand it and could see how the checks she was going to cash on Thursday would go undetected.

Once they all proved up, it was time to go.

Tony was the last to leave. He set the alarms and locked the door only to notice Shannon was still standing by her car. She came over to Tony and wanted to talk about Bonnie. She said her first reaction was that she was some kind of a pretty bimbo who was able to get jobs by her looks. And when asked about her background and her interests, she seemed to dodge the questions. But when they went to lunch, she opened up and told her about her childhood.

"Tony, are you aware of her background?" asked Shannon.

"I know her father died when she was very young and her mother never remarried," replied Tony.

"Did you know she spends time in cemeteries hoping she can connect to his spirit and meet him? It left a big hole in her life that she's desperately trying to fill."

"Do you know where her father is buried?" asked Tony.

"She said he was never buried. He was cremated and her mother never told her what happened to his ashes. Her mother ignored her and saw her only as a nuisance—a child she never wanted. I felt so sad listening to her. I almost started to cry!" said Shannon. "I guess that's why she's so reluctant to talk about herself. But she is a strong believer in the spirit world. She said there are a lot of people who aren't ready to die or die prematurely and their spirits stay among us until they finally accept their fate. She believes her father is among them and she wants desperately to communicate with him."

"Maybe she should see a psychic?" suggested Tony.

"I know, I thought of that too. But so many are phonies out there that could really take advantage of someone like her. Her mother ignored her all her life. She has an aunt that has been really good to her. But she really had no one to bring her up. No brothers or sisters. Just alone all her life in a house with an alcoholic mother. No friends growing up either. You would never know by looking at her. I guess it's no wonder she has taken to you. You're stable and have shown an interest in her. She thinks the world of you. Maybe the father figure she so desperately needs."

Hmm, thought Tony, *it would be nice to think so.* "But I'm only ten or fifteen years older than her!" said Tony.

"She needs an older man in her life and she really trusts you," said Shannon.

Just then, a firetruck went by on Route 1 with full sirens. It was hard to continue their talk, so Tony waved goodbye to Shannon, and they both left.

LATER THAT NIGHT
IN THE OLD PORT

Tony arrived at his favorite bar in the Old Port early, anxious to meet with Clyde. He got there first, and it seemed before he even sat down, Libby brought him his favorite beer in a frozen glass. The ice-cold beer was just what he needed. He noticed as Libby was walking back to the bar that she was wearing a black T-shirt with a big white question mark on the back—the logo for Pasami and Cheese.

Soon Clyde arrived and assured Tony he was ready to go. Tony gave him a cheap TracFone. This, he explained, was not traceable by the police. He also gave him a pair of latex gloves to wear. "Put these on before you arrive at the car dealer and don't take them off until you're back in your truck. The police are going to go through the car very thoroughly, looking for fingerprints. They'll also be looking for DNA samples so don't sneeze or cough," said Tony.

"Probably shouldn't fart either?" wisecracked Clyde.

"Hey listen, this is very serious," Tony responded. "If you follow all the instructions, you won't get caught and we can go on to bigger things."

"Like what?" asked Clyde.

"Some things I'm working on. No details yet. Let's see how this goes first," said Tony.

They had another beer then left. Outside the bar, Tony said, "next time I see you will be Thursday afternoon at the bank. Good luck!"

"I learned a lot when I was in jail. I'm pretty confident I can pull it off."

"You will," replied Tony. "You will."

BEWARE OF THE BANKER

As hard as he tried, Tony couldn't sleep. What had he done? Thursday, Bonnie cashed thousands of dollars of checks at his bank. If she got caught, she'd probably go to jail and if she ratted on Tony, he'd be in jail too. And he convinced Clyde to rob his bank branch and if he got caught, he'd be back in jail. He doubted Clyde would tell the police he was working with Tony, but it was still a risk. Tony began to feel really guilty about how he had taken advantage of these kids. At the very least, Tony himself was going to have to disappear before the bank finds out about the 5,000 and the 200,000 he diverted into his own fake bank account. Clyde could get him a fake ID and then he'd relocate to Las Vegas. He had the funds to lay low for a while then perhaps find a job where he could be paid under the table.

THURSDAY, THE DAY OF THE GREAT FALMOUTH BANK ROBBERY!

Tony stopped at a donut shop by the Expo and bought a dozen assorted potato donuts then continued on to the branch. He was the first one there, followed by Cindy. Tony had a canvas tote bag that he placed on the floor beneath Bonnie's teller station. Shannon arrived with a bouquet of mums for the office. About ten minutes later, Bonnie arrived, and they all began setting up their stations to prepare for the day. Tony was really nervous and hoped the girls couldn't tell. He went into his office and scanned his computer for messages. It was now 8:55 a.m., five minutes before opening and already there were two cars in the parking lot. His shirt had a perfume smell to it. He realized it was Jade's from the casino. Guess he hadn't washed the shirt he wore there last Friday night. Oh well. It smelled great and distracted him. Just what he needed as nervous as he was. Every now and then, throughout the day, he would pull up the collar and take in a deep breath. It was like she was standing right behind him! Then again, his collars always seemed to smell like Jade's perfume!

Tony passed around the donuts but no one was interested. So he took a chocolate sea salt donut then put the rest on a serving dish and set them on the customer counter. He asked if everyone was ready then unlocked the door. He greeted the first customers then went back to his office to enjoy his donut and continue reading his emails.

There wasn't much excitement, so he started scanning the Las Vegas apartment rental web sites. A typical quiet morning, then at 10:10 a.m., the armored-car service arrived with a delivery. Shannon signed off on the delivery then as Ralph was leaving, he motioned to Tony to speak with him in the parking lot. Ralph said he had been thinking a lot and would like to talk more about an insider job to rob his armored car. He asked again if it would just be Tony and two others and asked if they could meet this Sunday afternoon.

"I want to move on this quickly," he said, "before I change my mind. Behind the fire station, there is a baseball field. How about we meet there at 2:00 p.m. Sunday, right field dugout. That's a quiet place with no cameras or people around to see or overhear us."

As they were speaking, Shannon came out and told Tony he had a phone call waiting. Tony looked at Ralph and said he'd have everyone there and then looked at Shannon. "It's the Falmouth Police Department," she said. "Tony," she whispered, "is everything all right?"

Tony went in and picked up the phone. Couldn't imagine why they were calling. Did they get wind of the robbery? "Yes, Tony. I'm an officer with the Falmouth Police Department and we have a statement from a Mr. Hamilton alleging that you and the bank stole over a thousand dollars from him. Do you know him?"

Tony was relieved that this was all it was. "Yes," he groaned, "I know him."

"Well, he claims he has sufficient funds, but you continuously charge him overdraft fees. Anyway, I have to come over and make out a report. I'm free later this afternoon, okay if I drop by around 3:30 p.m.?"

Holy shit, 3:30? That's the time for the robbery. Oh no, no, no, no. Oh my god! "Uh, no, no, that won't work. I'll be out most of the afternoon. Meetings, you know. Sales calls too. Busy afternoon. Real busy afternoon. How about tomorrow morning?"

"Okay, probably better. Any documentation you may have would be helpful. How about 10: a.m.?" the officer asked.

"Perfect," answered Tony. "I have correspondence from Mr. Hamilton and can explain what he's upset about. Just a confused old man."

"Then it shouldn't take too long. See you in the morning."

Tony took a deep breath. Can you imagine if he just dropped by this afternoon? Shannon walked into his office. He thought she must have been outside his door, listening. "Everything okay?" she asked.

"Old man Hamilton wants his overdraft fees back. Filed a police report. I wish he'd just close his account and go to another bank and be someone else's problem."

"Maybe you should do it for him!" offered Shannon.

She was always so cheerful and had an easy solution to just about every problem. Tony felt bad knowing how later today, she'll probably be scared out of her mind when the bank is robbed.

It was now 11:17 a.m., and the day was moving along quickly. Tony looked up to see Steve at the counter and walked over to greet him. Steve was the president of an investment company based in the Salem, Massachusetts area. Chilmark Partners was a trust company that was established in the mid-1800s. It took in a lot of family money from wealthy cargo ship owners back then and even more when the Civil War broke out as people tried to safeguard their assets. Much of that money was still being cared for by Chilmark benefiting generations of New-England families. Steven and his wife lived on the ocean in Gloucester, Massachusetts and had a second home on Cumberland Foreside. His wife would live there all summer and Steve would come up weekends and vacation time. It had over an acre of heather planted alongside the driveway. Incredible sight!

"What brings you to Maine in October?" Tony asked.

"Had a meeting with some school board members and the superintendent at Greely High School. We have a fairly large trust from a Cumberland family and they have offered to use a good chunk of it to establish a STEM program in the old Greely Institute building. STEM stands for Science, Technology, Engineering, and Math. I'm proposing a top-notch research center with a resident working scientist. Will cost the school nothing, nothing! Can you imagine? Plus the scientist we're thinking of is already working on a way to desalinize salt water using magnetism. If she succeeds, which could take four or five years, it would give Greely High School worldwide notoriety! She will also help attract female students who typically haven't shown an interest in STEM careers."

"What was their reaction?" asked Tony.

"Well, it certainly took them off guard; but I'd say overall, they were pretty excited about my presentation."

"Steve, if I remember right, you went to Greely, didn't you?" asked Tony.

"Class of '76. But that was a long time ago."

"What a coincidence," Tony replied.

"Yeah, a coincidence," Steve answered. Then Steve thought to himself, *There's a lot more coincidences out there—we haven't even scratched the surface.*

Now 11:48 a.m.—time for Tony to take Bonnie to lunch.

While Bonnie was closing up her cash drawer and gathering her handbag, Shannon asked where Tony was taking her.

"Well," said Tony, "she's done a good job for us this week, so I guess it will either be Mexican or Thai."

Shannon winked at Tony. She knew that he was just hoping he'd be seen out with this knockout. "Enjoy," she said, "we'll be fine here."

Once outside, Tony asked if Bonnie had any trouble cashing the checks. "No, not at all," Bonnie replied. "I waited until Cindy had a customer then cashed one or two checks. But you know not too many customers go to her."

"Yes, I am aware of that. She gives off too much negative energy."

"Why do you keep her?"

"Number 1," Tony answered, "I would be inviting a heck of a lawsuit unless I had a strong case for letting her go and number 2, I knew her years ago and she was actually fun to be around. Not sure what happened to make her so miserable but deep down I think someday, she'll return to the person she once was. She suffers from some mental issues."

"Maybe that's why I like you—lots of patience and a big heart," said Bonnie.

"Do you have the canvas bag I gave you?" asked Tony.

"Yes, it's in my handbag, all wrapped up."

"Okay," said Tony as they walked toward the skating center. "We're going to put it under the front seat of the black pickup truck parked over there. I called the ice rink the other day. I told them my son's bike was stolen when he left it by the entrance and asked if they had cameras that monitored the parking lot. They said no, couldn't help me. But they asked for a description of the bike and said they'd keep an eye out for me. Otherwise they suggested filing a police report."

"I didn't know you had a son, didn't know you were married," said a disappointed Bonnie.

"I don't, not even married," answered Tony. "Just needed a story to find out if they had surveillance cameras in the parking lot."

"Wow," said Bonnie, "you are clever!" She was also relieved to hear Tony wasn't married.

"You can pick up the tote bag day after tomorrow and it's all yours," an enthusiastic Tony replied.

Then Tony got serious. "Tomorrow is your last day at the bank. The stolen checks you cashed today won't come back to us for three or four weeks. By then, you'll be long gone and when they start looking for a teller named Bonnie, they'll find there was no such person!"

"But won't they come after you for hiring me?"

"I'll just tell them there must have been a mix-up 'cause I thought you had been sent to us from another branch. I'll cover it best I can, not too worried. I think we're all going to look foolish when they find you never existed!"

From there, they walked over to a nearby restaurant. Bonnie looked over the menu then asked the waitress what she recommended. After the waitress left, she leaned over and whispered to Tony, "Don't ever order what they recommend. It's usually something that hasn't sold well and they have pressure to sell it or they have to throw it out."

"Oh," answered Tony, "I forgot you're a waitress and know all the tricks!"

"Well," she said, "guess I'll go safe with a salad, perhaps with chicken or walnuts."

Tony paused, not knowing how to approach the next subject. He had not really sat this close to her before. We've discussed how beautiful this girl is. He found himself staring into her eyes. There was almost a hypnotic effect, trancelike. There was a powerful force of some kind coming from those eyes. He was definitely lured in.

Just then, she giggled like a school girl and turned her head.

"What's so funny?" asked Tony.

"You were staring at me."

"Sorry, just thinking. Have something on my mind but can't discuss it in here—in case someone overhears me. I'll fill you in as we walk back to the bank."

"How intriguing! You're such an interesting person!" Bonnie was excited.

"Well, you said your lifelong dream was to be like Bonnie in Bonnie and Clyde. I'm going to give you a big chance next week!" teased Tony.

He noticed she began to eat a little quicker and when the bill came, she urged Tony to be generous with the tip. "That's how waitresses earn a living," she said.

On the way back to the branch she asked what he wanted to tell her. Tony teased her a little bit, almost flirting, but was also a little paranoid about someone overhearing him.

So in a hushed voice, he leaned close to her and told her there was a chance to rob an armored car like the one that delivers cash to the bank each week. With some inside help, they would not be caught. It would be one of the largest cash robberies in the history of the state of Maine and would certainly make her famous! She asked a few questions but seemed very excited. She asked if it was like the armored car Ralph arrived in this morning.

"It would make you a millionaire! With a million dollars in cash. And—not traceable!" exclaimed Tony.

She was excited and found herself even more attracted to Tony. Perhaps even starting to fall in love.

3:14 P.M., FALMOUTH ROUTE 1 CAR DEALERSHIP

Clyde parked his truck exactly where Tony had instructed him and waited until 3:00 p.m. On his way to the car dealership, he walked through a parking lot in front of a department store and was checking out the cars, something he always did. He noticed one that was cool-looking and he stopped to see what kind it was. Alfa Romeo Stelvio. He had never seen one up close so stopped to look in the windows. He noticed the keys were left in it. After checking it out, he continued his walk to the dealership then a thought came to him. If he was going to steal one car—why not two! If the keys were in it, no doubt the door would be unlocked. He thought he'd look good driving an Alfa Romeo! He had his hat and sunglasses on so even if there were cameras, they wouldn't be able to see much detail. He carefully put on the latex gloves. Then he walked back, no one seemed to be around, started up the car and off he went! Thanks for the ride!

Clyde parked in the lot where they sold the used cars. He stopped at the bright yellow Chevy SS. As he was getting out, he noticed a thick folder of papers on the passenger seat with a glossy photo stapled to the cover. He recognized the woman and then realized this was the car that the host of the *Maine Living* TV show drove. His favorite local program! He felt kind of bad but at the same time, he really only took it across the street. She'll get over it! He carried a plain white tote bag with no marks or logos. He tried to keep his back to the building as much as possible in case they did have surveillance cameras, but none were in sight.

It wasn't long before a young salesman noticed him and approached like they were old friends. "Looking at the SS?" he asked. "Quite a car! I'm Mark, can I answer any questions you may have? Like to take it for a road test?"

"Man, I'd love to take it for a test-drive. I've been watching this car for a couple weeks now and have the money in the bank to make it happen. Has it got the eight-cylinder engine?" Clyde asked.

"Do you know the definition of exhilarating?" asked Mark. "This car also has the high-performance suspension package for optimized handling. And we just dropped the price to $9,999!"

"Tell you what, man," said Clyde, "if I can take it for a quick spin and I like it, I can stop at my bank up the street and make a withdrawal, probably pay for it with cash today."

"Sounds good to me," replied an excited Mark who hadn't had a sale all week. "I'll just need to make a copy of your driver's license and hold on to the keys to your car. Let me get a dealer plate for you."

It's the Alfa Romeo Stelvio right there. I'll give you the keys but promise me you won't take it out for a spin! Sorry it's a little difficult to get the license out of my wallet. I burned by hands on my wood stove and have to wear these gloves."

"Sorry to hear that, you're not trading that in, are you?"

"No, it's my girlfriend's car," answered Clyde. Didn't he wish. He regretted saying it as soon as he did. Too much information.

"By the way, what do you do for work?"

"I'm a deckhand on a tugboat in Portland. Been there six years. Love it. Can't wait to show the other guys this bitchin' car. Would have to put some black racing stripes on the side though. Here's my license."

Mark held up the license. The photo was a little blurry. "Okay, Mr. Olson, I'll just make a quick photocopy of this and give it back to you. Be out with the keys in a few minutes."

3:44 P.M.

Tony was starting to get really nervous. Only sixteen minutes before closing and no sign of Clyde. Had everything gone okay with the car dealer? Did he chicken out?

Tony tried to act calm. He spread out some papers on his desk and took a deep breath. There were no customers in the bank. He tried not to keep looking out the window. Just then, he heard the door open and thought this must be it. But it wasn't. Wouldn't you know it, one of his nicest customers had just come in and was standing at Shannon's teller station. It was Isabelle, a beautiful older woman who Tony admired but now, he had to get her out fast before she's caught in the robbery.

He walked out in the lobby to greet Isabelle. "How are things up to the lake?"

"Oh, it's been a beautiful day. A nice, quiet fall day. Hated to leave but needed to pick up a few items for dinner. You've really got to stop by some time for a visit."

Just then, Phil walked in. A midfifties guy who made a living doing odd jobs for widows and older women. He stopped to introduce himself to Isabelle and asked if she lived alone and offered to help her rake her leaves and other odd jobs. Isabelle looked offended at his aggressive approach.

Tony interrupted him and told him Isabelle was in a hurry for an appointment. The he turned to Isabelle. "I've got a few things to do before we close today but had to say hello."

After Phil left, Tony told Isabelle he had once worked undercover for the CIA and was proud of his achievement of "taking out" five Mexican drug lords. When his father died, he left the agency

112

to come home and care for his mother. She passed away just a few years ago and left him very bitter about how life had treated him. He has tried to honor his mother by helping older women with chores around their houses. He told her he thought Phil was probably harmless.

Isabelle seemed to understand and as she walked out the door, she said, "Good to see you too, Tony." Now the branch was quiet again, and it was after 3:50 p.m. Tony was getting angry now. Where oh where was Clyde?

3:54 P.M., FALMOUTH DISPATCH

"Falmouth 9-1-1, what's your emergency?"

Clyde sounded out of breath. "I just witnessed a head-on car accident on Allen Avenue Extension, one car was going awfully fast and I guess lost control. Right on the bridge!"

"May I have your name please, sir?"

At that, Clyde had already hung up.

"Falmouth fire alarm on the air with an EMS call. Ambulance 2 to respond to Allen Avenue Extension two car accident, unknown PI. Dispatching police and fire, code 3, lights and siren."

"Ambulance 2 responding with crew of two. Have you notified Portland?"

"Ten-four, ambulance 2, they are responding with MEDCU 35."

"Car 21 responding."

"Ten-four, Car 21. Note that I am dispatching police and fire units to the scene," instructed the dispatcher.

At central station, David and Erik started up the ambulance. As the bay door opened, the red lights were snapped on. Snap, snap, snap. On went the overhead red lights, the front and side red lights, and the rear flashing lights. Erik turned on the hi-lo siren as they rolled out of the station.

Meanwhile Clyde put on a pair of ski goggles (Giro mirrored snow sport goggles) and hat then pulled into the parking lot to the bank. He could hear the siren from a police car in the distance, no doubt responding to the car crash and smiled. He grabbed his canvas tote bag, left the car running, took a deep breath, then walked quickly to the entrance to the bank. It was now 3:58 p.m., just a couple minutes from closing. Perfect timing!

Clyde kicked open the door which startled everyone inside. He stood in the middle of the lobby, all three tellers were staring at him, and then he announced at the top of his lungs, "My name is Clyde. Someday I will be famous and you can say you once met me. I want the teller in the middle to hand me all your twenties and the other two to lie down on the floor."

Then he walked over to Cindy and placed his tote bag on her counter. Although her hands were shaking, she put the cash in the bag, then he told her to lie down on the floor with the other two. He did not see Tony anywhere. He then walked around to the side of the teller counter where he could see all three of them. Two were flat out on the floor, but Bonnie was on her hands and knees with her butt up in the air. With her short dress, her thighs were exposed as well as the bottoms of her bikini underwear. For a minute, Clyde froze staring at the sight, almost forgetting what he was doing. *OMG*, he thought to himself, then he said, "You, the one on your knees. I want you to count out loud from one hundred backwards. When you finish, everyone can get up. Don't cheat as I have someone outside watching through the windows."

At that, Clyde began to leave. He opened the door but remembered the bomb pack so turned around and came back to the lobby, reached into the tote bag, felt for the bomb pack, then tossed it on the floor. "Oh, a gift for you to remember me by." Then he left, got in the car, and slowly drove out of the parking lot. His heart was beating with adrenaline like he'd never experienced before. Clyde was now a bona fide bank robber!

FALMOUTH DISPATCH

"Ambulance 2 to Falmouth"

"Go ahead Ambulance 2."

"We've gone all the way to the Portland line on Allen Avenue Extension and cannot locate the accident."

"There have been no other calls reporting an accident. You may return to quarters. Falmouth fire alarm to all units responding to Allen Avenue Extension. Return to quarters, report unfounded." The dispatcher had also heard from Portland Dispatch that they were not able to find an accident on the Portland side of Allen Avenue Extension. She was able to trace the call to a local cell tower but was unable to retrieve the cell number.

The Bank

Shannon whispered to Bonnie to start counting. But Bonnie was too scared to get the words out. She was shaking. Then Tony emerged from his office.

"Everyone okay?" he asked. "You can all get up now. I just pushed the alarm button in my office and will call the police now." Then he noticed the bomb pack on the lobby floor. "Uh-oh, we've all got to get out of here as soon as possible—he left the bomb pack on the floor!"

Once outside (before the bomb pack went off), Tony called the police on his cell phone and reported the robbery—one man, no one hurt and he used a bright yellow sedan to drive off, going south on Route 1. Just as he hung up, they heard the bomb pack go off, filling the branch with tear gas and spraying red ink everywhere. They all looked in the windows to see the mess.

Tony tried to calm them down, but they were all nervous someone was watching them. It looked like Bonnie was going to be sick. Tony went over and rubbed her shoulders in an effort to comfort her.

As they were catching their breath, a baby-blue Jaguar pulled into the parking lot. "Oh no, no," exclaimed Tony. "Can you guess who that is?"

The driver's window rolled down, and a thin arm started waving. "Tony," a woman's voice called. Of all the people to visit and with such incredibly bad timing, it was Mrs. Rosewater. Tony walked over and she said, "Tony, the arrangement on the back seat is for you. I wanted to thank you for helping me with my savings account the other day."

Tony opened the back door and lifted out a huge floral arrangement. "Wow, Mrs. Rosewater, thank you!"

"Oh, it's really nothing. I was just at the club for tea and it was a centerpiece. They said I could take it with me and I thought how nice it would look in your bank. You always watch out for me, and I never know how to thank you."

Tony complimented her on her lovely print dress and thought to himself that she just thanked him 200,000 times. "Thanks so much." Then he closed her car door and walked back toward the tellers. He heard her car behind him as she drove out of the parking lot.

FALMOUTH DISPATCH

"Falmouth Public Safety to all units, report of a bank robbery on Route 1. One subject, left in a bright yellow sedan, southbound on Route 1, was not armed."

"Falmouth 3 responding from Allen Avenue Extension."

"Falmouth 6 responding from Allen Avenue Extension."

"SP (State Police) units have been notified on statewide," reported the dispatcher.

CLYDE

Clyde drove cautiously but deliberately. His hands were shaking, he was sweating. He went down Lunt Road and pulled into the library, parking tightly between two cars. He was in the middle of the lot and almost hit the flagpole. He got out of the car and checked it carefully to make sure he had everything, then sprayed a whole can of Lemon Pledge into the car to hide his scent. He shut the door, making sure the car was locked, leaving the keys inside. He took off the latex gloves and put them in his tote bag. He took off his coat and reversed it so it was a different color. He turned and started walking briskly then looked back at the car to make sure he didn't drop anything then smack, he walked right into a young man, almost knocking him over.

"You okay?" asked Clyde. "My fault, I wasn't paying attention." It actually gave Clyde a touch of reality.

"I'm okay, didn't hurt at all," the kid said.

"Well, my name in Clyde and someday, I'm going to be famous, and you'll be able to tell your friends you once met me!"

"My name's Jackson and I'm going to the train exhibit at the library." His grandfather looked at Clyde with kind of an instinctive suspicion and asked if he was here for the exhibit.

"Hey, sounds like fun but maybe later." Then Clyde continued walking out to Lunt Road and found the path across that the street that would take him through the woods to the arena where his truck was parked. He took a deep breath, felt under the seat until he found the other tote bag Tony had said would be there, closed his eyes for a second, then could hear the sirens in the distance coming closer and closer.

He drove slowly out to Route 1, couldn't see any police cars yet at the bank, then continued on to Bucknam Road, then north on Route 9. He stopped just before the railroad tracks in Cumberland Center; there was a bridge there over a small stream and he tossed the TracFone into the water when no one was looking. Further up Route 9, a Cumberland police car was heading toward Falmouth at a high speed, lights and siren. It seemed like the validation he needed to convince him that he really had just robbed a bank.

As Clyde continued up Route 9 he came to Greely High School where he saw a sign announcing a home football game. He thought that might be a great place just to catch his breath and sit anonymously in the crowd for an hour or so. He pulled in and parked by the new Performing Arts Center.

MEANWHILE, AT THE BANK

Tony had gathered the tellers in a spot in the corner of the parking lot, trying to comfort them. Bonnie was in tears, couldn't speak and looked away, wishing she could be left alone. Tony placed the floral arrangement on the ground by the front door.

Just then a police car traveling at a high rate of speed turned off Route 1 but missed the parking lot entrance when he swerved to avoid a Jaguar sedan driving slowly in the middle of the road. He hit the curbing by the sidewalk. He was driving one of the new Ford Explorers and the front end bounced up in the air upon impact which in turn exploded the airbag. *Keystone cops*, thought Tony, then he began to worry the officer may be injured.

"Car 7 to Falmouth."

"Go ahead Car 7."

"FPD Car 2054 involved in a 10-55 accident, property damage only but will need a tow truck."

"Ten-four."

Another police car pulled in (FPD 158) and stopped quickly to see if his partner was okay, saw the thumbs up, and proceeded to the bank entrance. The officer practically jumped out of the cruiser and surprised them all at how big he was. Could have been an NFL linebacker!

"Everyone all right? Anyone inside?" His questions came quickly, then he asked if he could take a look inside.

Tony explained about the bomb pack and how the branch was not only sprayed with red ink but that it's also filled with tear gas. At that, Jimmy, the policeman, asked if he could at least open the door and begin to air it out. By then, his partner had climbed out of his damaged cruiser and walked up to the bank. Jimmy took out a cell phone and called the chief to give him an update.

Jimmy then asked for a description of the robber and his get-away car. He was surprised to learn the robber only asked for a few twenties. He was a white male, midtwenties, average build, about six feet tall, wearing ski goggles and a baseball hat, dark blue jacket, jeans and sneakers. No noticeable accent, wore blue latex gloves. No weapon visible. Seemed nervous. A half-dozen police cars were now combing the area searching for the yellow getaway car.

CLYDE

Clyde sat down on the bleachers and took a chance to take a deep breath. It was the start of the third quarter and Greely was ahead by ten points. He felt comfortable sitting in the crowd; even more, he really felt anonymous. He kind of wished he could go back to the bank and hide in the bushes to watch what was going on; how frustrated the police must be, trying to find him. He thought how easy it had been. How fun it actually turned out to be. How cool he was and how everything went exactly according to plan. Tony did a great job organizing this. Then he thought about the teller with her butt up in the air. That was his one mistake. He should have taken her hostage!

The scoreboard said it was the "Simon L. Berman Field." Clyde thought about that for a minute and thought it might have been named after one of his old math teachers.

There was a young man sitting next to him with his parents, most likely a high school kid. At one point, Clyde sneezed, and the boy said, "Bless you."

Clyde looked at him and said, "Hi, my name is Clyde. Someday I'm going to be famous, and you can say you met me!"

The boy looked back at him and said, "My name is Ethan."

"Well, Ethan, it's nice to meet you." Ethan's dad looked at Clyde and smiled.

POLICE DISPATCH

"Falmouth Public Safety, what is your emergency?"

An elderly woman responded, "I've been listening to my police scanner at home when I remembered I had an overdue library book. I'm now at the library and noticed there is a yellow car in the parking lot that may be the one you're looking for."

"Can I have your name and a number where I can reach you if I need to?"

At that, the dispatcher broadcast the information over the radio and an officer responded that she was in the area and would check it out.

"Falmouth Dispatch to Car 12."

"Car 12."

"Just had a report from the car dealership on Route 1. A customer failed to return a car from a test-drive. Been out for almost an hour. It's a yellow Chevy SS with Maine dealer plate 52."

"Car 12 to Falmouth base, I have the car in sight at the library with dealer plate 52."

"Car 1 to Falmouth. Any further information from the dealership?"

"Yes, they got a driver's license. Am running it now for criminal record. It's a thirty-eight-year-old Kennebunk man."

"Would you notify Kennebunk PD and have them send a unit to the subject's house?" asked the chief. "Also have everyone who contacted him at the dealership remain until we can get a detective over there to interview them. "Meanwhile I'll be responding to the library. Can you also request a tracking dog from Westbrook PD to see if the robber left a trail we can follow? He may still be in the area."

"Ten-four, Car 1."

"Car 12 to Car 1. Suspect vehicle is empty, doors locked. Looks clean inside. Will tape it off."

"Ten-four Car 12."

BACK AT GREELY
HIGH SCHOOL

Clyde sat in the bleachers, oblivious to the game. He kept thinking that now he was a bank robber, he had robbed a bank! He thought how impressed some of the guys he met in prison would be. When the game ended, it was starting to get dark and he walked out with the crowd. As he was walking, he realized his truck was on the other side of the building; so he took the long way around and by the time he got there, he was about the only one left. He unlocked the door and stood for a moment, looking back at the school. *Wouldn't the school be proud of this alum?* he thought. Then he gazed up at the cupola, lit up in the dark, and noticed an extension ladder to the roof. As he opened the door, he remembered the tote bag Tony had put there and remembered Tony asked him to hide it for a few days where no one would look for it. He looked up again at the cupola and decided to climb the ladder to the roof and tuck it inside the cupola. *Last place anyone would look for it,* he thought.

Afterward he drove home very carefully so as not to get stopped for anything. Once home, he quickly changed his clothes then visited his mother and father. She was warming up the big pot of chop suey she had left over (she mixed the tomato sauce with red wine), so he didn't hesitate to join them. It had a really rich, heavy taste.

His mother asked how his day was and he told her that he had stopped to watch a football game at Greely on the way home.

"That's not like you," she said. "How come?"

"Oh, I don't know, drove by on my way home and saw the crowd for the game, decided to stop, something to do I guess."

"You didn't go with someone else or meet someone there?"

"Nope, just me."

Then his father looked at his mother and said, "Bet there's a girl involved."

"You going out tonight?" asked his father.

"No, had enough excitement for today."

Then his mother spoke up, "The news said there was a bank robbery in Falmouth this afternoon. Police set up roadblocks and are looking for a yellow sports car. So best not to go out if there's a bank robber on the loose!"

Then Clyde (or rather, Blake) asked if there were any other details. "Did they catch the guy?"

"Could have been a woman," replied his dad, "but no, still on the loose. Did not appear to have been armed."

"You know," said Blake, "from Falmouth, he could hop on the interstate and be out of Maine in less than an hour."

"Or he could be hiding right in this neighborhood," answered his mom.

Imagine that, thought Blake, *right in our own neighborhood.*

BOOTHBAY GOLF CLUB

CT had been playing well. Remember CT? This is a story about CT, FBI special agent. He loved to play golf but wished he had more time for the sport. A round of golf took the better part of a day and he seldom had that kind of time. He and his wife had arrived in Boothbay Harbor around noon for a long weekend. He had been working some long hours lately and was looking forward to a few days at an inn overlooking the ocean. Despite a little fog, it was a good afternoon for a round of golf. His wife was going to enjoy the spa and then join him for dinner when he returned. They had reserved a table that overlooked the ocean that would also give them a great view of the sunset. Although he was living outside of Boston, his first love was the State of Maine.

The foursome playing ahead of CT's was really slow. Despite some attempts at intimidation, they wouldn't let CT's group play through. So CT sat down at the 15th tee to wait for them to move ahead. Just four more holes and he could meet his wife for dinner. The mistake he made was to check messages on his I-phone. He came across one marked "URGENT." You guessed it, the message concerned the bank robbery in Falmouth. He read the bulletin and realized that this wasn't a typical spontaneous drugee who needed quick cash. He called the Boston Field Office to learn more and his suspicions were confirmed. This appeared to be a professional job.

"Shit," he cursed out loud. "Sorry guys, got to go back to work. Something just came up." While driving his golf cart back to the clubhouse, he called the Falmouth police chief.

"Moose, just heard the news. Any updates?" he asked.

"We've got nothing," the chief replied. "This guy didn't miss a trick. He set us up with a phony call reporting a bad car accident on the other side of town, used a stolen car for the robbery and parked it a short distance from the bank, then disappeared. We found the car. He had sprayed the car with air freshener before he left so there was no scent for the dog to pick up on. He also knew about the bomb pack at the bank and tossed it on the floor before he left. Bank is a mess."

"Do you know what scent he used in the car?" asked CT.

"Might have been lemon, why?"

"Lemon disguises more odors than any other scent. This guy really sounds like a pro."

"Funny thing, though," added the chief, "is that he really wasn't interested in taking any money. Just got away with a handful of twenties."

"He could have done this in collusion with one of the tellers. It's an old trick, while the robbery is taking place, the teller he's working with fills her purse with as much money as she can. The teller gets away with it because it's assumed that any missing money was taken by the robber."

"So should we search the teller he approached?"

"Search them all. Everyone who was in the bank at the time of the robbery."

"Sounds like this may have been a practice run to test us," added CT. "Anyway, I'm on my way. Sounds like a challenge!"

ETHAN

Ethan's dad was working the night shift, so his mom was hustling in the kitchen to make dinner. Spaghetti, no doubt, Ethan's favorite. She left the TV on for him to watch and at 6:00 p.m., the local news came on. The lead story had to do with the bank robbery. Ethan wasn't much interested and started looking for a video game to play. But his ears perked up when they reported that the robber introduced himself as "Clyde" and vowed that someday, he would be famous.

"Falmouth police have released a physical description of the robber as well as surveillance photos," the television news reported. "Subject was described as a six-foot-man of slight build wearing ski goggles. Dark blue jacket. Introduced himself as 'Clyde,' not armed."

"Mom," Ethan cried out. "The man who sat next to us at the game was a bank robber!"

"What makes you think that?"

"Because when he robbed the bank, he told them his name was Clyde and that someday, he'd be famous. That's the same thing the man sitting next to me said. Mom, I met a real bank robber!"

His mother hadn't really heard the news report so was quick to dismiss Ethan's claim. Ethan must have heard it wrong. Oh well. "Dinner's ready—it's Mamma's famous spaghetti recipe!"

FALMOUTH POLICE DEPARTMENT HEADQUARTERS

Sitting around a conference table were the police chief, a detective, the security officer from the bank, the three tellers and the bank branch manager. The bank staff was asked to recall everything they could about the robbery with as much detail as possible, in the order things happened.

Shannon led off, saying how they heard a big bang as he kicked the door open just as they were about to close for the day. It had been fairly quiet in the building and this startled her.

"What was he wearing?" the detective asked.

"A hat, sunglasses and blue gloves," said Shannon.

Cindy piped in with, "A dark blue jacket, jeans and work boots. And I don't think they were sunglasses, more like ski goggles."

"So part of his face was exposed?" asked the detective.

"Yes. Probably six feet tall, white, slim guy. Maybe thirty years old," added Shannon.

"Any marks like scars, tattoos, facial hair?" asked the detective.

They all agreed nothing remarkable.

"Okay," continued the detective. "Sorry to interrupt, Shannon. Please continue."

"Then he stood in the middle of the lobby and said something like, 'My name is Clyde, I'm going to be famous. Really weird, I thought, for him to introduce himself."

"You sure he said his name was Clyde? Any strange characteristics or accents to his voice?"

They all nodded their head in agreement that his name was Clyde and no one could think of anything odd with his voice.

"Then what?"

"He told us all to lie down flat on the floor except for Cindy and asked her to put just tens and twenties in his bag."

"Did he seem to be confident or nervous?" asked the detective.

"I would say he seemed to know what he was doing but did seem a little nervous," said Shannon.

"Okay, Cindy, what happened from there?" asked the detective.

"He set his tote bag on my counter. I was really nervous and didn't want to make eye contact. I reached for my teller drawer and pushed the alarm button on the way. Then I took a deep breath and grabbed a bunch of twenties with one hand and the bomb pack with another then put them in his bag."

"Did he say anything?" asked the detective.

"No. But I kind of looked and still had lots of money in my drawer. Couldn't figure out why he only wanted some twenties and not the whole thing."

"Any guess as to how much you put in his bag?"

"Three, four hundred tops. I'd been carrying five to six thousand in my drawer all day. It had been kind of busy."

Shannon took over. "Then he told Cindy to lay down on the floor with us."

The detective looked at Bonnie. "What's your name?"

"Bonnie," she said. "I was on the floor at this time but wasn't flat out like the others."

"Why not?" asked the detective.

"Well," she said, now looking down, "I was so nervous I sort of wet myself and didn't want to lay down flat."

"Sorry," said the detective, "but can you add anything to what the others have said so far? Sometimes robbers come in to the bank a few days in advance to look around. Did he seem at all like someone you've seen before?"

"I just started this week so am not familiar with the customers. I remember just asking myself why would he introduce himself—why give us his name?"

"Yeah, not sure why he would have said that—could be he wanted to throw us of by claiming to be someone else. So what happened next?"

Shannon spoke up, saying, "He told us he was leaving and told Bonnie to count backward from ninety-nine to one before any of us could get up."

"And?"

Bonnie answered by saying, "I was so nervous I couldn't get any words out. I tried but just couldn't, then I started to cry."

Tony spoke next. "Then I came out of my office and saw the bomb pack in the middle of the floor. I told everyone to get out as fast as possible, and it wasn't long after we got out that we heard it explode."

"What does your bomb pack do?" asked the detective.

"It sprays red ink everywhere and spews out tear gas. So we could not re-enter the office and through the windows, we could see the red dye on the floor and walls of the office. Gonna be a mess to clean up. Wasn't too long after that when two police cars arrived. Oh, I forgot, I also called 9-1-1 to report the robbery and give a description of the getaway car."

"How good a look did you get?" asked the detective.

"I could see him pretty well by peeking out my office window. Noticed he kept the goggles on and his blue gloves. It was a yellow sports sedan and he drove out of the parking lot very slowly then turned up Route 1. That's when I went to check on the tellers."

"Did you get a license plate number by any chance?"

"No," said Tony, "didn't really think about it, sorry."

Then the detective looked at the crew and asked, "Can you describe the gun again?"

The tellers all looked surprised, and all shook their heads. "No," Shannon responded, "there wasn't any gun or weapon of any kind." It was a trick question as they had already told the detective there wasn't any weapon displayed. He was just trying to catch them off guard to make sure they stayed consistent with their story.

"Anything else?"

"Yes," said Bonnie. "He told us he had a partner outside watching us through the window to make sure we didn't call the police."

"Okay," replied the detective. "But, Tony, often times, these guys come in prior to the robbery to case the place and meet with a desk person. They might ask about taking out a loan or opening an account, all the while checking out the layout of the branch. So I want you to do your best to try to remember any contact you may have had in the last week or two with a stranger who never came back."

"Nothing comes to mind right away, but I'll give it some thought," answered Tony.

Just then, the chief got a call on his cell phone that CT was almost there and wanted to be briefed. "Why?" asked the chief. "A robbery of a couple hundred dollars without a weapon does not fall under the jurisdiction of the FBI!"

The chief asked the bank's security officer if the branch would be opening any time tomorrow.

"With the tear gas and paint, we've got to call a clean-up crew tomorrow morning. No, the branch will be closed all day tomorrow. Tony and I will go in first to secure the cash, I imagine the vault is still open?"

"Yes," answered Shannon. "Hope I didn't do anything wrong."

"No, under the circumstances, with that bomb pack on the floor ready to explode, you didn't have time to lock up like usual. So Tony and I will meet there at 8:00 a.m., lock everything up, and then call for the cleaners."

Then the chief instructed the tellers to stay in the area and plan to meet some time in the afternoon at the branch to answer some more questions. "It's been a long day for you all, I'm sure. Go home and get some rest and I'll see you all tomorrow afternoon. I have just learned the networks have been filming in the bank parking lot for the 11:00-p.m. news. If anyone from the press should try to call you, refer them to the Falmouth police detective. Do not offer any comments. See you tomorrow."

As they were all leaving, CT arrived. He looked at the chief and greeted him, "Hey, you guys slipping up? There hasn't been a bank robbery in Falmouth since the old Canal Bank at the Falmouth Shopping Center was robbed back in '62. This guy is dealing with Falmouth PD, so I'm sure you've caught him by now."

The chief responded, although somewhat annoyed to have CT butting into this. "We found the car fairly quickly at the town library just a short distance from the bank. Turns out he was taking it for a test-drive from a nearby dealership. The car was clean, very clean. We brought in a dog—couldn't find any scent, nothing to trail, nothing. He left a driver's license at the dealership. License was for a man in Kennebunk. Kennebunk PD sent two cruisers to the home of the man whose ID was used. Guess they surprised the shit out of him. He was playing bridge on his backyard patio with some friends. Well-known member of the community, president of the Plen Corporation, a secret defense contractor in Arundel.

"No witnesses have come forward. No cameras at the library, no one matching the robber's description entered the building around four. He either had another car parked at the library or someone picked him up. If his intention was to distract us with the easily spotted yellow car while he drove off in something that blended into traffic, it worked."

It was now CT's turn. "Okay, I think we have a real pro on our hands. He's either practicing for something bigger or playing with us, testing out the skills of the local police."

"Yes," replied the chief, "but what I can't understand is that the manager said they had received a large cash delivery earlier today. With the branch brimming with cash, why did he only ask for a small handout?"

"Hmm," wondered CT. "That kind of rules out that he might have been working with someone inside the branch. If he had been, the vault would have been open when he came in and he would have cleaned out the place. No, this guy is a pro. If he's as young as the tellers described, then he has someone teaching him, working with him. This could be a challenge! But you know, he could have been using this as a distraction for something else going on in the branch at the same time—a distraction to throw us off. Better search the tellers and the manager and do a thorough search of the branch. Let's also take a close look at the surveillance tapes during the robbery to see if there's any suspicious activity."

"Uh, CT?" the chief cautioned. "You don't have any business getting involved in this. It's my jurisdiction. If you want to help, fine, but remember, this is my town."

"You know I love stuff like this. And I've never left an unsolved case—never. So yes, I will respect the fact that it is your territory but let's see who gets him first! But for now, he's most likely still in the area—planning his next adventure. Oh and by the way," added CT with a little dig, "did you ever catch the 1962 bank robber?"

Just as they were on their way out, the chief got a call. A woman had just reported her car stolen from a nearby department store parking lot. An Alfa Romeo.

Friday Morning, Greely High School

It was just before 8:00 a.m., and the school buses were beginning to arrive. The boys from M & M Roofing were standing by their truck looking at the roof. They hoped to finish today and if they worked diligently, they could finish by—

"Lunch," said Mally. "I don't see why we can't finish by lunch-time, then pack up and have time to play nine holes before dark."

"I was really thinking we had a whole day's work ahead of us but looking at it now, there really isn't that much left. Maybe you're right. So let's get to work."

"Hey, Mark," Mally called out to him as he was starting up the ladder. "Why did six hate seven, eight, and nine?"

"You're kidding me, right? I don't know?"

"Because seven ate nine!"

"I'm not going to listen to this all morning, am I?" asked Mark.

"Would you rather listen to this?" followed by a loud fart.

Mally then started down the ladder.

"Where you going?" asked Mark.

"I dropped a nail, just going down to find it."

"You're kidding me, right? Those roofing nails are a dime a dozen and you're going to take five minutes to try to find one on the ground?"

Despite their joking around, they finished early and decided to have lunch in the cupola atop the roof. The view was extraordinary, and they decided they must be at the highest point in the town. Mark thought he could see Portland Head Light in the distance.

Then Mally stepped on something squishy and looked down to see it was a tote bag. He picked it up and looked inside.

"Holy shit! I mean, *holy shit!*" exclaimed Mally.

"What the hell?" responded Mark, sliding closer to get a look. "What you got?"

Then Mally reached in and pulled out a stack of twenty-dollar bills and more and more. Thousands of dollars!

Mally then said, "I found it, so it's mine."

"We should split it fifty-fifty, besides, it was my idea to eat lunch here."

"Take a look at these bills, take a good look," urged Mally.

"Okay, they look real to me."

"What I'm pointing out is that they're in good shape, doesn't look like they've ever been wet. Like they haven't been here in the weather very long."

"So, Sherlock Holmes, what you getting at?" Mark questioned.

"So, I think someone just put them here in the last few days. And they're going to be back soon. And I think whoever put it here meant to hide it and I don't think they're very nice people. Like drug dealers or something. And they can find out very easily who the only ones who've been on the roof recently are."

Mally began counting the cash. "There's over seven thousand dollars!"

"Then should we take it to the police?"

Mally thought for a minute then looked at Mark. "Look, we're honest guys. If we keep this and get caught, we're screwed. Possibly could be killed. There goes our business..."

"Oh shit, man, but I guess you're right. We can stop by the station when we leave today. I think it's just around the corner."

NOONTIME AT THE BANK

Quite a crowd had gathered at the bank—Tony and all the tellers, the bank security manager, a Falmouth police detective, the FBI's CT and cleaners. Tony unlocked the door and was immediately slapped in the face by the tear gas. The cleaner said he'd grab an industrial fan and put it in the doorway to mitigate the fumes. The gas was quickly escaping out the door and everyone smelled it. It was kind of like an adhesive that stuck to you. The police taped the area off from the public.

"Best back away until we get it under control," advised the policeman. But there was really no reason for him to say that as everyone was jumping to get away from the door.

As the cleaners carried several high-powered fans into the bank, they decided to meet in the parking lot. Occasionally a car would pull in to see if the bank was open but was turned away. Even the ATM was closed until they could count all the money in the branch to see how much was missing. The questioning involved how everyone felt (Bonnie confessed that she was still scared) to more descriptions of the robber to see if there were any discrepancies from yesterday. Also more probing questions to see if anyone had any thoughts of who it may be or if there had been any new customers lately that matched his description.

Finally they were allowed in, and they started with Shannon. She counted her cash with two men watching her. It made her nervous, but she came out right to the penny. Cady was next and at first came out $10 too much but counted it again and came out perfect. She was nervous because the stolen checks that she had processed were bundled with her work. Lastly they asked Cindy to count her

140

cash drawer, and she came out short $280. That would have been fourteen twenty-dollar bills, and Cindy felt that was right as far as how much she handed over to the robber, Clyde.

The bank security officer looked at Cindy and said, "So you had almost $11,000 cash in your drawer, and you only handed over $280?"

"He only asked for a few twenties, so that's all I gave him," Cindy answered.

"Good girl," he replied.

Then the policeman asked, "Are you all sure he did not have a weapon of any kind? A rifle, handgun, knife?"

They all shook their heads. "We could see both of his hands, and they had blue gloves on," piped in Shannon.

Then he looked at Cindy. "He didn't give you a note or anything?"

"No," answered Cindy. "He was quite clear in what he wanted, what he wanted us to do and that his name was Clyde."

Then the policeman turned to CT. "Ever run into this before?"

CT said they had a criminal personality profiler who stores information on crimes like this nationwide. "I've got her looking into this, but for me, this is a first as far as I know. Almost like all he wanted to do was scare the hell out of people and pretend he was a bank robber. And I don't think this is the last time we'll hear from Clyde. By giving us his name, he wants credit for this robbery which means he'll most likely strike again. He appears to be a real pro, but they all slip up at some point. Just a matter of time before we round him up."

So $280 was recorded as the official amount stolen. With that, they closed up and turned their attention to the cleaners. The bank would be ready to reopen Monday morning, but the carpet would have to be replaced and the walls touched up where the red dye sprayed. The bank security officer gave the okay to reopen the ATM so that customers could access it over the weekend.

As they were leaving, Bonnie thanked the other tellers for the training, and they all wished her good luck. This raised the eyebrows of the police, particularly CT, who were not aware she was just there for a week of teller training. The detective whispered to CT that as shaken up as she was, he bet she wouldn't come back. CT didn't react but took another deep look at Bonnie, not really sure what to think.

Midafternoon, Cumberland Police Headquarters

The M & M Roofing truck came to a stop at the Cumberland Police Headquarters but for a few moments, the engine continued to run, and they each looked at each other.

"Really sure we want to do this?" asked Mally. He held the tote bag in his hands then took a look inside at all the cash.

"Well, you know," replied Mark, "I've been thinking we should each take a couple hundred, you know, well, sort of as a reward for finding it."

"We're at the police station, the faster we get it over with, the better," Mally reluctantly replied.

Once inside, they were met by an officer named Spencer. He greeted them like they were old friends and invited them into a small office. "They tell me you found some cash, is that right?"

"Yes," Mark answered. "We've been replacing the shingles on the roof on the old Greely Institute building and found this tote bag filled with cash in the cupola."

Spencer looked in the bag and asked if they knew how much was in it.

"No, no idea." Then Mally looked at Mark then back to Spencer. "Yeah, probably around $7,000."

Spencer smelled the tote bag. "Did you guys notice this? Smells like perfume. Like it belonged to a woman. But how would someone get it up there?"

"We wondered the same thing," came back Mally who was somewhat proud of himself. "We used our ladders to get to the roof and it was quite steep. No other way up there far as we could tell without a ladder. And I don't think anyone could have thrown it up there."

Spencer said he would contact the school and get a list of everyone who would have access or potential access to the roof. Also to see if they have noticed any suspicious activity around the building.

Spencer was quiet for a moment while he sized up these two. He thought it was unusual for a couple of roofers to be turning in this kind of money. They were his primary suspects.

"There was a bank robbery in Falmouth yesterday afternoon, but only a couple hundred was taken, nothing like this. I'll give them a call and see if there's any connection, but I doubt it. Then I'll run nationwide teletype for information on recent robberies."

"What happens if no one claims it?" asked Mally.

"Well, you know," Spencer explained, "I really doubt someone's going to come in here to ask if anyone turned in a tote bag full of cash. There's definitely a story here and I'm not sure it's altogether legal. I would have some serious questions about this before turning it over. Looks like someone is hiding it and when they come back to get it, they're not going to be too happy. Probably won't call the cops either. Ever hear of hiding something in plain sight? This seems to be a good example. But of course, if they have a legitimate explanation, we'll hand it over to them, and perhaps they'll offer a reward."

"What do you think the chances of that happening are?" asked Mally.

"To be honest with you, pretty much nil."

Then Mark piped in, somewhat proud of himself, "We noticed the bills are crisp, like they haven't been exposed to the weather, so the bag probably hasn't been there that long."

"Good observation," replied Spencer. "It definitely wasn't up there during that heavy rain and wind storm we just had a couple weeks ago."

Mark smiled. Thought he was getting good at this detective stuff.

So again, Mally asked, "So what happens to it?"

"We'll hold it here for a couple months and if no one comes in, we have to send it to the state treasurer as abandoned property. If no one contacts them in seven years, it becomes state property."

That was really not the answer the guys were looking for.

Spencer counted the money in front of Mally and Mark and totaled it at $7,210. He then took down their names and addresses and thanked them for their honesty. Also took down their driver's license information. Spencer was still suspicious of these two and would do a background check on them then have the department detective do some investigating into their recent activity. He just didn't buy the story of two roofers finding this much money and turning it in. Maybe they found $50,000 and are only turning in seven. They were Spencer's number one suspects. He was sure there was much more to their story then they were letting on.

PREVIEW

It was now early Friday afternoon. The bank was closed until Monday while they replaced the carpet and repainted the walls. Tony was about to withdraw $2,000 from his account at the credit union and spend the night at the casino. Clyde was to pick Bonnie up Saturday afternoon and introduce her to the world of robbery. They would meet with Ralph Sunday afternoon to discuss the possibility of robbing an armored car of millions of dollars—potentially the largest robbery in Maine history. Don't forget to watch the *national* news Sunday evening; there might be a story from Portland, Maine! And Clyde may find himself at a pancake breakfast tomorrow morning!

SATURDAY MORNING

Clyde woke up to a bright sunny day. He had a sleepless night; planning what he would do with Bonnie today. He also wondered what she would be like. Tony hadn't told him much, just that she was a quiet girl who was excited about the opportunity to assist him with a robbery and would be dressed appropriately. He also told him she was a knockout and that he'd enjoy her company. He was to pick her up at her apartment at 12:30 p.m.

Clyde looked down toward his feet and saw that his cat, Whiskers, was sleeping with him. When he made eye contact, Whiskers began to purr. But she wasn't lying at his feet because she loved him; no, it was because she knew he was usually the first one to wake up in the morning and would be the first one to feed her. Clyde knew the game. The sun was shining on the bottom half of the bed and Whiskers was stretched out in the warm sunlight. Clyde reached down to pat her and just as he was within an inch of her, she zoomed off the bed and was on top of his chair in no time.

He put some food in her dish then walked into the bathroom for a quick shave and a shower. The steamy hot water felt great, like a sauna, and he relaxed as it massaged his back. Then he unscrewed the cap to the shampoo bottle, poured some about the size of a quarter in the palm of his hand, then put the bottle on the edge of the tub. Lather, rinse, repeat. But no sooner had he started to work it into his scalp when Whiskers reached up and knocked the bottle over, spilling the shampoo all over the floor. The cat jumped to get out of the pool of shampoo and caught the shower curtain with her claws. At the same time, Clyde was opening the curtain to try to catch the shampoo before it all spilled out and between the two of them, the curtain tore of its hooks. Now water from the shower was spraying all over the bathroom and Whiskers was nowhere to be seen. No doubt she was already in the house with his parents, looking innocent as all get out.

Clyde cleaned up the bathroom, well, sort of. He toweled off then looked in the mirror before getting dressed. He threw on a pair of jeans and a hoodie. Looking out the windows, he could tell it was going to be unusually warm; it was supposed to be in the 70s, and it had probably already reached that; unusual for October.

He walked into the big house for breakfast. His parents were reading the paper in the family room with Whiskers lying on the floor between them. Whiskers gave him kind of an I-dare-ya look. Great pet. Anyone want a cat?

"We were just going out to breakfast. Want to join us?" invited his mom.

"Where to?"

"The Methodist Church in West Cumberland. They have a pancake breakfast the second Saturday of every month. It's really good, why don't you come with us?"

Clyde thought for a moment then agreed. "Okay, but only if I can drive."

His F-150 pickup truck had a bench seat in the front and he liked it when the three of them crowded together.

On the way over, his mom noticed a farm stand with lots of pumpkins out front. That time of year, Halloween wasn't too far away. They talked on the way over. His dad was going to be driving his motorcoach later today for a group attending a barn wedding in Buxton and probably wouldn't be home until after 1:00 a.m. His mom was going to work the four-to-midnight shift. Clyde didn't offer any details other than he was going to call some friends and see what they were up to.

Clyde parked in the church lot then walked around to help his mother out of the truck. As they approached the door, an elderly couple were coming out and his father asked if they left any for us. Boy, never heard that joke before! Once inside, Clyde looked around and wondered if he needed an AARP card to get in. His dad paid while he helped his mom find a seat. It was actually hard to find three seats together. But once Clyde got in line for breakfast, his attitude changed. Stacks of big fluffy pancakes, baked beans, scrambled eggs, bacon, sausage, blueberry muffins, fresh fruit and on and on. And it smelled *so* good!

Clyde sat down, followed by his mom and dad. He looked at his plate and wondered if perhaps he had taken too much. Easy to do! Even his dad took a look and kind of raised one eyebrow. "I guess someone's hungry!"

Clyde attacked the pancakes first, practically drowning them in syrup. He heard the door open and looked over to see who was coming in. He almost choked when he saw it was two state troopers in uniform. He looked away but couldn't help but wonder if they were there for him. How did they figure it out? Did they follow his truck? What else would they be doing here if they weren't after him? He looked away, then dropped his napkin on the floor and bent down to pick it up and hide until they settled down.

And sure enough, one of them addressed the crowd. "Does anyone here own a black Ford-150 pickup truck?"

Clyde stood up, ready for them to put him in handcuffs. Practically shit himself. How, oh how did they find out? It had all gone according to plan, flawless.

Then the trooper said, "You left your lights on."

Clyde let out a long breath of air. Then polite as hell, he said, "Thank you, sir."

When he got back to his seat, his mother commented on how nice it was for the officers to let him know. "They're probably turnpike highway patrol, they can get off at the Burger King and access a gate to Blackstrap Road," observed his dad. "They seem to know about places like this."

But as they continued eating, Clyde felt they were staring at him. He didn't dare look their way but felt like the man in Edgar Allen Poe's *The Telltale Heart* who collapsed under the pressure and confessed to a murder as the cops sat in his living room with him.

Clyde was glad to get out of there and back in his truck heading home, his parents none the wiser as to his anxiety.

Once home, he checked the clock and began to get his stuff together for the afternoon.

Saturday Afternoon: Bonnie and Clyde Go on a Spree

Clyde was to meet Bonnie at her apartment in New Gloucester at twelve thirty and it looked like he would arrive about five minutes early. As he turned up her street, the house came up quicker than he expected. Tony told him it was shortly after the railroad tracks, but it was like right on the tracks with a big number 512 on the mailbox. He had to brake hard, producing a little squealing and then kind of slid into the driveway. He expected her to come right out but despite three cars in the driveway, no one seemed to be home. He waited almost ten minutes then honked his horn a couple times to let her know he was in the driveway (not the classiest way to make a good first impression).

A woman came out who did not match Tony's description of Bonnie. She came over to the truck and asked if she could help him. He asked if she was Bonnie and she said no. Then he told her he was there to pick up Bonnie and was surprised to hear there was no Bonnie living at this address. But just then Cady (aka Bonnie) came out walking quickly and told Viktoria he was here to pick her up. Viktoria looked again at him and watched Cady get in the truck—her instincts told her this was not good. Her first impression of Clyde was not at all favorable and she worried about Cady. She couldn't imagine what this was all about; and Cady had never mentioned that she had any male friends.

As they pulled out onto the road, Clyde looked at her and said, "Hi, my name is Clyde. Someday I'm going to be famous and you can say you met me."

Taking the cue, she responded, "Hi, my name is Bonnie and someday *I'm* going to be famous and you can say you once met me!" She paused for a few moments then asked, "Are you the one who robbed the bank the other day?"

"Yup, that was me. Tony tells me you were one of the tellers, but I don't remember the faces very well. It happened so quickly. But you are just the way he described you."

"How did he describe me?"

"Something to the effect that you were darn good-looking."

"Hmm, I didn't think he'd noticed." Suddenly she was a little flustered. She felt tingles in places she'd never felt before. So Tony mentioned that she was darned good-looking.

But then she turned her attention back to the robbery.

"Well, you really took me by surprise. But after it was over and I had a chance to think about it, I thought you did a great job. Like you really knew what you were doing!"

"Let me ask, were you questioned by the police?"

"Yes, twice."

Clyde was getting nervous. "What kinds of things did they ask."

"Mostly asking for a description of what you looked like and if we thought you may have come in earlier in the week to look the place over. You know, like did we recognize you? But overall, they seemed very frustrated about the whole thing."

"What kinds of things frustrated them?"

"That you introduced yourself as Clyde and that you really didn't seem interested in robbing the bank 'cause you didn't take much money. They wondered what your motive was. I guess I do too."

"Well, someday I do want to be famous as Clyde and I followed Tony's instructions, also added a few things I learned while I was in prison."

"Prison, you've been in prison? For what?"

"Well, I stole some construction equipment, not much, thought I could sell it quickly but turns out, I sold it to an undercover cop. But there had been some other equipment stolen in the area and they claimed I stole that too so they could look like they had solved all kinds of crimes."

"But that's not fair!" replied Bonnie.

"Welcome to the real world."

Changing the subject, Bonnie asked, "So you have my seven thousand, right?"

"Seven thousand?"

"Yeah, it was in a tote bag that I put in your truck to hide it, this truck, under the seat. Tony told me to."

"Was it cash? I didn't know what was in the bag, just told to hide it for a few days."

"The day you stole a couple hundred bucks from the bank, I stole over $7,000, so there!" bragged Bonnie.

"Well, our first stop, which is about five minutes away, is to get your tote bag. But how'd you manage that to steal that much?"

"Tony got me a job as a receptionist in an old-folks' home and when the Social Security checks came in, I took a few of them. Then he got me a job posing as a bank teller for a week and I cashed the checks while I was there, $7,210 worth! I put the cash in a tote bag and on my lunch break, put the bag in your truck. I got it out of the bank just before the robbery."

"Okay, we're almost at the school where I hid the bag."

Clyde parked his truck by the pool entrance in between two other cars. He looked around for cameras but couldn't see any. He asked Bonnie if she was ready for their first robbery together; the first one as Bonnie and Clyde. He then checked her disguise and she showed him a wool hat to hide her hair under and a smiley-face Halloween mask. She was wearing a black sweatshirt and matching black pants. She also had a change of clothes. She wore a pair of sneakers that Clyde had suggested as they would be doing some running.

He decided to leave the keys in the truck and made sure it was pointing out so they could drive off without any delay. "Okay," he said, "it's about a half-mile walk to our first stop. Most likely, we'll encounter some people on the sidewalks, perhaps walking dogs, and there'll be fairly steady traffic. Let's try not to look directly at the cars or speak with anyone. We just want to blend in."

"But, Clyde, you said we'd get my money first."

"I'll show you where it is, but I can't get it until after dark; I don't want anyone to see me."

As they walked, there was a lot of awkward silence. Clyde finally said, "This is the school where I graduated from. It's kind of amazing I graduated. I wasn't the best student. Only had one teacher I actually liked."

"I bet it was chemistry," Bonnie guessed sarcastically.

"No, no, no, it was actually an English reading class. Teacher's name was McCann. He made the class really fun. I think I was learning something but wasn't aware of it at the time. We read lots of short stories. I can only remember one, a really bizarre story called *"Bartleby, the Scrivener."* McCann did all kinds of crazy things to keep us interested. It never seemed like I was in school when I was in his class."

"You should drop by some time and let him know that."

"Sorry I can't do that. He passed away not long after I graduated. I did visit him at Maine Med just a few weeks before he died. I think I was able to give him the message then that I thought he was the greatest."

"Oh, well I went to Oxford High School and hardly ever went to class. They thought I was autistic, so they didn't force me to do anything. But like you, there was someone who was very special; her name was Eileen. I really wasn't very nice to her most of the time but she was always patient. She's really the only reason I went to school every day. She treated me like the mother I didn't have. She actually cared for me. She read lots of short stories to me. That's how I learned about Bonnie and Clyde. And you know what? Just like your teacher, she passed away shortly after I graduated. I felt guilty that I never thanked her for all the attention she devoted to me."

Just then, the cupola came into view atop the old Greely Institute building. Clyde stopped walking and pointed to the cupola. "That's where I hid your tote bag, up there."

"How'd you get it up there?" asked Bonnie.

"I climbed a ladder then walked up the roof and placed it in the cupola. But if I went up there now, I'm afraid someone will see me so will have to come back after dark."

"Why did you put it up there?"

"Tony said I should hide it in a place where no one would find it. I thought that was the best spot. Kind of like hiding it in plain sight!"

Clyde looked around and saw that the ladder was gone. How was he going to get up there now? He changed the subject and said that he had chosen to rob the public library. They close at two on Saturdays. As it was getting close to two, most of the patrons would be gone.

"But how much money does a library have?" asked Bonnie, somewhat disappointed. She thought robbing a library was moronic.

"Well, that's not the idea. No one who works in a library would ever think they'd be robbed; so they aren't prepared for it and it would make a nice practice for you. Let's make it fun! Besides, it was Tony's idea to do something easy for practice."

"But your truck is a long way away; what are we going to do after the robbery?"

Clyde had it all figured out. "There aren't too many roads out of here so chances are my black truck would be easy to spot. If we leave on foot no one in the library can identify a getaway vehicle. There's a path through the woods out behind the library that comes out on Blanchard Road across the street from an apple orchard. We can go through the orchard and cut over to Main Street; cross right into the schoolyard. Then get the truck and head off toward North Yarmouth and take the back road down to the interstate. Just follow me!"

"Guess I'll have to trust you. Sounds like you've thought this through. Let's go for it. Instead of taking out a book, we'll just take out their cash drawer." Then she stopped when they walked past an old cemetery and asked Clyde, "Hey, do we have a minute to walk into this cemetery?"

"Yeah, I suppose, why?"

"I never met my father. My mother said he died when I was very little. She never liked to talk about it, so I don't really know anything. I believe that some people aren't ready to die or die by surprise like in an accident and their spirits are still out there all around us. They exist in a world somewhere between life and death. Even though technically they're dead, their spirits can still communicate with us. So when I see a cemetery, I try to communicate with the spirits hoping to connect to my dad."

"Okay, we've got about ten minutes. But it sounds kinda weird to me."

As they walked into the cemetery, Bonnie was drawn to a tall monument with a small iron fence around it. "Must have been someone very special," she said, almost in awe. It was the biggest marker in the cemetery and stood right in the middle.

"I think all of the early settlers of the town are buried here," Clyde said, trying to impress her with his bullshit knowledge of the town history.

"Hmm," she observed, "Eliphalet Greely. Born in 1784, died in 1858. That was about 150 years ago!" Then she knelt down, closed her eyes, lowered her head, took a deep breath, then began to whisper, "I am water, I am earth. Life and death leap and bite, bring them close within my sight. I have no fear, come now near."

"What are you doing, what are you saying?" asked Clyde, wondering what the hell she was doing. He found it a little spooky.

"Someone taught me to say this whenever I am in a cemetery if I want to reach out to the spirits."

"Does it work?"

"*Look*! Look, Clyde, look at his stone. This just happened, look at the stone carefully—Greely's profile just appeared: he's looking at us!"

Sure enough, if you looked at the stone closely, you could see his profile. He seemed to be looking up toward the bell tower on the church across the street. You could see the outline of his face, his nose, his chin and his right eye. His head was tilted back slightly. If you stood with your back facing Main Street his profile was very clear. It was as if he was trying to communicate with her.

Clyde was just beginning to tell Bonnie that he was the man whom the school was named after when she whispered, "Look, over there, an old man is watching us."

Clyde looked but didn't see anyone. Bonnie was already heading toward where she saw the old man. "I'm sure I saw something. Looked like a man dressed in a black suit. But as soon as I saw him, he disappeared. He was right next to that grave over there."

Clyde had no doubt now that this girl was really wacko. "I'm sure it was just an apparition," Clyde commented.

"Oh, big word, Mr. Professor," replied Bonnie. "Look, I know what I saw, and it was real. This is where I thought I saw the man. He was standing over the grave of Captain Blanchard who lived about the same time as Greely."

Bonnie continued, "My last name is Blanchard. I could be related to him!"

They left the cemetery and walked quickly toward the library. It was getting close to two o'clock, closing time. Bonnie talked all the way about how exciting it was to see the profile appear on the gravestone. She said she couldn't wait to come back and spend more time in the cemetery. She wanted to learn more about Blanchard to see if she was somehow related.

When they got to the library there was a sign outside that said, "Volunteers needed, free training!" There was always a clever message posted. Clyde looked at Bonnie who was still excited. She was pumped and ready to go. He started putting on his blue gloves and goggles and she began to put her hair up under her wool hat. They nodded at each other and approached the door. Clyde gave the door a good kick which startled everyone inside then walked up to the counter with Bonnie next to him.

"My name is Clyde and this is Bonnie. Someday we're going to be famous and you can say you met us. For now, this is a robbery so hand over all your cash."

A woman in the bookshelves heard what was going on and quietly called the police on her cell phone to report the burglary in progress.

The librarian, a pretty gal named Sally, didn't seem phased at all. Annoyed, if anything. She looked at Clyde and said, "Shhhh, quiet, you must lower you voice, this is a library!" Then she asked, "Do you have a library card?"

"A what?" he whispered.

"A library card. Without a library card, you cannot take anything out of the library."

"Ma'am, this is a robbery. Hand over all your cash, *now*! I don't need a friggin' library card to rob you! What about this don't you understand?"

"Again, sir. No library card, no withdrawal. Now, are you a Cumberland resident? I also don't mean to embarrass you, but you're standing in front of the book-return desk. You really should be at the check-out desk."

"Huh?" asked Clyde.

"Well, I would be happy to help you with an application for a library card. That's the first step. It's procedure, you understand."

At that, Clyde looked around and ordered everyone to lie on the floor. He told Sally to count out loud from ninety-nine to one, then everyone could get up. He said they had a man posted outside, looking through the windows to make sure no one got up too soon. From there, he told Bonnie to follow him and they ran to the front room and then out the front door. There was a loud police siren that was getting close to the library, so Clyde motioned Bonnie to follow him to the other side of the building just in time to hide before the police cruiser arrived. Bonnie slipped and fell on some chestnuts on the ground but got up quickly. During her fall, an ID case fell out of her back pocket which contained her driver's license and bank debit card. The case fell in some leaves close to the front steps.

The policeman blocked the parking lot exit with his cruiser so no one could get out. He got out of the Explorer, leaving it running with the blue lights flashing and ran up to the front door.

Clyde got an idea. "Want to go for a ride?"

He took Bonnie's hand, and they ran toward the cruiser. Clyde jumped in behind the wheel and Bonnie climbed in the passenger side but had hardly closed the door before Clyde had already squealed the tires for a quick getaway.

He told Bonnie to keep her mask and gloves on as the car no doubt had a camera recording everything inside. "This is so cool," he said. "Look at all this cop equipment—it's real cop stuff!" He was very excited.

The blue lights were still on as Clyde zipped up the street toward Cumberland Center. He grabbed the microphone and in a very professional voice called out, "One Adam twelve, one Adam twelve, robbery in progress, requesting backup. It's a 10-80, we're in pursuit. Car 54, where are you?"

The dispatcher interrupted. "Sir, please identify yourself." Clyde made a sharp turn on Blanchard Road, almost rolling the top-heavy Explorer. He dropped the microphone as he needed both hands on the wheel to prevent an accident.

At this, Bonnie grabbed the mic and said, "This is Bonnie and Clyde. Someday we're going to be famous and you can say you once spoke with us!"

The dispatcher started saying something again but Clyde skidded the car up against a farm stand. The blue lights startled the woman inside who appeared to be a teenager.

Bonnie and Clyde got out and this time, Bonnie announced, "I'm Bonnie, and this is Clyde. Someday we're going to be famous, and you can say you met us. But for now, this is a robbery so hand over all your cash."

The girl reached into the cashbox and took out about $70. Bonnie told her to get on the ground and count from ninety-nine to one before she called for help. Then Clyde noticed some whoopie pies on the counter and asked Bonnie if she'd like one.

"Oh, they're from Chipman Farms, not too far from where I live. They're the best ones around," she observed.

So Clyde grabbed a couple and put them in the bag with the cash. The cashier said that for two of them, the total would be $3.98 plus tax.

"What don't you understand about this?" Clyde asked with a raised voice. "This is a hold up, and we're taking the damn whoopie pies along with the cash. Now don't tell anyone what just happened and we won't harm you."

Clyde took Bonnie's hand again and started out behind the farm stand into an apple orchard. He looked back to see the police cruiser that he had just stolen then heard sirens off in the distance. They continued running through the orchard; a worker off in the distance gave them a friendly wave for who knows what reason, then they climbed a fence into someone's backyard. They came out to the corner of Lawn and Maple.

They took off their disguises. Bonnie took off her sweatshirt and pants to reveal a striped shirt and short shorts underneath. She looked like a totally different person. Clyde showed Bonnie where to cross Main Street then follow Village Way to get back to his truck. Said they should go back separately; walking like nothing had happened. Just walking to the school. And if they saw a police car, to hide. So they split up, and Clyde gave Bonnie a head start so they wouldn't be seen together.

So Bonnie headed off to the school entrance and Clyde cut through a restaurant parking lot and over another fence right into the pool area of the school. No one seemed to be around, so he walked briskly to his truck and started it up. He could see Bonnie walking around the corner and drove over to pick her up. When she got in, he asked her to lie down on the front seat so no one would see them together as they'd be looking for a man and woman together. He then drove over to Greely Road then to Route 1 and started toward Portland, being careful to drive the speed limit and give the police absolutely no reason to stop him.

He told Bonnie he couldn't figure out how that police car got to the library so fast and wondered if they had some kind of alarm system like ADT that just required a push button. Regardless he congratulated Bonnie on a job well-done. He said stealing the police car wasn't something he originally planned but thought it was too tempting sitting right out front. "Nice of them to provide a lift for us! I was afraid, however, that I was going to roll it when I made that fast turn onto Blanchard Road—wasn't expecting it to be so top heavy."

"Well, you did take that corner awfully fast." Bonnie was sitting up now in the truck; and Clyde couldn't help checking her out. With those shorts, he couldn't help but stare at her long legs. She could tell he was staring at her, and it made her uncomfortable.

"What's next?" she asked.

"A guy I work with tends a bar on weekends on High Street in South Portland. Thought we could drop by there for a sandwich—my treat."

"Remember," Bonnie added, "I've got killer whoopie pies for dessert."

"Oh, yeah, that was funny when we're robbing the place and the girl said that will be three ninety-eight for the whoopie pies. Did she really think we were going to pay for them with the money we just took?" Then Clyde sat silent for a minute and asked Bonnie how she met Tony.

"Oh, seems like I've known him for a long time. I work nights as a waitress at Lenny's over by Hadlock Field in Portland. Not sure if you know it or not, but Tony comes in two nights a week, same days of the week, same time. Always orders spaghetti and takes half of it home with him. He always seems kind of lonely, almost sad. He's been very sweet. He's an older guy and without ever having a father, I kind of enjoy his company. He seems to fill that void in my life. We've become close friends and I look forward to speaking with him when he comes in. I try to save him the same table, number 4, every time he comes in."

"Lenny's. Hmmm, haven't been there for a long time," replied Clyde. "I have a couple beers with him once or twice a week at the Leaping Fish in the Old Port, and I know he spends weekends at a casino in Connecticut but never really wondered what he did the rest of the week."

"He once confided in me that he had figured a way to embezzle from the bank where he works and I thought that was really cool, that he was so smart to know how to do that without getting caught.

I guess I sort of told him I had always dreamed of how exciting a life in crime must be."

"Forgive me," Clyde asked, "but you don't give me the first impression that you would be interested in being a bank robber. But you seem to be good at it—a natural."

"What do you do for work?" asked Bonnie.

"I haul trash."

"Like a neighborhood door-to-door trash truck?"

"Yup, and we're getting a brand-new one pretty soon. Did you know that being a trash man is one of the five most dangerous jobs in the US? More trash men are killed every year than police and firemen combined!"

"No, never would have guessed," answered Bonnie. "I never hear of a trash man being killed."

"Just not as sensational as when a cop gets killed, I guess."

Just then, they pulled up to Maggie's, a neighborhood bar in South Portland. "Remember, order anything you want and it's on me. But chances are my friend won't charge us."

They walked in and almost instantly, Bonnie felt uncomfortable. The crowd was mostly men, tough-looking, rugged guys and there was a woman tending bar. The music was deafening. Clyde asked if Jason was working and the bartender said he was out back in the kitchen but should be out soon.

"This place has been here a long time, a neighborhood kind of place," explained Clyde.

"It's kind of creepy," whispered Bonnie into Clyde's ear.

Just then, a man came out and hollered over to Clyde, "Hey, Blake, good to see you!" It was Jason who apparently did not know of Blake's alias, Clyde. "How's it going?"

"Living the American dream, Jason, living the dream. Hey, thought I'd stop in for a quick bite to eat and introduce you to my friend, Bonnie."

Jason looked at them in disbelief. There was no way they could be together, no way. "Great to meet you. Can I get you anything?"

"Can I see a menu," asked Bonnie.

"For food, all we serve is hotdogs."

Clyde spoke up, "They're the red ones, the best!"

The thought of a hotdog had no appeal at all to Bonnie. And looking around, she found most of the guys were staring at her. "You know what?" she said. "I'm not really hungry. Nice to meet you, Jason. We got places to go so let's get back on the road." She felt used, like all Clyde wanted to do was show her off to his friend. They left the bar together and headed toward Clyde's truck.

"Not a hotdog lover?" asked Clyde.

"They're disgusting. Do you know what a hotdog is made of?"

"I hope you don't believe all that crap about ground up rats and intestines and stuff..."

"Plus that music was ear-shattering. Why *so* loud?"

"Hey, that was one of the best heavy metal bands out there," answered Clyde. "I'm surprised you didn't like the lyrics."

"Lyrics?" Bonnie was amused. "You're telling me they were actually singing something? Just seemed like a lot of screaming to me."

"Ya, it was a song about eliminating man from the planet and giving it back to the birds and animals. They claim that man has abused his privilege to live on the Earth. Time to give it back to Mother Nature, see if she can do better. Kind of a message to save the planet."

"You're making that up. There's no way that's what they were singing. But why do you think I would like those lyrics? You don't know me. Look into my eyes," Bonnie commanded.

Clyde turned and did as she asked. He began to feel lightheaded. She had him in a trance.

"What do you know about Mother Nature? What made you say that? I'm offended by your sarcastic remark about Mother Nature. What do you know about me?"

"Nothing at all. Sorry, I just met you, but thought you may be the type who is concerned about climate change and all that stuff." Man, he thought this girl was weird. She was scaring him. What did he say that ticked her off like this?

She turned away from him and asked that he take her home. There was silence in the truck. Then, as they pulled onto Sawyer Street, Clyde noticed people going into a theater and he got a crazy idea. "Bonnie, look at the theater across the street. What do you think about robbing the box office? Doubt if they'd ever expect it, doubt if they have security cameras. How 'bout one more before we head home?"

Bonnie looked at the entrance and thought about it for a moment and said, "Let's go for it!"

Clyde parked on the next side street and left the truck running. Bonnie started putting her black clothes back on again and Clyde reminded her to put her blue latex gloves back on. Then he laughed when he realized they would be a bigger show than the one people were going to go see!

They walked about a block to the theater, then he looked at Bonnie and asked, "Ready?"

She nodded her head, they put their masks on and Clyde kicked open the front door. He took a quick look around and estimated about a dozen people in the lobby and a box office to the right. He told Bonnie to go tell the people in the lobby to sit down and he would go to the box office.

Everyone was looking at Bonnie, not knowing what was going on. Then she announced, "We're Bonnie and Clyde. Someday we're going to be famous and you can say you met us. For now, I want everyone to sit on the floor and don't move. This is a robbery."

Sarah was in the crowd and looked at her husband. "Skip, this is part of the show, sit down." Then she looked at the others in the lobby and told them it was part of the show, "Sit down and play along." The others smiled and all sat down on the floor. They were all very excited at how the mystery show was opening.

Meanwhile Clyde walked up to the box office and demanded all the money in the cash drawer.

The clerk shook his head. "Cash drawer is empty, not a single dollar. This show has been sold out for weeks, so we have no cash sales tonight. Whenever Wendy brings her *Murder for Hire* cast here, it is always a sell-out. Can't even give you a couple tickets, sorry, man."

Clyde looked at Bonnie and urged her to follow him out quickly. Then he told the people in the lobby to count to one hundred before getting up. He turned and started out then ran smack right into a guy just coming in. He knocked him into one of the posts that held up the roof over the entrance. Then the man fell over a hedge next to the steps. The man's wife, Marilyn, was upset. "Derry, you okay?" Clyde took off as fast as he could toward his truck.

Derry's first inclination was to chase after him but instead, he merely yelled out, "You better run, kid, you better run and keep running and never look back!" Marilyn examined him to make sure he wasn't hurt. He was a little shook up but otherwise fine but couldn't understand why the guy was wearing ski goggles and so rude. That was until they went inside and learned of the attempted burglary. The box office manager was on the phone to the police and Derry took the phone and added his description and direction that Clyde headed toward. Hopefully they'd catch the bastard. Derry could outrun just about anyone but tonight, he had been asked by the theater manager if he would come in early and take a special seat right on the stage! But if he had known he was a robber, there's no doubt he could have outrun him.

Clyde took some backstreets through the waterfront neighborhood, trying to avoid Broadway as best as he could. Again he told Bonnie to duck beneath the dashboard as police would be looking for a vehicle with a young couple in it. He decided to take Cottage Road out to Route 77 then around to Scarborough and get on the interstate there. But they did not see any police cars and did not hear any sirens. They did see a state police car parked in the median as they approached Exit 10 in Falmouth, but that was it. He took Route 9 on his way to Bonnie's apartment. They talked about robbing the armored car. It really sounded, from what Tony told them, that it would be a piece of cake and they could easily get away with it!

Although Bonnie was disappointed Clyde was not Tony, she was excited and really had enjoyed her crime spree today!

SUNDAY AFTERNOON, LEGION FIELD, FALMOUTH

They were to meet with Ralph at 2:00 p.m. in the right field dugout at the Legion Field baseball park. Tony parked at the library then decided instead to park by Staples where his car would be just one of many rather than all by itself at the library lot. He got there about half past one; he wanted to be the first. He kind of felt like the host. He had also heard on the noon news the rash of robberies Saturday afternoon by a young couple calling themselves Bonnie and Clyde. The news story, however, cast them as somewhat crazy for consistently robbing places where there was no money to steal. It was pointed out that they were not armed and not considered dangerous but most likely still roaming at large in the immediate area.

Before Bonnie left her apartment, Viktoria stopped her and asked who the guy was who picked her up yesterday. Bonnie thought fast and said he was a new guy she worked with. "Kind of a creepy guy. Not my type, not my type at all. He lives in the area so asked if he could give me a ride to work. I don't think he's going to last long though."

Viktoria sighed. She agreed that he was creepy and was not at all impressed. Hopefully she wouldn't see him around anymore. He looked like trouble.

Bonnie arrived at the baseball field next and was glad to see Tony alone. She wanted to tell him she was disappointed in Clyde, was hoping for someone a little more compatible, was really hoping Tony would be Clyde.

When Tony saw her, he stood up and greeted her, "Bonnie, you were just on the news, you're already getting famous!"

"What?" she asked.

"You were on the twelve o'clock television news today. A story of how Bonnie and Clyde robbed a library, a farm stand and a theater. Also theft of a police cruiser! Busy day for you, huh?"

"It was a lot of fun. I liked surprising people; seeing the look on their faces. I liked the power of having people scared and willing to do anything I told them to. I've never had that kind of power in my life."

"How about Clyde, did you two get along okay?"

"Well, I have a lot of confidence in him but robbing a public library, I mean, really? It was almost embarrassing. Don't get me wrong, I enjoyed it and all but if you're going to rob something, then rob something of value."

"I think he wanted to see how you would do, a couple of practice jobs where the chances of getting caught would be slim. And look, you didn't get caught, did you? And you have great publicity now. You're already famous!"

"Well, it just seems a little strange to go from robbing a farm stand of a few dollars to robbing an armored car of a few million." Bonnie seemed frustrated and Tony could sense it.

"Well," Tony paused, "we're all going to work together on this next one. Ralph is going to lead the way to literally open the doors for us on the truck—open the doors to millions of dollars!"

Just then, Clyde seemingly appeared out of nowhere. But he also had a new attitude, a super ego if you will, that he was a hero and couldn't be stopped. "Afternoon, Bonnie, Tony." He looked at Bonnie and asked, "Have fun yesterday?"

Bonnie looked at him with a serious eye-to-eye stare. "Did you bring my tote bag?"

"I did stop there after dropping you off last night, but the ladder to the roof was gone and I couldn't find one on the ground anywhere. Then I thought I'd go back this afternoon and see if there is a fire escape to the roof. I'll get up there somehow."

Bonnie clenched her teeth, and Tony was quick to change the subject. "Clyde, I just watched the news on TV and there was a story about Bonnie and Clyde and your adventures yesterday."

Clyde looked at Bonnie. "See, we're already getting famous!"

"Well," Tony added, "but not in the best way. They kind of made you look foolish by robbing places with no money. They did say they thought you were still in the area though. That you remained at large."

It was now almost two o'clock and no sign of Ralph. They spoke among themselves about the robbery and Tony wanted to make sure they were all in with no hesitations. Bonnie confessed that she was very nervous didn't know what she would be expected to do and was worried what would happen to her if she got caught.

"All reasonable questions. Ralph will have the answers."

Just then they saw Ralph making his away across from the outfield. It kind of looked like a scene from *Field of Dreams*; and this was, in fact, a dream. Ralph spotted them and waved. He was carrying what looked like a small briefcase.

"Sorry to be a little late but to be honest with you, I wanted you all to gather together before I got here to discuss any concerns you may have. Then he introduced himself as one of the drivers for the armored-car company. Bonnie, Clyde, and Tony then introduced themselves. Ralph took a good look at Bonnie and Clyde. They looked very young to him.

"I just heard about you two on the radio and Clyde, I have a question for you. Were you the one who robbed Tony's branch?"

He looked first at Tony, almost to ask permission to answer. "Yes, that was me. But I couldn't have done it without Tony's help."

"And I'll tell you, there's no way you could rob an armored car without inside help either," replied Ralph with a stern tone.

"So here's the deal. Wednesday night, we pick up 11 or 12 million, mostly in currency from the Federal Reserve in Boston. We have to leave there at midnight for the trip back to Maine. People are waiting for us at our garage to begin packaging the money for our Thursday morning bank branch deliveries. The currency we get from the fed is packaged in white canvas bags. Each bag is tied with twine and then crimped tight with a lead seal to secure the bag. Inside each bag is an ID code that is sewn into the bag. The ID has a number similar to a barcode and the tag has a tracking device similar to a GPS. So if you take a bag and put it in the trunk of your car and drive off, they can follow you. So each bag we take will have to have the twine cut and the bundles of currency dumped out, a time-consuming process but very important. Discard the bags after you empty them! Just toss them on the side of the road. Twenty-dollar bills are bundled in stacks of one hundred, making each bundle worth $2,000. They put 100 bundles into each bag, making each bag of twenties worth $200,000. When we load the truck in Boston, I will stack twenty bags of twenties by the rear door into two piles of 10 bags each. This would total 4 million dollars which we'll split four ways, a million dollars each! Each bag weighs twenty-two pounds so you should be able to carry two bags at a time from the truck to your car. Bonnie, it may be best if Tony and Clyde run back and forth with the bags of cash and you stand by the car, cut the bags, then dump the cash into the trunk. Now if our truck idles for five minutes, dispatch is notified. So we have to work fast, very fast."

Clyde interrupted and looked at Tony. "A million bucks! Is that enough to call CG at the investment planning office? Imagine, me working with an investment planner! But why only one million each with so much in the truck?"

"Time is a big factor. You just won't have time to carry all the bags to your car, open them, empty them and cut the GPS tags out. You've got to move really fast, and there just isn't time for more. By taking twenty bags of $200,000 each, it can be done quickly, and you're out of there. I can have the bags stacked by the back door so just have to pull them out and go," responded an annoyed Ralph. "I really think that's the best plan if we don't want to risk getting caught."

Ralph cleared his throat and continued. "We come up the Maine Turnpike then transfer to I-295 in South Portland. We then continue north to Exit 20, Freeport. We take a left on the Desert Road. Five-tenths of a mile, maybe six-tenths, there is a bridge over some railroad tracks. The bridge has guardrails on either side. If you set up some kind of a roadblock there or park your car perpendicular across the street we'll have to stop as we can't turn off the road with those guardrails. We'll be trapped. There are also no streetlights there so it's a perfect spot for the holdup. It will be very dark. Also hardly any traffic at that hour on that road. Now there are two of us in the truck and both of us are armed with handguns. I'm scheduled to be the driver. My partner is fairly new so I am the senior crew member. I will instruct him not to draw his gun and to do as he is instructed. He'll be shittin' his pants so he will listen to me. Don't let on that you know me. Order us both out of the truck and to lay flat on the ground, then instruct me to open the back door and start unloading the bags of cash. I'll pull the twenty bags out and drop them on the ground, then order me to lie flat on the ground again next to my partner.

"As soon as your car is loaded, take off. We will then radio our dispatch to report the robbery and wait for the police to arrive. I will, of course, act nervous and completely surprised. We should arrange a place to meet the next day to divide up the cash."

Tony said he was going to rent a storage container nearby and they could go there right after the robbery to store the cash. He then commented on the cash. "Look," Tony said, "we're each going to have 50,000 $20 bills and every law enforcement group in the northeast is going to be searching for it. Banks have to fill out what is called a Form 104 Currency Transaction Report with all the details on anyone who deposits $10,000 or more in cash. They also have to fill out Suspicious Transaction Reports for anyone who deposits less than $10,000 but the source of the cash seems suspicious. Put the cash in a safe deposit box at a bank or even open up two safe deposit boxes at different banks. So I wouldn't deposit more than $1,500/$2,000 a month into your bank account. Also don't go out and buy a new car with the cash. The car dealer would then have to deposit it and will be questioned as to what customer used cash for a large purchase. Best to take it to the bank in several small trips. Be damn careful. Spend it slowly, make it last!"

"Oh man," exclaimed Clyde. "But this will take forever."

"Yes, but think of it this way. You will never need money again!"

"I plan to quit my job after the robbery," said Ralph. "Continuing on for just a little above minimum wage doesn't make sense. I plan to tell them I just can't get back in the truck after the trauma of the robbery. What are you all thinking of doing after the robbery?"

Tony said he planned to fake his death here then move to Las Vegas using a new identity.

"Fake your death?" asked Bonnie, "How you gonna do that?"

Clyde said he couldn't wait to tell his boss to shove it. He would tell his parents he lost his job and would continue living with them. Perhaps get a part-time job as a bartender or something.

Bonnie said she had decided it would be her last robbery and she'd give up being Bonnie but not sure what to do next. She then looked at Tony hoping he would have the answer, but he didn't respond. No reaction at all. She needed his advice.

The National Sunday Night Weekly News

"Our last news story tonight comes from Portland, Maine where a young couple calling themselves Bonnie and Clyde are on a wild-robbery spree. But the odd thing is they are robbing places with little or no money to steal. They have robbed a town library in Cumberland, a nearby farm stand, a theater box office and Clyde robbed a bank but only asked for a few twenties. An unusual story which we will continue to follow."

"My name is Chester, we appreciate your spending part of your evening with us. From all of us at the *Weekly News*, thanks for watching."

MEANWHILE, IN A TOWN JUST OUTSIDE OF BOSTON, MASSACHUSETTS

"Mom, doesn't Aunt Sally work in a library in Cumberland?" asked Martha.

Her mother was in the kitchen trying to squeeze one more night out of leftovers. "Yes, I think so, why?" In all honesty, she really had no idea. She hadn't kept in touch with her sister-in-law.

"The *Weekly News* just reported that a library in Cumberland, Maine was robbed by a young couple calling themselves Bonnie and Clyde.

'Was anyone hurt?"

"No. Seemed like more of a joke than anything else."

"Well," said her mom, "I'm sure we'll hear about it if it was Aunt Sally.

CLYDE GETS AN UNEXPECTED VISIT

Clyde searched the internet Sunday night for used guns for sale but for the most part, he wasn't comfortable with the ads he saw. Suspicious they could be a trap. Then he looked through an *Uncle Handy's* magazine and found an ad for a used AR-15 machine-gun offered by a licensed gun dealer in Temple, Maine. He called the man and after convincing himself the guy was legit and not an undercover policeman, they agreed to meet Monday afternoon, halfway between North Yarmouth and Temple at a donut shop parking lot in Auburn that is now out of business.

While he was on the phone, he thought he heard a knock on his door. He hung up the phone and looked outside to see a man standing there. He recognized him instantly and let him in. It was Big John.

"How long you been out?" Blake asked.

"About three weeks now," answered Big John. "Not a bad deal, I served three and a half years of a ten-year term. Guess they needed the space. I don't know, but I'm not complaining."

"How'd you find me?" asked Blake.

"Wasn't that hard. Nice place here. You livin' with your folks?"

"Kind of. It's kind of like a duplex and they live on the other side. Hey, they still serving those blueberry muffins?"

"Every morning. Why, you miss them?"

"No way, I'll never eat another one in my life! Is Razor Ray still there?"

"Oh, yeah. He's still got at least five more years before he's out. But remember that big fat guard Arnie? He got cancer and quit. Didn't miss him either. What a mean bastard he was!"

"Like a beer Big John?" Blake asked.

"Sure! Got something to tell you about, something real exciting."

"What's that?" Blake handed Big John a bottle of Molson from his refrigerator.

"Well, listen to this. Until I find a place, I'm living with my mother. An antique dealer came to the house a couple weeks ago to look at an old desk and a couple lamps she has. This guy is connected to some very wealthy people in the area and even overseas. When he found out I just got out of prison for grand larceny, he asked to meet with me. He told me he'd give me fifty grand if I could steal a painting from a house in Falmouth. Am looking for a partner and thought of you. What do you say? I'll split the fifty grand with you!"

Blake looked at him and shook his head no. "Didn't you learn anything in prison? No way do I ever want to go back there again, even for one day, no way. I'm seeing a P.O. (parole officer) now who is keeping a close eye on me and I have a good job. Nope, no thanks. Besides, I'm not a crook. I just stole some construction equipment once, that's all. I don't know anything about breaking into a home and stealing a painting."

"No, listen to me. I've already cased the place. Should be a piece of cake. Probably won't take more than a couple hours and we split fifty grand. Looking at this Tuesday or Wednesday night while the owner of the house sleeps."

At this Blake choked on his beer. Tuesday or Wednesday? He liked Big John and had an incredible urge to tell him about his plans for Wednesday night but didn't breathe a word. They continued to talk for a while and reminisced about times in prison. But when Big John decided there was no way he was going to get Blake to help him, he called it a night and left.

MONDAY MORNING
AT THE BANK

Tony arrived at the bank first and was instantly hit with the fresh-paint smell and the glue used to hold the new carpet down. They had repainted all the lobby walls and replaced all the carpet in the branch. It looked great—you could never tell that just a few days ago the lobby was sprayed with red paint and reeked of tear gas. Kind of amazing they could do all that in just a couple days. It was a very bright sunny day and as Tony was glancing outside, Shannon drove up. She got out of her car and started walking toward the front door, carrying a small box. Tony held the door open for her—not only to let her in but to let some fresh air in as well.

Shannon instantly remarked, "Wow, it's so much brighter with the new paint!" Then she sat the box down on the teller's counter and said she had made everyone a treat to help settle back in after the robbery. Tony opened the lid on the box and looked inside.

"They're cherry fritters with dark chocolate drizzled over them," Shannon explained.

Tony grabbed one quickly, took a bite, then closed his eyes. "Oh my god," he said, "these are truly incredible!"

"Well, you guys are my guinea pigs, I kind of dreamed this up and wanted to see what they would taste like. You really think they're good? I made one for everyone."

"Oh, for sure!"

Cindy came in soon after for the day and Claire would be in later, a ten-to-two shift today. Tony pointed out Shannon's pastries to

Cindy, but she didn't seem interested. "Just had breakfast," she said, "maybe later." She was always so cheerful.

Tony thought the morning would be busy from customers curious after the robbery. But instead, it was dreadfully quiet, the phone didn't even ring. It wasn't until almost ten thirty that the first customers came in. Tony looked up to see two women at Claire's station, both women had on jackets with the Camp OLS logo on the back. It was Kelsey and Linda, codirectors of the summer camp. Before managing the branch in Falmouth, Tony managed a branch in Windham where the camp had their account. The camp was just a short distance away on Sebago Lake and either Kelsey or Linda brought in their deposits regularly. So whenever they would be in the Falmouth area they always made it a point to do their banking business at the Falmouth branch and say hi to Tony.

"What brings you to Falmouth today?" Tony asked them.

"Hi, Tony," they both seemed to say in unison. "One of our summer staff members, Sarah, lives in Cumberland and we're going to meet her for lunch today. In fact, we're going to offer her a full-time job."

"But I thought it was just you two?"

"Well," said Kelsey, "we also have a full-time office staffer. But we were just awarded a government grant to help us become a 'green' summer camp, a camp with zero waste and self-sufficient energy."

"We're even looking at a treatment facility so that we can convert waste water to drinking water!" exclaimed Linda. It was obvious they were both excited about the possibilities.

"Not only is Sarah a summer staff member but she has considerable expertise in this area," added Kelsey.

"Once we accomplish our goals, we can use our camp as a model for others and offer consulting services to help them," Linda explained.

It was quiet in the bank, so Shannon walked around the lobby to tidy things up. There were a couple chairs off to one side of the lobby and the morning paper was spread out on the coffee table. She picked it up to straighten it out and began to read a cover story. The Mannequin Murderer had struck again. This time at a farm stand on

Route 201 in Windham called the Oh My Gourd Farm. An older woman was manning the pumpkin stand and was sitting under an umbrella holding a sign advertising pumpkins for $5. She had been strangled and posed there on the side of the road. She had several pumpkins in her lap. A woman had stopped by with her two children to purchase a couple pumpkins and found the old lady. It was similar to the one before with the woman posed in a lounge chair by the side of the road in Pownal just a couple weeks before. Both had been posed with scarves around their necks to hide the strangulation marks and wearing sunglasses. Shannon summarized the story to the other tellers then commented on how creative this killer is. It appeared that the purpose was to startle people when they realized the body was dead—not so much to kill people. There did not appear to be any connection between this victim and the last one. The only similarities are they were both elderly women living alone.

Report from FBI Forensics

Forensic Report. Subject: Analysis of Falmouth Bank Robbery

*Good images from bank camera showed robber at almost exactly six feet tall. Hat and goggles left nose, cheeks, and jaw exposed.

*Hat was well-worn. Goggles appeared new. High-end goggles, most likely recently purchased from a sporting goods store or ski slope. Not sold in department stores.

*An examination of dark blue coat showed inside of collar a plaid pattern indicating it is a reversible jacket. Sharp crease on left arm indicated it was still quite new. Close look at zipper showed a piece of the string from the price tag remaining. Most likely purchased at department store. Not at a high-end clothing store.

*YKK initials on zipper, a Chinese company that makes 92 percent of the zippers in the world. If you look at the pull on your own zipper, chances are you'll see the YKK initials. So nothing extraordinary. It's an onomatopoetic zipper with a single slider. Used on low-priced budget clothing.

*Films showed he carried the tote bag in his right hand and put the cash into it with his left hand. Also tossed the bomb pack on the floor with his left hand. Conclusive evidence showed him to be left-handed.

*Examination of automobiles used in robbery showed no hairs or fibers, no physical evidence of any kind. Subject left no trace.

CT read the report and immediately sent out a directive to search the films of all department stores within twenty miles of Falmouth to see if they have films of the bank robber purchasing the blue jacket.

THE STORAGE BROTHERS

After work Monday, Tony went to see if he could rent a self-storage unit. He had seen ads on TV for the Storage Brothers. They seemed to be fun to work with, so he decided to see what the deal was. He drove slowly through the main gate to the office. There was only one car in the lot, a '72 Cadillac Eldorado in a somewhat sad shape. He thought to himself that must belong to one of the Storage Brothers. He wasn't quite ready for the greeting he got when he opened the door.

"Hi, welcome to Storage Brothers. I'm Kim and this is Julian. If you can't remember which is which, you can just call either of us KimandJulian. One word, *KimandJulian*."

Then Julian introduced himself. "I'm KimandJulian."

And Kim piped up, "And I'm KimandJulian."

"If you can't tell, we're obnoxious. So obnoxious, we're often referred to as *abnoxious* cause obnoxious just isn't enough. A special word had to be invented to describe us."

"Hey, Kim, I don't see a wedding ring. He must be planning to hide something, perhaps a body?"

"Hey, my name is Ton—"

Tony was interrupted before he could finish. "We don't want to know your name. Everything here is assigned by account numbers. We are praised for our discretion which is very important to our clients. So if you want to hide a body, that's none of our business."

"No, I'm moving," said Tony. "I just need a place to store my furniture for a year or two."

Kim looked at Julian. "Right, of course. We've never heard that one before, have we, Julian?"

Tony was getting irritated and tempted to leave, but there was something kind of corny that he liked about these guys. They obviously enjoyed what they were doing. Plus Kim was wearing a Pasami and Cheese T-shirt. Any fan of Libby's must be okay. What Tony didn't know was that Kim was the lead guitar for the band and without argument the best guitar player this side of the Mississippi! He could transcend the stereotype of what a guitar could do and was often compared to Jimmy Page! And Julian performed the group's vocals with an awesome voice. They would often finish their concerts with an encore performance of the Blues Brothers' "I've Got Everything I Need (almost)" with Julian doing an amazing impression of Elwood Blues. He was almost a dead ringer.

"Okay, here's the deal. You pay us the first month's rent in cash. After that, credit card or check is fine. Miss twelve payments and we turn your stuff over to the state, abandoned property. You have a combination lock that has a password that only you know. There is also a security fence around the property that also requires a password so you can have access 24-7. The password is 'Galveston' but don't tell anyone. Every storage unit has surveillance cameras recording all the comings and goings in case someone tries to break into your unit. You can store anything in there, and I do mean anything."

"As long as it fits," added Kim.

Tony agreed to all the details and signed a contract. He also couldn't wait to get out of there. On his way out. he complimented Kim on his T-shirt.

"Oh, so you've heard of us," replied Kim.

"Yeah, we're both in the band."

"No kidding. I know Libby from the Leaping Fish."

"Libby is an amazing drummer." Julian jumped in. "Did she tell you what she has lined up for us?"

"We're flying out soon for a recording session at the Les Paul Studio in California. He developed a revolutionary overdubbing technique. With the sound-over-sound multitracking, it will sound unbelievable. It will sound like there are two Libbys playing the drums! It will give us a new ambient electronic sound. Way cool."

"But didn't Les Paul pass away some time ago?" asked Tony.

"About ten years ago. But his recording studio is still going strong. The sonic textures manipulate sound like nothing you've ever heard before. It's going to be very cool when it's finished. Can't wait!" said Julian.

Then Kim added, "But do you know what the coolest thing is?"

"Ah, no," answered Tony.

"She's been talking with Apple about putting our song on voice commerce. People will be able to just ask their HomePod to play our song and it will! Libby is really taking the band to new levels. We'll be a nationwide band soon!"

"Oh man, good luck with that. I'm anxious to hear it." At that, Tony headed for the door.

"We also have a new agent: ever hear of Rocco Mars Productions?" asked Julian.

"Sorry, can't say I have," replied Tony.

"Well, he's very aggressive and can take us to places we've only dreamed of!"

"Hey, Tony, a quick joke before you leave." Kim jumped in. "Two men walk into a bar and order a clown for dinner. But after a couple minutes, one man looks at the other and asks, does this taste funny to you?"

They showed Tony a container; he signed the papers and paid the first month's lease payment.

After he drove out, Kim looked at Julian. "Did you notice his beady little eyes. He's definitely planning to use this for some illegal purpose."

"Oh, no doubt," Julian agreed. "But then again, they all do."

Northeast Guns and Ammo

When Clyde found the old donut place in Auburn, he noticed a fairly nice Ford van in the lot with "Northeast Guns and Ammo" painted on the side. This helped ease his suspicions. The cops wouldn't go to that much trouble. Standing next to the van was a fairly rugged guy with a beard. He came over to Clyde and shook his hand with a very firm handshake. "You're early," he said. "I'm Ben, brought some other stock with me for you to look over as well."

"You're even earlier," said Clyde. "Nice to meet you. I'm anxious to see what you have."

As Ben was getting out the AR-15, Clyde noticed what looked like an Uzi. "S'cuse me, sir, but is that an Uzi?"

"Yes, and I could give you a good deal on it. For a submachine-gun, see how light it is. I don't know how much you know about them, but it's made in Israel and was used by their assault forces. Only one and a half feet long and lightweight, perfect for quick use. A favorite of our Secret Service. You can see it's an open-bolt weapon. It can fire 600 rounds per minute. It's so lethal and so small, it's nicknamed *a machine pistol.*"

Clyde asked if it was in good working condition.

"I have a range out behind my shop," replied Ben, "and just tested this out last weekend. She's a beauty, not much of a kick to her. No, I wouldn't shit ya, it's one fine item."

Clyde noticed a pistol in the back of the van and asked if he could see that too.

"This one? This is a 9mm Glock G-43 pistol—the preferred handgun by law enforcement across the country. In fact, it is used by 65 percent of the cops and is also great if you need a concealed carry.

Nice grip fits all hand sizes and has a six-round magazine. Cops are real comfortable having this between them and the problem! Tell you what, you can take both the Uzi and the Glock for $999. What do you think?"

Clyde looked at him. "If you take cash, it's a deal!"

"Good for you. By the way, do you carry?" asked the dealer.

"No."

"You should, everybody should. Second Amendment right, you know. Better get your permit before they take it away from you!"

Late Monday Night, at a Falmouth Foreside Oceanfront Estate

Even though there was only a sliver of the moon, it seemed fairly light out for quarter past three in the morning. A dark figure was moving slowly in the yard, casting just a minimal shadow. He had been observing the house and watched as they turned the lights out from their second-floor bedroom, just about 10:00 p.m. He waited patiently until he was confident this was the time. He crept up to the back porch and paused to look out over the water to admire their view. He was impressed that he could put all his weight on the floor without any creaks. He had a light strapped around his forehead, similar to the ones joggers use, which he turned on just as he was getting to the porch door. There was a window on the door. He planned to break the window then reach in and open the door. This, no doubt, would wake them up, so he would have to move very quickly.

But back in burglary 101, he learned to try the doorknob first and guess what—it wasn't locked. Before going in, he prepared himself to be greeted by their German shepherd. He had observed it when he cased the place out by pretending he was with the gas company and needed to take a quick air sample from inside the house to make sure there weren't any gas leaks. He gave the man the gas company's phone number which the man did call (the number was phony and was answered by his girlfriend who assured the wealthy entrepreneur that the service man was legit and shouldn't even be there five minutes). So he pulled out a juicy extra thick steak, opened the door and proceeded quietly into the house. Sure enough, he was met within seconds by the dog who started growling but quieted down in no time when given the steak. So with the dog preoccupied, the man shined a flashlight over the fireplace mantle and there she was—a priceless Renoir.

He reached up with both hands to slowly remove it, but it seemed glued to the wall. He gave it a jerk and not only did it come off, but it set off an ear-piercing alarm. He tossed a smoke bomb on the floor and hurried back to the door, stepping over the dog (who had already passed away from trying to eat the steak which was filled with small sharp pieces of glass). Before going out the door, he tossed a card on the floor that said, "We'll take good care of it." It was signed by Bonnie and Clyde. The man made his way down to the dock and climbed into a dinghy that would take him out to a boat that he could hide in. As he climbed into the Boston Whaler, he could see several lights on in the house. The alarm was still sounding, so he started up the boat (they wouldn't be able to hear the noise) and slowly cruised over to Long Island. His planning paid off; it was so easy. He couldn't believe the door was left unlocked!

Police were quick to respond. Falmouth had a unit at the Foreside Fire Station just up the street and a state police unit was observing traffic from a median strip crossing near Falmouth Exit 10. They found the home owner to be very distraught but not about the stolen painting (it's insured)—but the bastard who killed his dog. "If I ever catch him, I'll serve him the same dinner he served my Ranger!"

It wasn't for about forty-five minutes before a Falmouth detective found the note from Bonnie and Clyde on the floor and by that time, there were probably half a dozen cops in and around the house. Once he saw the note, he called the Falmouth police chief who said he'd be right over. The chief called CT before he left his house to let him know that he was right, his poster boy was a pro and was testing them out before pulling off the big one.

A tracking dog was brought in and was able to find a trail that led him down to the dock. And that's where the trail ended.

Tuesday Night at the Leaping Fish

The art robbery filled the news on radio and television state-wide and even on national cable news. Tony couldn't imagine Bonnie and Clyde would do this and would even do it without letting him know first. Tony was pissed; it was such a huge risk just before their big heist. But on the other hand, he gained much more confidence in Clyde's abilities.

Tony took a seat at an empty table at the Leaping Fish. Libby was waiting on another customer, so he gazed out the window to look for Clyde but also to watch the people going by. He was kind of lost in thought then looked over at Libby behind the bar. When she looked over his way, he waved to get her attention and she pointed at his table. He turned and was surprised to see a cold pint of beer waiting for him. She must have served it while he was looking out the window. He looked back at her and gave her the thumbs up. He watched her for a while trying to imagine her as a member of a well-known band. Who would have known? He was anxious to see her play at the Garden. Tony had recently purchased one of her CDs and loved to listen to the drum solos. It was a CD titled *Door to Infinity*. She was wearing a T-shirt that promoted Zildjian Cymbals, illustrated with an amazing drum set.

Finally Clyde walked in with a big smile. Before sitting down, he leaned over to Tony and asked, "Did you hear the news about the art theft?"

"Clyde, tell me, what the hell were you thinking?"

"Sorry to disappoint you, but if the truth be known, it wasn't me."

"What?"

"Whoever he was or whoever they were, they pinned it on us to throw off the cops. And you know what? I hope they get caught!"

"Oh man, I have to think about this one. Didn't that happen to you once before?"

"Well, sort of. I once stole some construction equipment and got caught. But there had been some other equipment robberies in the area that the police hadn't solved, so they pinned them all on me. Officers got to close the case and look good in the community. And I paid the price with a nice jail term. But that was the cops pinning the other robberies on me. Last night was another burglar setting me up for his theft. I'm still seeing a P.O. (parole officer) once a week. You can't win."

Then Tony asked, "Did you share with him your plans for tomorrow night?"

Clyde laughed. "The P.O.? No, guess I haven't asked him for his opinion. But hey, I have a gift for you. I was able to pick up an Uzi submachine-gun for you."

"What?"

"I found it listed by a dealer and bought it yesterday afternoon. It's fairly small but will make you look like something out of the movies. I picked up a pistol for myself, so we're going to look wicked cool. I parked next to you on Church Street so will give it to you when we leave."

"Man," said Tony, "I was going to get a cheap BB gun. So it sounds like you're ready to go!"

Clyde looked at Tony. "All systems go, man, all systems go!"

LATER AT LENNY'S

Tony dropped by Lenny's on his way home just to check in on Bonnie. She wasn't expecting him but as it turned out, his favorite table—number 4—was open, so he walked down and took a seat. She was picking up an order and acknowledged him. But rather than the usual smile, she looked sullen. Something told him something was wrong.

He fumbled through the menu without really looking at anything; he was getting very nervous. Finally she came over and sat down next to him. Before he could say anything, she started whispering.

"Tony," I'm getting really, really scared. Ralph told us this could be the biggest robbery in the history of the state of Maine and that the police won't stop until they solve the crime. You're leaving for Las Vegas and I have nowhere to hide. I worked in the senior home and at the bank without any disguise and there must be tons of pictures of me while I was working at the bank. I identified myself as Bonnie at both places. I don't mean to sound vain, but I have a very distinctive look. I won't be able to work here anymore and if any of the photos of me are publicized, my landlady will be able to spot me in a second. Tony, you got me into this. I trusted you. I don't want to continue with Clyde, just don't think we make good partners. Tony, I've known you for a while now and have grown to like you, I mean like you a lot. Tony, you have to take me with you to Las Vegas."

Tony did not see this coming. He just looked at her, not knowing what to do or say. Most guys wouldn't hesitate, but he wasn't sure he wanted her around him all the time—perhaps even the rest of his life.

"Tony, let me put it this way. If the police catch me or should I say, when they catch me, they will put pressure on me to tell them everything I know, and I'm afraid they'll get it out of me—everything I know about you. Tony, you have no choice but to take me with you to Las Vegas."

Tony took a deep breath. She was literally sitting against him. He looked into her eyes; she was so beautiful and those eyes so hypnotic. "I think I understand," is all he said.

Bonnie stood up and said she had to get back to work then walked off, obviously upset that he didn't openly embrace the idea of her going with him. Tony felt bad but really didn't know what to tell her. He had to think this one over.

Bonnie went over to another waitress and asked her to cover while she went to the ladies' room. Sarah was an amazing waitress and had a memory for what customers regularly ordered. A man had just sat down at the counter, and she asked him if he wanted the usual: two pancakes, blueberries, and bacon instead of sausage and eggs scrambled. The customer nodded his head and smiled. She did this all shift.

Bonnie went into the ladies' room, bunched up a few paper towels, and threw them at her reflection in the mirror. She didn't know whether to lose her temper or break down and cry. How could Tony just sit there and not say yes or no? If he didn't take her with him—well, she couldn't think what would happen. She sat down on the floor with her back against the wall and began to sob quietly with her eyes closed.

Tony left the restaurant quietly. He really hadn't thought much about what would happen to her. Clyde would be okay, but Bonnie?

A Restless Tuesday Night

Tony couldn't sleep. The armored-car robbery was now only twenty-four hours away. He kept thinking about Bonnie. She was right. Once those checks came back, the bank could see she cashed them, then to find out there wasn't even a person named Bonnie employed by the bank! If they asked Tony about her, he could fudge his way through it by saying he thought she was sent from the main office. Then when they looked at her application, they could see it was all phony. And they would have photos of her. Lots of photos from the time she was there. If they publicized them—TV, newspapers, etc., lots of people would recognize her. Customers at the bank, the bank tellers, customers at Lennie's, residents at the senior housing, her landlord, etc. There is no way she can stay in the area and if she does get caught, she might rat on Tony in exchange for a lighter sentence. Most guys wouldn't hesitate to take a girl that looked like her with them.

Of course in Las Vegas, she would go back to being Acadia and could cut her hair to alter her looks somewhat. Plus she comes with a million bucks. She could easily get a job as a show girl or perhaps a high-class call girl! So yes, he decided he'd take her with him. He had no choice. He had to.

He didn't worry too much about Clyde. He should be able to pull this off with ease and hopefully won't do anything foolish with the cash. Even if the police caught him somehow he wouldn't tell. Clyde doesn't really even know who Bonnie is but does know where she lives.

Ralph seemed to have thought this through. An ambush on a back road, armed robbery, just pull out a fraction of the cash in the truck, then take off. Cash bags are trackable so felt the crooks would be apprehended within minutes. Just worried about his own personal safety. Robbers were disguised so couldn't identify them or even how many there were. Too dark for much detail. No, Ralph isn't much to worry about.

But what had he done? This wasn't a game anymore. If caught, they'd all go to jail for a long time. If only one of them got caught but broke down and identified Tony—they knew my plan to move to Las Vegas. Could the police find me there?

Then he started to sweat. Maybe he should call it off. But it would still leave Bonnie vulnerable to getting caught for the stolen checks. How could he protect her?

Clyde was having a tough time falling asleep. He was about to take part in the biggest cash robbery in the history of the state of Maine, and he was working with three completely inexperienced people. Ralph knew his job, the security measures on the truck, and how to overcome them but was he really going to be able to convince his partner that it was only a drill? Bonnie had absolutely no experience except that she had some enthusiasm for being a famous robber. Tony was a nice guy, a friend, but a thief? Not so fast. He didn't seem like a real aggressive type—not mean enough to be a robber. Not for something like this. The FBI would be all over this until the case was solved. If just one of them was suspected, it wouldn't take much for them to force a confession and turn them all in.

Tipping off the police in exchange for immunity from prosecution may be the way to go.

WEDNESDAY MORNING, 7:55 A.M.

A phone call to the Freeport Police Department was forwarded to Chief Doyon on a recorded line. The caller claims to have knowledge of a crime to be committed in Freeport tonight and will only give the chief the details if a deal could be made. The chief invites the caller to meet with him as soon as possible.

Chief Doyon was new to Freeport, having come from a lifelong law enforcement career in the Bucksport, Maine area. He was very much a hands-on, old-school cop, getting out on a patrol for an hour or two every day and being visible at most community events including high-school sports and drama. He treated the patrolmen more as brothers than subordinates. He was well-respected for his good judgement. Crime in Freeport was almost nonexistent—limited pretty much to an occasional domestic disturbance and a shoplifter at the outlets. Numerous accidents and traffic violations on the interstate that went through town, but those came under the jurisdiction of the state police.

The informant arrived at 9:07 a.m. Chief Doyon promised complete confidentiality. The chief was given a quick summary of the plan before going into more detail. The chief realized that a lot of work would have to be done quickly in order to prepare for this. The informant was visibly nervous but credible. The chief didn't make any promises of immunity but from his experience, convinced the source that most likely prosecution, if any, would be minimal. The robbery was planned for 2:00 a.m. on the Desert Road, just off the I-295 Exit 20.

The informant left, and the chief sat back for a minute and closed his eyes, then picked up the phone and called the FBI regional office in Portland.

It didn't take long for the message to go up through the ranks all the way to CT. He was in the middle of a briefing on a surveillance assignment, investigating rumors of smuggling going on with containers coming in from the Mediterranean. Word has it that a lot of stolen weapons were coming into Boston Harbor. CT didn't want to take the call at first, but his instincts told him he should. He was glad he did! He immediately called his meeting to an end so he could call Freeport and then get in his car and book it to Maine.

CT requested a listing of all the resources Freeport had available. In addition to the standard things a small-town police force had Doyon mentioned that nearby Brunswick had a military-armored Humvee (a High Mobility Multipurpose Wheeled Vehicle). CT asked if there was nearby helicopter available equipped with search lights. The forestry service did have a helicopter, but it was out of service. The state police had a fixed-wing aircraft, but that wasn't what CT had in mind.

Doyon had made arrangements with a private school on the Desert Road to use their community hall as a communications center. CT asked to set up a briefing there at 5:30 p.m. with representatives from Freeport PD and the state police. In addition, CT had requested twenty-five members of the FBI's special forces tactical team including one on-scene commander, highly trained men and women who would position themselves at the location of where the robbery was to occur. They would have advanced weaponry with enough firepower to stop a small army. They would wear suits that could absorb bullet fire and they'd be wearing night-vision goggles. There would be twenty men and five women comprising the team.

CT's office called and had a recording of the conversation between the informant and the Freeport police chief. CT put his phone on speaker and listened to a person who you could tell was very nervous. Doyon was very skilled in the questions he asked and how he led the informant to reveal much more information than was planned. But what caught CT's attention were the names of those involved: three men and a woman named Bonnie.

There was the armored-car driver, Ralph, then Tony, Clyde, and Bonnie. Clyde and Bonnie. Bonnie and Clyde! Then it hit him. Could Bonnie be the same woman as the bank teller? Was she in on it and if so, why didn't Clyde choose her to rob from so he could get away with much more money? She was the one who said she was so scared she pissed herself. That bitch! What an actress? The branch manager's name was Tony. So you had Tony the branch manager, Bonnie a teller, and Clyde the robber. No wonder it went off as smooth as it did. No wonder Clyde had made it look so easy, so professional!

CT immediately pulled over and sent an email to the Boston office. He wanted them to contact the bank and get the full names of Tony and Bonnie then run them through the NCIC records (National Criminal Information Center).

Meanwhile CT had received two emails. The Freeport chief had confirmed that Brunswick PD would send their armored Humvee. The state police would be sending their mobile command post to coordinate communications between the departments and agencies, and the Massachusetts state police had replied that they could send up their stealth helicopter.

The helicopter was a prototype Sikorsky built for the military. The Comanche has a top speed of 201 miles per hour with composite rotors that made it almost silent. The stealth technology made it almost impossible to be picked up on radar. It could carry some really badass weapons, making it one of the most lethal choppers in the sky. The government cancelled the RAH-66 program after only a few were made. One was sent to Boston to help search for the Boston Marathon bomber and was left with the Massachusetts state police. But CT wanted it for its search lights and almost silent presence. Looking at Google Earth, he could see there was a field where the copter could land. Just need to make sure the ground is dry so that it wouldn't sink into the mud when it landed.

As CT drove to Freeport, he made notes. He would want a state police unit standing by at the York Toll, Mile 32 median, I-295 medians at Mile 9, 16, and 20. Also to block northbound Exit 20 and southbound Exit 20. One to block roads off of Desert Road, Hunter Road, and Campus Drive.

Freeport chief texted that the director says he will have school cleared by 4:30 p.m., and there will be a caretaker to let everyone in to the community hall. Director wants to know if they can proceed with school tomorrow morning as scheduled or if FBI sees need to continue using it as a command center.

It wasn't much longer before CT pulled into the Freeport Police Headquarters. Two policemen came out to greet him; they had never seen a cruiser like the one CT was driving. It was called a police federal sport cruiser, a high-speed interceptor built on a Porsche 911 Turbo. Complete with a full set of blue LED visor lights and hide-away strobes with a one-hundred-watt phaser siren.

"If I join the Feds, do I get a car like this?" asked one of the cops.

"All you have to do is confiscate one in a drug raid and have it modified to police interceptor specs," answered CT

"It must go like hell!"

"Boston to Freeport in less than an hour," joked CT. "Just kidding, but it was one fast little ride!"

CUMBERLAND PUBLIC LIBRARY

As part of the opening procedure Wednesday, one of the librarians emptied the night drop. There were quite a few books that had been returned plus a wallet with a sticky note on it. A man from public works found it while raking the lawn Monday and placed it in the night drop. The wallet contained a driver's license issued to Acadia Blanchard of Oxford, Maine, as well as a debit card and $21 in cash. No one seemed to recognize the name, so the director decided to hold it in his top desk drawer for a few days and if no one calls, he would mail it to her.

8:45 A.M. AT THE BANK

Tony did not know how to reach Bonnie, so he called Lenny's. Sarah answered the phone, and he asked if he could leave a message for Bonnie; even more important, could she forward a message to her at her home? Then he realized they know her as Cady.

"Who is this?" Sarah asked.

"My name is Tony, I'm a regular. Cady knows me."

"Are you the one who came in yesterday afternoon?"

"Yes, I saw her yesterday."

"I'm not so sure she wants to speak with you," Sarah replied.

"I understand, but I think she will like this message. Please let her know she's welcome to join me this weekend and if she has any questions, she can call me today at the bank. Tell her she can start packing her bags."

"Okay, if you're sure. We have her cell phone number, so I will call her and pass on your message. It was Tony, right?" asked Sarah.

"Yes. So important you reach her this morning. Should clear things up between us. Thanks *so* much!" Tony hung up and hoped she'd get the message.

CHIEF DOYON, FREEPORT POLICE DEPARTMENT

Chief Doyon was very cordial and had a cup of coffee ready as soon as CT sat down in his office. He had a friendly appearance. CT's first impression was that he was also a tough cop and had been tested on many occasions. He was also very methodical and asked questions almost like he was following an outline. He was able to compartmentalize the task at hand. His concentration was 100 percent. He also had a very dry sense of humor. CT instantly liked him and thought that he could use him in the future as a Maine contact. This all decided in the first few minutes.

Chief Doyon immediately pledged that he would assist CT in any way possible with as much manpower and resources as possible.

CT began by giving a description of Bonnie and Clyde and how much he wanted to nail these kids. Coincidentally a call just came in from CT's office with an update on Bonnie and Tony.

"I have good news and bad, CT, about what I found out from the bank on Tony and Bonnie."

"Go ahead, good news first, please."

"Tony has been employed at the bank for seven years, the past three as manager of the Falmouth office. A somewhat average employee, lacks aggressiveness. Prior to joining the bank, he was a car salesman. Not involved in any community organizations except for the Falmouth chapter of the Chamber of Commerce. Drives a 2016 navy-blue Subaru. Resides in Portland. Minor infractions on driving record. No criminal history."

"Okay," replied CT, "what did you get on Bonnie? I suspect that's the bad news."

"Yes, indeed. The bank has no record of a Bonnie working at the Falmouth branch or any Bonnie for that matter as a teller. I asked them not to call the Falmouth branch to ask who she was, did not want to raise suspicions."

"So who was she?" CT hung up the phone. That little bitch pouted and said she was *so* scared during the robbery she wet her pants. And she was in on it all the time. And Tony organized the whole thing. He planted her there without the bank knowing. Clyde was probably supposed to rob her. As a teller, she could have loaded up her cash drawer and given him most of the cash in the bank. So why didn't he?

So why did Tony orchestrate a robbery on his own bank? With a clean record—no criminal history? Why was he suddenly willing to risk it all? But you know what they say? *"Beware the banker, Beware the banker!"*

CT turned back to Chief Doyon. "So we have four people involved that I know of. From your information and mine, we have the armored-car courier Ralph, a bank branch manager, midthirties, no criminal history, a trash-truck driver, late twenties, Clyde, and an early twenties woman who goes by the name of Bonnie. Bank has no record of a Bonnie working at the Falmouth branch. Looks like the manager is the one who has planned this out. The biggest cash robbery in the history of the state of Maine planned by a complete amateur. Boy, I can't wait to get my hands on these people and find out just who they think they are!"

"Come on." Motioned the chief. "Let me give you a tour of the area and the layout of the land." Then the chief looked out the window at the parking lot and walked down the hallway to a wall where the keys to the vehicles were kept. He looked at the hook for cruiser 307, but the hook was empty, even though the car was parked right outside.

"Anyone know where the keys are to 307?" asked the chief to no one in particular.

A voice came from a locker room. "They're in the car."

The chief, somewhat embarrassed, answered, "Keys are never to be left in an unattended vehicle. Find out who did this, put a note on my desk, and I'll be sure to assign him to chaperone the next middle-school dance!"

They both walked out to the cruiser and sure enough, the keys were in the ignition. "Why don't we just put up a sign and let everyone know that the cars are here for the taking?"

CT felt bad for the chief. He obviously wanted everything to go professionally.

"You know," added the chief, "these new patrolmen come out of the academy and think they know everything. I treat them just like I would bring home a new puppy. I give them lots of love, and how do they repay me? They piss all over my floor."

CT was interrupted by a call from Katie. "Have been reviewing the report from the art theft."

"Go ahead, what do you think?" asked CT

"I'd bet my bottom dollar this wasn't your Bonnie and Clyde. Doesn't fit their profile at all. Can give you more thoughts when you have some time?"

"That was kind of my gut reaction. But am on to something big they have planned for tonight. Talk to you in the next day or two," responded CT

As they pulled out onto Main Street, the Freeport chief pointed out a sandwich shop across the street. "If you or your men need a quick bite to eat, I wouldn't hesitate sending them over there."

CT asked Doyon for a little background. The chief replied that he had begun as a security guard at a paper mill and after a few years attended the Maine Criminal Justice Academy. He then got a job as a patrolman in a fairly quiet midcoast town then was promoted to detective. From there, he continued up the ranks then was contacted to see if he'd be interested in the chief position in Freeport. He had built up a reputation for community policing where the police are very visible in the town and the schools. Apparently Freeport wanted more police presence in the area.

CT was asked about his background, and Doyon was surprised to learn that CT was from Maine. "My father loved to hunt and taught me a lot about the woods. I wanted somehow to be able to make a living protecting the forests and eventually became a game warden. I worked in the western Maine mountains and broke up many poachers as well as smugglers running stuff into Maine from Canada. Conducted a lot of searches for missing persons lost in the woods. The warden service was offered a couple slots in the FBI training school at Quantico and they submitted my name for a position. Quantico to the FBI is like Parris Island is to the marines. It is one very tough school. I loved the training and was able to transfer my skills from the woods to the streets. The FBI offered me a job, and I took it, eventually being transferred to Boston to head up the New England office. Been there ever since.

They then drove by Exit 20 off I-295, and the chief explained the robbery location would only be one-half mile away. He pulled into the Maine DOT maintenance facility where the robbers intended to hide until they heard the armored car was nearing the exit. CT made note of the buildings and heavy equipment parked in the lot. From there, it was just a short distance to the planned robbery site. There was a bridge over a railroad line with heavy guardrails on either side. The robbery would take place just after the bridge as the road sloped down. This would make it possible for them to block the road with their car and the armored car wouldn't see them until they were right on top of them. There was a yellow sign that warned of an intersection 500 feet ahead. This is where the robbers would stop the armored car. They pulled over and got out to look around. CT noted his agents could take a position across the street and hide behind the guardrail and also take advantage of a clump of thick trees.

From there, they proceeded a little further up the street to the private school. The chief noted that the population along the road included two families that could be potential hostages. He offered to post officers in front of those homes. School was in session, and the appearance of a police car drew some interest from students outside on recess.

The Chief explained that the New Harmony Academy attracted the brightest and most talented students. It had a reputation of harder to get into than Harvard!

"Why's that?", asked C.T.

"It's an environmental school where the students work together trying to come up with solutions to save the planet."

"Like global warning?"

"Ya, they're inspired by the respect for Mother Nature."

They parked the cruiser and got out. It was now almost 11:30 a.m. The chief pointed over to the high-school building and the field that he thought would be a good landing spot for the helicopter. CT paused as he watched several birds flying overhead, then he looked at the chief and said he could sense two men coming toward them. The chief looked around and didn't see anyone, then saw two men walking around one of the buildings. He asked CT how he was able to tell the two men were coming even though they were hidden behind one of the buildings.

"I had a good teacher," CT replied.

The two men approached and greeted them with big smiles. The chief introduced them to CT as the director and caretaker of the school. Their smiles immediately disappeared when CT spoke. CT stood 6'4" with a muscular frame. With an attempt to intimidate them, he looked each one directly in the eye. He then introduced himself as the field director of the Boston FBI office and thanked them for their cooperation. He stressed that the FBI operation was based on insider information and that their presence must be kept a very close secret. "No one, I mean no one, can know that we are here tonight!"

CT was effective. Both men nodded that they would not breathe a word. "Now we need this school completely evacuated by 16:30 today. Completely, no exceptions. Is that possible?"

The caretaker pointed out that one teacher lived upstairs in one of the school's buildings across the street. "Lady Athena."

"You'll have to put her up in a local hotel tonight. Also buy her a nice dinner in town. Don't worry, we'll reimburse you as well as make it worth your while for us to use the school tonight. If all goes well, we'll be out of here by daybreak so you can operate as normal tomorrow. The teacher can come back any time after 6:00 a.m. And if all goes well, you should be able to learn why we're here tonight on tomorrow's morning news!"

"Now we have a helicopter coming, so I would like to take a walk over and look at the condition of the field. I understand this is the high-school building?" asked CT.

"Yes," replied the director. "It's our newest building."

They walked out into the middle of the field. About three acres, fairly smooth, recently mowed, dry soil. Should be perfect. "We'll set up a compass rose and place a flare at the south, east, and west points, about a hundred feet apart. At the northern point, we'll place two flares, each about six feet apart. The pilot will use those to guide his way down. Hopefully it won't attract too much attention from the neighbors."

Then the chief asked the director, "Do you have anyone in community hall right now?"

The director looked at his watch, gazed over at community hall and said, "No, it should be dark right now."

"Then let's head over and take a look," suggested the chief.

As they walked in, they passed a couple students carrying musical instruments but for the most part, they went unnoticed. One young student was struggling with a heavy cello case. They entered the dark space, and CT gazed around until the caretaker flipped on the light switch.

It was like an auditorium with a stage; a capacious space well-suited for their use. "This is perfect," commented CT. "Do you have any chairs you can set up?"

"Yes, sir," replied the caretaker. "How many should I set up for you?"

"Oh, let's say about forty or fifty. And half a dozen tables if you can. We'll need a couple for the caterer and a couple for gear. Bathrooms?"

"Yes, right outside the door on the left."

"Okay, this is a perfect setup for us. Thank you so much for your cooperation! So if you can have the school completely evacuated by 16:30, we'll begin arriving for the evening at 17:00." Then CT looked at the caretaker and asked him for a cell phone number in case something came up. CT reminded them once again that they had to keep this a tight secret; not a word to anyone.

The four men shook hands, then the chief and CT went back to his cruiser. They drove out of the school lot slowly then continued west on Desert Road to further familiarize themselves with the road.

They stopped at the corner of Webster Road then turned back to the school. CT commented that the Freeport police should set up a spike mat closer to Campus Drive. In addition to the spike mat, they should block the road with cruisers.

Back at Freeport Police Headquarters, they offered the conference room to CT for his use for the afternoon.

12:10 P.M., FALMOUTH BANK BRANCH

A navy-blue Crown Victoria pulled into the bank parking lot and parked within inches of the passenger side of Tony's car. The driver opened his briefcase and took out a small box about the size of a cell phone. It was a vehicle tracking device or more specifically the Silver Cloud Model 20 GPS tracker. He switched it to "Active" and waited briefly for the green light to come on. Then he got out of his car and, very subtlely, stuck it on the inside of the right rear wheel of Tony's car. It had a very strong magnetic attachment. The device would allow the FBI to know where Tony's car was located at all times.

The man, an FBI agent from the bureau's Portland office on Middle Street, then took off his sunglasses and walked into the branch. As soon as he entered the branch, Claire asked if she could help him. He asked Claire if he could speak to someone about a car loan. Claire told him to wait just a sec while she called Tony then she sent him into Tony's office. She watched him, or perhaps stared at him, while he walked across the lobby. He was very muscular and was dressed in very expensive tight-fitting clothes. You could tell he was proud of his body. As he entered Tony's office, Claire looked at the other two tellers then commented, "Did you see that guy?"

The man introduced himself and shook Tony's hand. While shaking hands, he stared hard into Tony's eyes. He couldn't help but wonder if this was really the man who was the mastermind behind the attempt tonight on the biggest armored-car robbery in Maine history.

"I'm new to the area and just moved here with my wife and daughter. My daughter recently turned twenty-two, and I told her I would help cosign a loan for her so she can buy a car. Would you be the one to speak with?"

"Yes. My name is Tony, branch manager. Does your daughter have a job?"

"She's going to be starting a new job soon as a dental hygienist. She'll have a good income but no track record yet. That's why I'd like to cosign for her."

"You are aware, I imagine, that if she stops making payments, they become your responsibility?"

"Yes, sir. Do you have an application I can take home with me and bring back in a couple days?"

"Sure, I'll attach my business card to it so you can call me if you have any questions." Tony handed him the application and asked, "I'm sorry, I didn't get your name?"

"Oh, sorry, it's Colson. Nice to meet you, Tony, I'll see you soon."

On his way out, Colson thanked Claire for her help and she replied that she hoped to see him again some time. She regretted it as soon as she said it, but what the heck.

At that, Agent Colson left the office, got back in his unmarked car, and confirmed with CT that the tracking device was now transmitting from Tony's car. Also in his email to CT, he mentioned that his impression of Tony was not one of an experienced thief. Looks more like the type of guy who should be leading a group of Cub Scouts on a hike.

12:45 P.M.

CT sent a text to his Boston office, which was actually located across the river from Boston in Chelsea, not too far from Logan Airport. He asked for an update and got a reply that the helicopter was confirmed, and the bus with twenty-five agents would be leaving soon. They would be traveling on a fairly new Prevost motorcoach privately chartered from VIP Tour & Charter. The FBI needed a company they could rely on and VIP was the best. Everything on schedule. CT gazed at his watch then decided to have lunch before meeting with Captain Barrison from the Maine State Police.

Chief Doyon told him that an order had been placed with a local store to deliver hot coffee and lots of energy bars to the school for snacks tonight. "A couple cases of ice water would also be good," added CT. At that, CT began walking up Main Street to find a spot for lunch with no particular place in mind.

The walk was good for him. It gave him a chance to get some fresh air and go over the plans. He was surprised at the number of people on the sidewalks and the percentage of those that were carrying shopping bags. He couldn't help but notice people; that's what he was trained to do. Eventually he found a restaurant not only advertising lobster rolls but also WIFI. Didn't take much persuasion to convince him this was the place.

After placing his order (with a request for a toasted, buttered roll), he opened his laptop and first checked the tracking device on Tony's car. Still hadn't moved, still parked at the bank. "Looks more like the type of guy who should be leading Cub Scouts on a hike." That was the message from the agent who met him earlier.

207

Apparently he has known this armored-car driver for some time and between the two of them figured out how to pull off the robbery. We don't know much about Clyde except what he has shown us. He is a skilled thief and seemed to enjoy making a joke out of the police. But who is he, and how did he become involved with Tony? CT couldn't wait to catch him tonight and interrogate him until he knows this kid's entire background. And who is Bonnie? The bank has no record of her as an employee, yet she was working as a teller the day the branch was robbed. She was credible when they investigated the robbery and was convincing that she had nothing to do with it. If she was in on it, Clyde would have gone to her teller station and she could have handed over a ton of cash. So what was her role? And why, after that, did she start a crime spree with Clyde? Obviously Bonnie and Clyde weren't their real names; so who were they, and how did they get involved with Tony, or how did Tony get involved with them? What is Tony's motivation?

CT finished his lunch; it was damn good, nothing like a generous portion of fresh lobster packed into a hot buttered roll. He left a nice tip for the waitress. He made a mental note that her name was Lauren. He would make sure to ask for her the next time he came back. Then he began walking back to the police station, pausing to look at the overcast sky. He passed an ice cream vendor and decided to purchase a cone to enjoy on the walk back. He was thinking about Clyde. Who was he? What was his background? What's next? Could they have crossed paths before?

CT was going over the first incident with Clyde, the bank branch robbery. How clever he was to call in a bad car accident on the other side of town that diverted the police away from the bank, giving him lots of time to get away before they could respond.

CT stopped in his tracks and almost out loud, said to himself, "Holy shit!" Was this "inside" information about the robbery tonight the same ruse? Were they playing him for a fool again, diverting all his resources away from the real crime location? Was CT being set up once again? At least they had a tracking device on Tony's car. But was Tony even involved or was that part of the story to throw them off?

CT's instincts were all over the place. He really felt that this kid was getting the best of him.

He continued walking, but his mind was going crazy. He couldn't let this kid get the best of him again! He needed a backup plan but didn't have one. This had been too easy. Boy, this kid was good.

Barrison hadn't arrived yet, so he found a quiet place where he could sit with his laptop. It was midafternoon and in less than twelve hours, this would all be over—hopefully. But just an hour ago, he thought he had this completely covered; now he wasn't so sure. Who was Clyde? CT couldn't let on to anyone that Clyde was getting to him.

CT had never met Captain Barrison in person but had several conversations with him over the years. So when he arrived, CT took a good look at him. Average height, broad shoulders, looked very physically fit. He had a reputation for being a leader, someone you could look up to, and someone who didn't need to be told twice what was expected of him. The people under him showed great respect, and it was well-deserved. He gave CT a great first impression. This would be a guy playing an important role tonight, and he gave CT the confidence that he was a true professional and would exceed what CT expected.

They met in Chief Doyon's office, and CT filled in Barrison on just about everything he knew. He asked Barrison to park a cruiser at the York Toll booth near the Maine/New Hampshire border and have him notify the command post when the armored car passed through. Also a cruiser parked in the median at Mile 32, then on I-295 at the median on Mile 9, Mile 16, and Mile 20 (the Freeport exit to Desert Road where the robbery would be). Once the armored car passed Mile 20, that cruiser should follow it and block the ramp to Exit 20 northbound and another cruiser to block Exit 20 southbound. For the purpose of radio traffic, the armored car will be known as the "bluebird".

CT also let Barrison know that the FBI planned to tail the armored car from the Hampton, New Hampshire toll. "We have a guy who is excellent at it. What I'm concerned about is they may

209

be throwing us off with the Desert Road location so if they pull off sooner, I want to be all over it as fast as we can get there."

"Should we have more units ready?"

"No, we'll have a high-speed chopper standing by in Freeport that can reach York in less than ten minutes. So if there are no further questions, I'll see you at the briefing at the school tonight. But hey, I'll most likely be here all day tomorrow. Can I buy you lunch?"

"Sure, I'd be very interested. There's a new place just down the road on Route 1 if that works for you?" asked Barrison.

"Sure. I'd like to talk with you about some things you've got going on; perhaps things we can help you with. What's the name of the restaurant?"

"The Circle Bar X Tavern. It's a craft brewery—brew their own beer on the premises and offer fantastic barbecue-pulled-pork sandwiches. Can't even get your hands around them."

"Sounds like you've been there once or twice before!"

1:55 P.M., AT THE BANK

Tony heard Lucy in the lobby joking with the tellers. She was here to give Claire a ride home. She was a little bit early so stopped in to visit Tony. He was starting to get really tense and needed a little Lucy.

"I heard Bonnie quit?" she asked, hoping it wasn't true.

"Yes, kind of rough to be involved in a holdup the first week on the job. Guess it scared her to death."

"At least no one was hurt," she said.

"Well, I really miss her working here. She was one good-looking gal. I'm sure you must miss her too!"

"Got to admit, she was good for business."

"Suppose you'll ever hear from her again?" asked Lucy.

REPORT FROM FBI FORENSICS LAB

"CT, we were able to get some good footprints from the library that matched those we found in the apple orchard," reported John from FBI Forensics.

"Go ahead, what have you got?" asked CT.

"Work boots most likely worn by Clyde. Chippewa Utility Boot, approximately size 11, round toe, well-worn Vibram sole. Woman's walking sneakers, new condition, New Balance 877s, standard women's size 9."

"Thanks, anything else?"

"Yes," replied John. "My guess is they aren't exactly boyfriend/girlfriend."

"Why do you say that?" asked CT, somewhat amused by the observation.

"Crossing the apple orchard, they walked about six feet apart from each other. Doesn't suggest they were very close or even carrying on a conversation."

Interesting, thought CT, *very interesting*. A relationship that is all the more puzzling.

3:25 P.M., AT THE BANK

Tony was deep in thought, looking at Las Vegas apartment rentals on his desktop when something occurred to him. Should he look for a one-bedroom or two-bedroom place now that Bonnie would be joining him? A mischievous smile came across his face. For the first time, he actually thought what it would be like to sleep with Bonnie. In just a few hours, his life was about to make a big turn for the better!

His daydreaming was interrupted, however, when he heard a knock on his doorframe. A sing-song voice called out, "Tony-O, oh Tony-O!"

He looked up and sure enough, it was Glenna. For a little background, Glenna started a new job at a second-hand store across the street and opened a checking account with Tony. On her next trip in, Claire waited on her, and she asked Claire about Tony and confided she had the hots for him. Claire, being Claire, could tell Glenna wasn't exactly Tony's type, not even close, so encouraged her, saying that Tony was single and looking for someone. Glenna took that as a green light and had been coming in regularly ever since.

"Tony-O, I made you a pan of blondies." Then she took the aluminum foil off the pan to show him, and they looked and smelled awesome, made with tons of chocolate chips. "Just out of the oven, still warm!" she exclaimed.

"You shouldn't have," Tony answered, more than willing to take them but trying not to look at her bright red hair. She was a full-figured woman, you might say.

"Well, Tony-O," she continued in her sing-song voice. "I'm having some friends over to my apartment Saturday night to play charades. I found some really funny gag gifts for prizes. It will be *so* much fun. I'm hoping you can join us! Seven, Saturday night, you don't have to bring anything. I'll see you then!"

Tony was repulsed at the thought. Saturday night at seven, he planned to be on the road to Las Vegas with the most beautiful girl in the world, not playing charades with Glenna. This, of course, didn't stop him from enjoying one enormous slice of a blondie. He looked out at the teller line and could see Claire smiling at him.

"Oh, Tony-O, why don't you go to her party Saturday night?" Claire teased.

"I'll never forgive you for encouraging her," shot back Tony.

4:55 P.M.

The twenty-five tactical team agents on their way to Freeport were under the command of Debbi Grenier. She had served in the Army's 3rd Armored Division and had received the Medal of Honor, the highest personal military decoration.

CT received a call from Debbi. She had just copied a radio transmission from a Maine State Trooper on the Maine Turnpike requesting a back-up. Two men with outstanding warrants. As the bus was only five minutes away from the Kennebunk stop, she was asking permission to stop and assist.

CT glanced at his watch and approved the request. He them instructed her to order the whole team to disembark the bus on arrival and surround the car with weapons drawn. *Can you imagine,* thought CT, *being surrounded by twenty-five FBI Special Forces in full assault gear with weapons!* Who says the FBI doesn't have a sense of humor!

He then checked the tracking device on Tony's car and found that it was now parked in Portland at his apartment on Stevens Avenue near Congress Street. So far, so good. He sat down in his Porsche interceptor and started to head over to the school for the evening. He had just finished a burger and shake and was so preoccupied, he couldn't remember if it was good or not.

The parking lot was empty, and he found the door to the community hall unlocked. Lights were on. The command center should arrive in about an hour, the chopper in a couple hours, the bus in about an hour, Freeport police chief and the state police captain any minute now. Would be nice if the caterer delivers soon. Then we all wait.

CT set up his laptop then opened his briefcase and spread papers out across the table. While he was reviewing his notes, he heard a car pull in. It was Chief Doyon followed by a van—the caterer. Probably a good thing that no one else was here yet as he didn't want the caterer going around town, spreading the word about a big police presence at the school.

CT offered to help the caterer carry things in, but the caterer said he was all set. CT looked in the back of the van and saw several cases of water, coffee carafes, what looked like finger sandwiches, assorted pastries, and lots more. He looked at Doyon and nodded his head, "This looks good," he said. "Could be a late night."

"Well, if you think of anything else to add, just let me know."

CT didn't hear him, however, as he had just received a text from the bus in Kennebunk. "Two young men from Lawrence, Massachusetts, they shit their pants when they saw us, confessed to heroin hidden in trunk. Now on their way to jail. Bus is back on the road and GPS says will be in Freeport in fifty-two minutes."

"Good job, always nice when we can help out the locals!" CT responded.

A check with the local weather showed an overcast night with a chance of scattered showers or even snow flurries. Low 30s, two-thirds moon. Tony's car was still parked at his residence in Portland. State police mobile command center to arrive soon. It was all coming together. It wouldn't be long before he could close this case!

7:20 P.M., COMMUNITY HALL

Almost everyone was here now, gathered in the community hall. State police command center parked out front, Brunswick police Humvee and FBI bus in the parking lot, Freeport police chief and state police captain sitting at a table together. Massachusetts police helicopter just minutes away. Freeport also sent over a fire truck and an ambulance to stand by.

The tactical team were specially trained to intervene in high-risk situations. They carried Remington 700 sniper rifles equipped with laser-pointed sights. In addition, they also had a waist belt that held a Springfield .45-caliber pistol and ammunition. They wore Kevlar helmets for head protection, goggles to protect against flying debris, bulletproof vests. They each had a radio with earpiece and microphone linked to the command post. They wore military-issued fatigues with flame-resistant Nomex fibers. The team consisted of twenty men and five women. The team commander was a woman.

CT made his way to the front of the gathering. "Good evening, ladies and gentlemen. I would like to get started first with some introductions, and then I want to give you some background into why we are here and talk about the plan for tonight."

As mentioned earlier, CT was a tall man, broad shoulders, rugged build. He had a commanding appearance and had no problem getting people's attention. So you could hear a pin drop as soon as he started speaking. "First I would like to introduce our host, Chief Doyon of the Freeport Police Department." Doyon stood up, and then CT added that Chief Doyon should also be thanked for providing the snacks which was met with spirited applause. Then he introduced Captain Barrison of the Maine State Police, Lieutenant

Smithner from Brunswick Police, and Agent Grenier from the FBI special forces unit.

"First let me mention that as you can see, we have several different departments all using different radio frequencies. These will all be coordinated through the command post using the Maine statewide police radio frequency. I will call for a signal 1,000 at midnight, keeping this cleared as an emergency channel only to be used for this operation. The command post will be known tonight as the Big MACC. MACC stands for Multi-Agency Communications Center."

"Weather looks like a cool night in the 30s, overcast, chance of a shower, and possible flurries. Typical Maine fall weather. There are no streetlights at the scene, so the overcast skies will make it very dark."

"Tonight," CT continued, "an armored car will be leaving the Federal Reserve in Boston at midnight with approximately ten to twelve million in cash, bound for their main office in Pownal where the cash is sorted and assigned to trucks for delivery tomorrow morning to bank branches around the Portland area. This armored car is expected to take Exit 20 off I-295 and head west on Desert Road toward Pownal, passing through Freeport at 2:02 a.m. We have credible information that an attempt will be made to rob the truck as it exits 295, about six-tenths of a mile west on Desert Road. Just down the street from where we are now. Four people are involved, an insider from the armored-car company and three others—two men and one woman. One man and the woman go by the names of Bonnie and Clyde." This drew some snickers from the crowd. "The other man is a branch manager of a local bank—the bank that was just robbed recently by Clyde. When Clyde robbed the bank, the manager was there who is also one of the four as well as Bonnie, working as a teller. The armored car will be known as the "bluebird" on all radio traffic.

"Here's what we know about them. Bonnie was interviewed after the robbery. Claimed to be in training, her first week at the bank. Said she wet herself during the robbery, she was so nervous. Very believable, I fell for her story." At that point CT showed a slide of her at the bank from the bank camera taken during the robbery. "It's not a great photo, but you might be able to notice she's an exceptionally beautiful woman—perhaps midtwenties. A check today with the bank's human resources department claims no knowledge of anyone named Bonnie working at the branch that week or any other branch for that matter. So she obviously has some relationship with the manager. Again she fooled me completely. The manager, Tony, has worked for the bank for a few years and sold cars prior to that. No criminal record, no motor vehicle record.

"So since he's been manager of the Falmouth branch, he interacts with the armored car service once or twice a week whenever it makes deliveries. The armored-car driver, Ralph, has been with the company for a little less than two years. Just enough time to think he's figured out how to rip the company off for millions and not get caught. No criminal history. That brings us to Clyde. Now it's getting personal. He has made us look like fools over and over. He is in his midtwenties. We can't find any clue as to who he is. He covers his tracks very well, acts very professional, and his crimes are well-thought-out. No idea what his connection is to Tony or Bonnie. We have searched databases around the country and can't come up with anyone with a similar profile. From my experience, someone that young doesn't work that well without an older, more experienced teacher. And that isn't Tony. So I am really looking forward to capturing him tonight and interrogating the shit out of him until he squeals like a pig!

"His first crime that we know of was the Falmouth bank robbery. Again Tony was in the branch and no doubt worked with him on the details. Bonnie was working in the branch on the teller line at that time. The branch had an armored-car delivery that morning by Ralph, a Thursday morning, so it was flush with cash for the weekend. Estimated at 75–80,000 dollars in the vault which Bonnie had access to. When he entered the branch, he announced that his name was Clyde and that someday, he'd be famous. Then he went to one of the other tellers and asked only for a few twenties then left. He didn't go to Bonnie and didn't make any connection to her. He did ask her to get on the floor with the other tellers and to count from one hundred to one backward before they could get up. He then took off in a bright-yellow car which he drove all of two hundred yards, abandoned it, and that's the last we saw of him. Car was filled with lemon air freshener. Dogs unable to pick up any scent due to the heavy lemon smell. The robbery occurred as the bank was closing. Just before entering the branch, he called the police to report a bad accident on the other side of town. Both police units on duty responded so when the dispatcher was notified of the bank robbery, both cars were out of position, giving him plenty of time to drive away. An old trick, but he pulled if off brilliantly. A lot of work went into this robbery, so I ask myself, why did he only ask for a few twenties when he could have grabbed tens of thousands of dollars and get away with it?

"His next robbery came two days later. A town library, in the town of Cumberland, robbed at closing time. All the library had in the cash drawer was overdue book fine money. Like less than ten bucks! This time, he had Bonnie with him and again it was announced to everyone in the library that they were Bonnie and Clyde. A police cruiser arrived in less than a minute which I'm sure took them by surprise. When the officer went into the building to investigate they stole the cruiser to use for their getaway. He made a few wisecracks on the radio then ditched it at a nearby farm stand."

"They then went in to the farm stand and robbed that, again announcing that they were Bonnie and Clyde. From there, they left Cumberland and drove to South Portland where they attempted to rob a theater box office where a show was just about to begin. Problem was, the show had been sold out for some time and there was no money in the cash box! Again they introduced themselves to the patrons as Bonnie and Clyde and one patron, when interviewed by the police, thought they were part of the show!

"Then I think it was three days later, they broke into a private residence during the night and stole a valuable Renoir painting. They left a thank-you card, signed Bonnie and Clyde. It was their first serious robbery that we are aware of. Again a very professional job, apparently with lots of preplanning. Painting is worth millions.

"None of the robberies involved weapons, and all were done very professionally. We have been unable to find any evidence—fingerprints or DNA samples from any of the locations. The media has enjoyed making the police look bad while these kids commit one crime after another and get away with them. This, of course, only makes me want to nail the bastards even more!

"This morning, the driver from the armored-car service met with Chief Doyon and confessed to the plans for tonight. He was one scared kid who thought the foolproof plan would fall apart, that one of the others would get careless with the cash and get them all caught. Got thinking about it and felt they weren't experienced enough to keep this quiet. Didn't want to spend the best years of his life in prison. Asked for some kind of immunity if he gave us all the details. He was very thorough. Said they will have a toy rifle but no actual weapons. We'll be following the progress of the armored car from the time it enters Maine until it arrives here. It will be referred to on the radio as the Bluebird. We have a tracking device on Tony's car and right now, it is parked at his home in Portland. No idea where Bonnie and Clyde are at this time.

"Now just to review FBI policy on firearms. We do not fire warning shots. We do not shoot to wound. We only shoot to kill. We do not fire at any target unless there is a clear threat to our lives first."

The meeting was interrupted to announce the helicopter was just about to land. It was already dark, so the flares would be a big help in assisting the landing. The meeting was stopped so they could all go out and watch the helicopter land.

The stealth helicopter was so quiet nobody saw it until it was literally almost on the ground. The wash from the rotors was powerful though. Landing lights illuminated the landing area and soon it landed. Then the pilot opened the door and jumped out, dressed in an orange jumpsuit and white helmet. The landing lights were still on, creating quite a profile. She took the helmet off and shook her long hair over her shoulders.

Then CT went over to introduce himself to Cat, captain of the helicopter. Cat was an army veteran, having served tours of duty in Afghanistan and Iraq. She was a tough young woman with lightning-fast reflexes.

"Cat, I'm aware of your reputation but have never had the opportunity to meet you. I appreciate having you here tonight."

"Actually I love to fly missions with this. Glad to help out, sir."

"What's it like to fly a chopper like that?" asked CT.

"I feel like James Bond. It's faster than anything I've ever flown. and it's like driving a Ferrari, a sports car in the sky. It's also loaded with special features like a Bond car. Too bad the army discontinued the program. I was briefed on tonight's operation on the way up."

"Sounds like you're having too much fun. I'll fill you in on the details, but what I want you to do tonight is hover as low as you can over the armored car and turn on your flood lights to illuminate the scene just like it was daylight. There are some telephone wires, but nothing is higher than the telephone poles. The lower you can get, the better. Don't come in until I give you the order. It should happen about 2:00 a.m."

"This machine has stealth technology and you truly cannot hear it even when it is above you. But if I come in too low, the wash from the rotors will knock you over! You may have had a little preview of that when I just landed."

"Okay. You judge how low you can get without stirring up a sandstorm."

"Yes, sir. Done it before…"

"Okay, come on in and relax for a while. We've got plenty of snacks, and I'll fill you in. Also want to drive you to the location where this will all happen so you can plan accordingly."

As they went inside, CT watched Cat closely. She stood straight with her shoulders back and answered every question with yes sir or no sir. Obvious military background. She was all business and showed no signs of a sense of humor. She was here to do a job and was completely focused on the mission. He could also sense that she was one tough young lady who didn't take any shit from anyone! CT even wondered who would win if they were to arm wrestle! God he loved working with people who had army experience!

9:27 P.M., TONY'S APARTMENT

Tony had been very nervous all evening as the big event drew nearer. He tried to mentally go through every detail step by step but didn't have the patience. He tried packing some things but found he couldn't do that very well. He paced, he wiped the sweat off his forehead, he even tried some stretching exercises. So when the doorbell rang, he was glad to have company.

It was Bonnie. They had agreed to meet at his apartment then pick up Clyde at the Yarmouth Visitors' Center on the way to Freeport. He invited her in and took her coat. He wanted to compliment her on how stunningly beautiful she looked but instead just asked her if she found his place without any problems. He felt awkward but at the same time really excited to have her as a partner—a partner in crime!

She looked around his living room, taking it all in. "I've never been in a man's apartment before," she confessed. "Will I be safe?" She then offered a Mona Lisa-type sly smile.

Oh the thoughts that ran through Tony's head. "With me?" he asked innocently.

"Just kidding. I trust you completely! But you know what they say, 'Beware of the banker!'"

"Here, have a seat. I'd offer you a glass of wine, but we shouldn't be drinking any alcohol. How about some grape juice? I've also got some crackers and some French onion dip we can share."

"Sounds great, let me help you."

As they walked out to the kitchen, he noticed that she was looking at everything along the way, particularly artwork that he had hanging on his walls. When they got to the kitchen, Tony opened the refrigerator and told Bonnie where she could find a couple glasses. Tony grabbed the dip and took a box of wheat thins out of the cupboard then invited her back to his living room. On the way, she asked about one of his paintings. It was a watercolor of a lobster boat during a storm.

"I painted that in the third grade, and it won an award," he said. "Not sure what inspired me, or what the judges saw in it. But I've always kept it. Always meant to frame it at some point but never got around to it."

"Taking it with us to Vegas?" she asked.

"Yeah, I suppose I should. You like it?"

"I know what the judges saw in it. There's a hardworking lobsterman who is trying hard to support his family and despite the storm, he's out there working. You can see his determination, and you've painstakingly painted every raindrop and the waves that show the danger he is confronting. If you look hard at it, your eyes are drawn to him and his struggle in this storm. It's really an emotional work of art."

"Really?"

"Let me tell you a little about myself before we take off for Las Vegas," she suggested.

Tony sat back on the couch, fairly close to her, and encouraged her to share what was on her mind.

"You think you know me, but you don't. My mother had me when she was still in high school and never married. I don't know who my father is and whenever I asked my mother, she would change the subject. All my life, I've wanted to meet him. Growing up, my mother never really paid much attention to me. She seemed to see me as a nuisance, a responsibility she didn't want to accept. Her older sister, my aunt, treated me more like a mom than my own mother did. I was diagnosed early on with autism, although many disagreed. I did have some kind of complex medical fragility. My mom used it to get state aid which she spent on cigarettes and other things for herself. In school, I was called a 504 student, and an ed tech was assigned to me. Her name was Eileen. Although she was a grandmother, she really treated me like her little sister. She was with me throughout school and went with me to class or sometimes, we would just hang out in a resource room. When we were alone, she would help me with my schoolwork or just read stories to me. She's the one who read the story of Bonnie and Clyde to me, and it pretty much changed my life. I wanted to be Bonnie so bad. I was envious of her fame and the excitement she must have felt robbing banks. I used to go to bed at night dreaming of a life like Bonnie had. So when you told me you were going to rob your own bank, I got very excited. I thought that I had finally met my Clyde!"

"So what did you think when I introduced you to Blake?"

"Was that his name? Oh, but I have to be honest and tell you, I was *so* disappointed. I wanted you! He just didn't have the excitement I was looking for. Did you know he stole my $7,000!"

"He did? You never got it back?"

"He took me to pick it up and showed me a cupola on top of a school and said he hid it up there. But he couldn't have because there was no way to get up there!"

"Well, in a couple hours, you'll have a million bucks, so you can put it behind you."

"Anyway, I'll have you!"

"Well, I think we'll have fun together! But I never would have guessed you were autistic?"

"I've always been off the charts on intelligence tests, can't you tell? But my thought processes are not always accurate. In school, I was very antisocial and could be very uncomfortable at times around other students. I would often have unpredictable emotional responses. I was supposed to see a cognitive therapist, but my mother never took me to the appointments."

"But now you're a waitress. That isn't for someone who is antisocial."

"Oh, I've come a long way. But there are times at the restaurant that I need to excuse myself and hide in the ladies' room for a while. Something else I gotta tell you, Tony," she continued. "I have this weird thing that I have to sleep with my body lined up with the poles. Head toward the north pole, feet facing south."

"Are you serious? That to keep your body in alignment or something?" Tony shook his head, paused for a moment, then asked, "So, are you gonna be okay during the robbery tonight?"

"This is kind of what I'm getting at. Something like tonight I'm really looking forward to. It's my Bonnie and Clyde dream. It's the adrenaline. I know what's going to happen. I'll be fine. But in some unknown social settings, I could freak out."

"Freak out?"

"Well, not really, I just withdraw and want to be left alone."

At that, she leaned over and put her head on Tony's shoulders. She was quiet for a long time. It really felt great to Tony to feel her resting on his side.

"Tony?"

"Yeah?"

"When I was a kid, I used to ask my mother all the time about my father. She would usually ignore me or change the subject but once she told me he had died unexpectedly, so she didn't want to talk about it. I thought she just made that up so I wouldn't ask anymore, but I sort of believed her in a way."

"You'll probably never know."

"So I spend a lot of time in graveyards and cemeteries. Looking at last names, looking at dates of birth and death to find someone who would have died when I was just born. Then once, I met a woman in a cemetery who told me about the spirit world. This may sound corny, but she said there are some people who die accidentally or who just aren't ready to accept the fact that they are dead and their spirits linger until they eventually cross over. As I said, it sounds weird, but she said the spirits surround their loved ones. That they are really out there trying to communicate with us."

"Okay, sounds like you believe this."

"Well, I want to. But I've got to tell you what happened. Have you heard of a song called 'Strange Snow?'"

"No, afraid not."

"I saw a performer last summer who picked up an old guitar at a garage sale at an abandoned home which was rumored to be a haunted house. One of the strings on the guitar could only be heard by spirits."

"Oh, come on, you don't believe that, do you?"

"Well, I sure wanted to. I listened to the performer play his guitar and the string that only the spirits could hear. That night, I dreamt I was back in high school and met with the principal. He showed me a drawing of a banker, then he crossed his arms over his chest and shook his head back and forth as if to say no. As if to say, 'Beware of the banker.'"

"Oh, give me a break."

"No, I'm serious. Spirits communicate showing signs and symbols. I was visited in my sleep by a spirit!"

"But I thought you said spirits wanted to communicate with loved ones. Was your principal a loved one?"

"Well, I guess I don't know who it was."

Then Tony whispered, "So I guess I'm the banker he wanted you to be aware of!"

"Well, you are the only banker I know."

At that, Tony reached under her arm and started tickling her.

"Stop it, stop it, stop it," she squealed.

Then Tony said, "Look, it's just about time for us to pick up Clyde and have some fun! Ready?"

They both stood up, and Bonnie stood very close to Tony. She looked down and whispered, "Will you kiss me?"

Tony was and he wasn't quite ready for this, but somehow it seemed right. He gave her a quick kiss and could only react with an OMG! But it wasn't enough for Bonnie. She pressed her body tightly against his, looked him in the eyes, and asked him again to kiss her, really kiss her.

Tony looked her in the eyes, those seemingly hypnotic eyes, he put his arms around her lower back and pulled her even tighter against him. He slowly moved his face toward hers until he met her lips. She put her hands behind his neck and pulled him tight to her. Wow! Tony felt a little dizzy, like he was spinning. She opened her mouth slightly and lightly outlined his lips with her tongue. Tony responded with his own tongue, and the kiss seemed to last for several minutes. He had never, never, never felt anything like this. She slowly ground her hips against his, and he responded in the same manner. His body was tingling until she released him. They both seemed to be out of breath.

"That was absolutely awesome," Tony whispered. "I don't think I've ever experienced anything quite like that."

"Tony, I have to be honest. You are the first person I've ever kissed in my whole life. It was okay?"

"Good, ah, oh yeah! But there's no way that was your first kiss!"

"I'm not kidding." She leaned forward and gently licked his ear. Then she whispered, "You know what? There's a lot more where that came from. I can be good at being bad."

Tony actually felt weak. Oh thank you, God!

Then they left the house to pick up Clyde. On the way, Tony remembered his indecision as to whether he should rent a one-bedroom or two-bedroom apartment when they got to Las Vegas. Guess she just answered that question!

The ride to Yarmouth was actually quite quiet. It was now after midnight, and the armored car should have already left Boston. They talked about Saturday afternoon. Bonnie said she planned to pack a backpack with all her necessities and leave her apartment for a walk, making sure Viktoria saw her leaving and leaving alone. Then she would walk up to the cemetery where she would wait for Tony and once Tony arrived, she would get into the car with him and two million dollars in the trunk then head off for Las Vegas!

When she didn't return to her apartment or show up for work, she assumed Viktoria would notify the police and tell them the last time she saw her, she was out walking all by herself. Police would presume a stranger picked her up and abducted her, never to be seen again.

It was quiet again in the car and as they approached Yarmouth, Tony felt her hand on his shoulder. Then she giggled, and her hand slowly slid down to his lap.

YARMOUTH PARK 'N' RIDE

Tony and Bonnie pulled into the Park 'n Ride about thirty minutes past midnight. Clyde was standing next to his pickup truck; he had been pacing back and forth as he watched the time. He was getting very nervous and thinking about everything that could go wrong. When he saw Tony, however, he acted very cool and confident.

"Ready to do this thing?" Clyde asked.

"Won't be long now," Tony answered. They decided they'd wait in Tony's car until 1:00 a.m. and then drive to Desert Road. It was only five minutes away.

12:15 A.M., BIG MACC

CT observed that Tony's car left his home shortly after midnight and headed northbound of I-295. He followed it with the tracking device until it stopped in Yarmouth at 12:25 a.m. This must be their meeting place. He alerted the Big MACC communications center that the robbers were parked less than four miles away. So if they manage to escape somehow, this is where they will most likely go first to get their cars. Better position a state police car there shortly after they leave. May also be a good idea for the officer to run the license plates of all the vehicles parked there to see if we can learn more about these folks.

At 12:30 a.m., CT ordered the twenty-five tactical team to begin walking up the street to take their positions.

At 12:56 a.m., "SP unit 722 to Big MACC. Positive confirmation on the Bluebird. Just passed York toll plaza."

At 1:04 a.m., CT checked the tracking device and saw that Tony's car had left Yarmouth and was headed toward Freeport. CT gave the word for state police to send a car to the rest area to run the plates on all the cars parked there.

At 1:09 a.m., "Unmarked FBI car parked at DOT maintenance lot off Desert Road confirmed a sedan pulled in and parked, left motor running. Three subjects inside."

At 1:19 a.m., "SP unit 711 to Big MACC, Bluebird just passed Biddeford Mile 32."

At 1:27 a.m., state police called with a positive ID on one of the cars parked at the Yarmouth Visitors' Center. "I think I found your boy, CT. Black Ford F-10 pickup, registered to Blake Donahue, born May 12, age 27, current address Route 115 North Yarmouth, numerous traffic violations, license under suspension, sentenced to three months' prison for theft of construction equipment. Now serving two years' probation."

"Great work," CT responded. He now knew what he needed to know about Clyde. Local boy, probably with lots of connections made while in prison. Probably working with someone he met there.

At 1:32 a.m., "State police unit 742 to Big MACC, Bluebird just passed through I-295 Exit 44 toll plaza."

1:38 a.m., "State police unit 524 to BIG MACC, Bluebird just passed Mile 9."

1:43 A.M., ABOARD THE ARMORED CAR

"Hey, Towhead." Ralph broke the silence. It had been a very quiet drive. Very little traffic. The radio was tuned to a talk show.

"The name is Sheldon."

"I'm the senior guy here. If I want to call you Towhead, I will." Sheldon had thick blond hair that was almost white. Ralph liked to pick on him; mostly to keep reminding him who was boss.

"Okay, what's up?"

"They called me in early before our shift today. There's going to be a drill tonight," Ralph announced.

"What kind of drill, when?" asked Sheldon.

"Robbery drill. We have one once a year. They said it would probably be on the Desert Road, about five minutes from now."

"You're just telling me now? You asshole!"

"I know you're new and haven't been through one of these before. It was covered during your training, and you're not supposed to have much advance notice."

"Yeah, but five minutes?" He paused for a few seconds. "Okay, so what's going to happen?"

"So somewhere on the Desert Road, someone, probably more than one person, will stop us. I don't know how. They are professional actors and will be carrying BB guns. We are to follow procedure. Do everything they ask, 100 percent cooperation. The fed was also aware of the drill. There are twenty fake bags of twenties loaded by the back door. I will turn those over to the robbers then close the doors. They will load the bags and take off, then we can continue on. They will be driving to the vault building where we will meet them for a brief review. Don't worry, they won't keep us too late. When they stop us, I will push the alarm button. Do not, under any circumstances, draw your weapon. Me neither, just like in training. Just do what you're told and follow any instructions I may have. No need to panic or be frightened. Just remember, it's a practice activity we do once a year."

1:45 A.M.

"SP unit 732, Bluebird confirmed at Mile 16."

1:48 A.M., FREEPORT DISPATCH

"Freeport Public Safety, what's your emergency?"

A man out of breath started yelling into the phone, "I'm driving on the Flying Point Road and see a fire up ahead—looks like it could be a barn. I'm gonna check and see if anyone is around and will call you back."

"May I have your name, sir?"

But the phone went dead. "Freeport fire alarm transmitting Box 215, unknown address on the Flying Point Road. Reported working fire. Dispatching Engines 2, 5, and Ladder 1."

"Freeport police dispatch to Car 1."

"Car 1, go ahead."

"We have report of a structure fire on Flying Point Road. Two engines and the ladder have been dispatched. We have no police units on that side of town. Please advise."

"Request a unit from Yarmouth PD."

1:49 A.M.

Reported that the black sedan with the three occupants left the DOT parking lot, turned west on Desert Road.

1:51 A.M.

Black sedan parks on Desert Road just beyond the railroad tracks, two people get out.

1:52 A.M.

"State police unit 742 to big MACC. The Bluebird now signaling to take I-295 Exit 20. As soon as they take the ramp, I will position and close the exit."

"State police unit 720 to Big MACC. I will block Desert Road west of site and place spike mats in the roadway."

C.T. whispered into his microphone, "looks like it's show-time!"

1:55 A.M.

Tony positioned his car across the road making it impossible for the armored car to pass by him. He popped open his trunk and left the car running and the driver's door open. Just as the armored car approached, he waved his arms signaling them to stop and displayed the Uzi machine-gun. Bonnie and Clyde stood next to him. They could be seen clearly in the headlights. The brakes squealed as the armored car slowed to a stop, and there was a hiss of air from the hydraulic brakes.

Tony aimed the Uzi and fired four shots into the front right tire. The truck is immobilized. The Uzi was louder than they expected, and the tire also exploded with a bang. It certainly woke up the neighborhood.

"My name is Clyde, and this is Bonnie," Clyde yells out. "We have you completely surrounded with other members of my gang. Someday we're going to be famous and you can say you met us. For now, get out of the truck and do as I say."

Sheldon looked back at Ralph as if to ask what he should do. Ralph whispers, "Just get out of the truck and do as they ask. Be sure to hit the panic button first."

Ralph opened the door and was immediately told to lay flat on the ground and keep his hands where they can see them. After Sheldon got out, he was ordered to lie on the ground next to Ralph. Ralph was then told to open the back door. Once opened, he started pulling money bags out and dropping them on the road. Clyde and Tony began grabbing the bags and ran them to Tony's car. Ralph looked around, hoping the police will get there soon. Bonnie was standing next to the car's trunk with clippers to cut the string on the bags.

After Tony and Clyde carried about ten bags to Tony's car, sure enough, the FBI turned on their spotlights. Everyone froze, trying to figure out what was going on.

"This is Agent CT of the FBI. I want everyone to drop what you're holding and lie face down on the ground. Everyone down, *now!*"

The bright spotlights blinded them as they got down on the ground. Tony, Bonnie, Clyde, Ralph, and Sheldon all fell to the ground and FBI agents started toward them with handcuffs. Cat was given the word to turn on the bright overhead spotlights to illuminate the scene below.

Tony slowly stood up then ran toward his car. The others stayed on the ground. There was a misty rain now in the air. Just as Tony was about to get into the driver's seat, a shot rang out. A bullet hit Tony directly in the balls from a low-powered rifle. Tony fell to his knees in excruciating pain and put his hands on his crotch to try to ease the pain. His hands were instantly dripping in blood. He looked up in disbelief and confusion and just as he did, the bolt on the rifle slid into place and another shot was fired; this time, it hit Tony in the forehead through his left eyebrow, killing him instantly. The shots were fired from a rifle that was not an FBI weapon. Even though the scene was illuminated from the helicopter and FBI flashlights, no one saw the shooter.

Bonnie screamed out, "Tony!" And again, even louder, "T-O-N-Y!" She started to get up to run to him but fainted and collapsed on the ground. Clyde slid over and pulled her body onto his lap.

"My name is Clyde," he yelled toward the spot where CT's voice was coming from. "Someday I will be famous, and you can say you met me." Then he slowly pulled the pistol from his pants. "I have a hostage. Let me get to the car, and she won't be hurt."

"Put the gun down, Blake. Put the gun down, *now!*" ordered CT.

He slowly raised the pistol and started to aim it toward CT. "I am…"—pause—"ready to die." At that, he pulled the trigger. The shot missed CT but did hit one of the agents standing next to him in the shoulder. Clyde was preparing to fire a second shot. The agents trained their red laser beams on Clyde's head.

Before Clyde could get a second shot off, CT ordered the agents to fire.

Clyde was hit with seventeen shots from close range. Although no shots were aimed at Bonnie, she was hit twice from the crossfire.

The force from the high-powered rifles was enough to push Clyde backward into the guardrail. His head was nothing more than a bloody stump, and his spinal column was severed.

The helicopter was now hovering directly overhead, and its powerful lights illuminated the scene below like daylight. Bonnie was writhing on the ground; one ankle twitching. An ambulance was called to transport her to the hospital as fast as possible. She was losing a lot of blood. Most likely, she was dead, and the ankle was moving due to muscle spasms. She was wearing light-blue New Balance 877 sneakers.

A tracking dog was brought in from Yarmouth PD to try to follow the tracks of the person who shot and killed Tony. The dog was unable to pick up a scent. Cat searched for the shooter and also used infrared heat imaging but after twenty minutes with no luck was sent back to Massachusetts. She did identify two coyotes in the area, however.

The armored car was sealed with police tape, and the two men were taken to the community hall to be questioned. An hour later, the armored car was towed to a police garage for study. Tony's car was also towed to the same garage.

A state police evidence technician team surveyed the scene and reconstructed the event with CT's help. The drizzling rain changed to snow flurries and then to light snow.

A medical examiner was called to certify that Tony and Clyde were deceased. Their bodies were placed in black-zipper body bags and taken to the morgue.

The bus with the FBI agents was sent back to Boston.

The fire department came with a tank truck and washed the blood out of the road.

CT thought to himself that if Ralph hadn't informed them of what they'd planned, they probably would have gotten away with it. But it would be hard for all four of them to have that much cash and not slip up somewhere. No matter how careful they were, at some point, someone would make a mistake. Only a matter of time.

CT was the last to leave the scene. It was now very quiet and very dark outside. He picked some wildflowers from the roadside and tied them to the "Intersection 500 Feet" signpost. It was almost directly over the spot where Clyde's body had lain. He thought about Clyde's last words. "I am ready to die." He probably figured out he was looking at a minimum of ten years in a federal prison and wanted to go down as a tough guy. Pulling that trigger was pretty much a suicidal decision. The light snow was beginning to cover the ground like a white blanket, covering up any evidence of the crime scene.

Just as the original Bonnie and Clyde died in an ambush resulting from an informer, Blake and Acadia met a similar fate.

The falling snow seemed to have a peaceful quietness to it. CT thought to himself that it was strange for it to snow in late October. The wind was beginning to pick up, and it was causing the snow to swirl around and around on the road. CT looked at it and thought it was, *Strange snow.*

THE AFTERMATH

Shelden-

Sheldon suffered a traumatic mental breakdown as a result of the robbery. The gunfire, the FBI, the sight of Clyde's dead body and the interrogation was too much for the 19-year-old, who had only been with the company for four months. He spent the next three months in the hospital for acute psychiatric care (in the P-6 ward). He then relocated to Orlando and got a job as a costumed character at a theme park. Hiding in the costume gave him a sense of safety and security.

Ralph

After a long discussion, the police and the armored-car company decided not to prosecute for his role in the robbery. He was, after all, the informer who exposed Clyde and ended his string of burglaries. His employment was terminated, and he moved to New Hampshire. He is now working as a medical billing clerk at the Dartmouth-Hitchcock Hospital in Hanover. He was not injured during the robbery. He found a small apartment within walking distance to the hospital and to keep him company, adopted a rescue dog that he named Wesley.

Tony

He was not a dishonest person, and he was not a thief. He was just heavily addicted to casino gambling (slot machines). His addic-

243

tion led him to desperate measures. Like most of his casino visits, Lady Luck was not on his side this night either. He did have second thoughts about doing this and felt guilty talking Bonnie and Clyde into being part of this scheme. His mother wrote his obituary and mentioned that Tony went to church on a regular basis. Two bullet-shell casings were found on the ground 19 feet from his body. They were traced to a semiautomatic rifle, a 22-caliber Marlin 50. This is an antique rifle that is considered a rare collector's item. The shooter was never found. It would be two years before the bank discovered that he had stolen $200,000 from Mrs. Rosewater. On his nightstand in his apartment were two tickets to a November Pasami and Cheese concert at the TD Garden in Boston—tickets that will never be used.

Bonnie

Bonnie fainted when Tony was killed. Clyde tried to take her with him as a hostage. She was hit by two stray bullets when the agents shot at Clyde. One entered just under her right ear and exited through her chin essentially blowing her lower jaw off. A second bullet entered her upper torso just below her right armpit, traveled through her right lung and ripped open her left anterior descending artery, pretty much a death sentence. Despite several hours of surgery, chances for her survival were almost nil. She was placed in intensive care in critical condition. There was a faint blip on her EKG which was only possible due to artificial heart pumps. Doctors agreed that if there was no improvement by noon, they would remove the life-support equipment. Her heart beat was slowly deteriorating.

Police went to Tony's apartment where they found a car registered to Acadia. It still showed her address as Oxford, Maine. They had the Oxford County Sheriff's Department visit the house to try to reach a relative, but the house was empty. Apparently no one had lived there for several months. At the hospital, however, she was listed as Jane Doe.

Doctors found that by playing music in intensive care, the beat sometimes was beneficial for the patients. They tuned the radio to a local radio station that played recently-released popular music. But the music did not help Cady. She was slowly fading into death. The life-support equipment was removed at noontime and her EKG went to a flatline.

CT

Another criminal off the streets. CT hadn't seen it ending this way and hoped that he would have a chance to sit down and really analyze Clyde. Nothing that Clyde did deserved him to pay for this with his life. The presence of the Uzi machine-gun was a game changer and once Clyde aimed and pulled the trigger of his pistol at the FBI, there was no choice. It was suicide, plain and simple. Could his death have been avoided? Or all three of them for that matter? Of course. There was no reason for all three of them to die. CT just shook his head in disbelief. Did he let it go too far? The informant told him they had no weapons, so when Tony started firing the high-powered Uzi machine-gun, things took a turn for the worst very quickly.

After lunch with Barrison, C.T. sat in the driver's seat of his car and paused before starting it. He looked around and noticed the light snow that fell last night had melted and the bright sun felt good. He was looking forward to being home and getting some much needed rest. He called his wife to let her know he was on his way.

"You OK?" she asked. "I've been worried about you since I heard the news."

"News?"

"Yes, it's been on the cable networks. How Bonnie and Clyde died last night in a shootout with the police. It's national news!"

C.T. really wasn't expecting that, nor would he refer to it as a shootout. "Well," he said, "I'm fine. They wanted to make the national news and I guess they did. One of my agents took a bullet to his arm but has been released. I'm on my way home now, should be there in a couple hours and will fill you in."

"Always so good to have you home, safe and sound, after these things. How 'bout if I meet you at the door with a big hug and a martini?"

"Jane?"

"Yes," she responded.

"Shaken, not stirred."

He first met Jane in fifth grade. Perhaps the luckiest day of his life. They had been childhood sweethearts. She was a very pretty girl and was even more beautiful now. Jane was used to him being in harm's way but was never comfortable with it. When he was a game warden, he went after people hunting off season and was often out all night. In the FBI, he would often be out on dangerous raids. Early in his career as a game warden, he was wounded by a man who had been breaking into cabins in the Moosehead area. He set traps that would snare any law-enforcement officer closing in on him. CT walked right into one and was seriously wounded. It taught him a valuable lesson. From that time on, he analyzed every possible situation he was in to not only protect himself but also the people he was leading. Jane was always confident in his abilities and never doubted he'd come home after the dangerous situations he found himself in as a game warden in the woods and as an FBI agent in the roughest neighborhoods in the Boston area. To come home safely after being in a dangerous, life-threatening situation and get a big hug from Jane made CT realize how lucky he was! To her, there was no better sound than to hear the front door open late at night and hear CT undo the Velcro closures on his vest.

CT was looking forward to the two-hour car ride back to Boston for some quiet time to sort out exactly what happened and organize his report. He wasn't aware of the fact that he would soon be back to Maine to investigate another crime. Not too far from Freeport, another woman had been killed by the Mannequin Murderer. She had been placed in a rocking chair and positioned on a second floor next to a bedroom window with an overhead light on to illuminate her at night. No doubt inspired by the movie *Psycho*. This was the

Mannequin Murderer's third murder which now classifies him as a serial killer. The FBI always investigates serial killers.

Desert Road, Freeport

Some time, when you get a chance, take a drive to Exit 20 off Maine I-295, the Desert Road exit in Freeport, head west about a half-mile. You will go over a bridge with railroad tracks underneath, then about 200 feet after a yellow fire hydrant, you will see a sign that warns of an intersection 500 feet away. That is the site of the armored-car robbery. You may even see flowers left on the signpost. You are encouraged to hang some flowers on the post as well in honor of Bonnie and Clyde! And when you see the site, you may find yourself wondering, *Perhaps this story really happened?*

BONNIE PARKER AND CLYDE BARROW

This book was inspired by the true story of Bonnie and Clyde who were, next to Jesse James, the most notorious bank robbers in United States history. Most of their robberies, however, were small stores and gas stations. They enjoyed making fools of the police. At that time (1930s), police were not permitted to cross state lines. So they planned their robberies to be as close to a state line as possible. After their robbery they would cross the line into another state and stop and wave at the police who had to stop at the border. Police did not have radios to notify the police in the next state over.

The father of one of the Barrow gang members told the police that Bonnie and Clyde would be spending the night at his house. The police set up an ambush and killed Bonnie and Clyde as they arrived. Just like in *Beware the Banker*, they were ambushed and killed as a result of an informer. Bonnie was only 24; Clyde 25.

Roy Thurston married Bonnie when she was only 15. When he heard they had been killed, he replied "I'm glad they went out the way they did. Much better than being caught."

Bonnie kept a diary which was filled with writings about how she suffered from loneliness throughout her life.

Celies no kapa, pievienojies garu aplim

To Be Continued

QUIZ

E-mail your answers to: bsomes@netzero.net Your responses will help shape the plot of the sequel to this book.

- A. Any idea who Acadia's father is?
- B. Any idea who the Mannequin Murderer is?
- C. Any idea who the mysterious old man in the dark suit is?
- D. There are three women in this book who are witches—members of the Daughters of the Enlightened coven. Can you name them?
- E. Do you have a guess as to what is hidden in the basement of the old Greely Institute building?
- F. Who killed Tony?
- G. Who do you think the main character of this story is?
- H. Have you been to the Desert Road in Freeport where the book ended?

Email your answers to bsomes@netzero.net. They will be taken into consideration when the sequel to this book is written.

SOUVENIRS

A. Pasami and Cheese tour T-shirt (S, M, L, XL)

B. Framed twenty-dollar bill with police evidence tag attached from Clyde's Falmouth Maine Bank robbery (only fourteen available)

C. Compact Disc single recording of "Strange Snow" (If there is enough interest we'll finalize the lyrics and produce a CD).

D. *The Witches of New Harmony*, the sequel to *Beware of the Banker*. Already in the works; will let you know when it is available.

E. If you would like information on *Beware of the Promoter*, the next book in this series, will let you know when it is available.

F. Would you be interested in a tour from Portland, Maine with the author driving by locations which were used for this book?

For more information on these souvenirs, contact bsomes@netzero.net and full details/prices will be sent to you as soon as they are finalized.

THE STORY OF BONNIE AND CLYDE

(A poem written by Bonnie Parker in 1934)

You've read the story of Jesse James,
of how he lived and died.
If you're still in need of something to read,
here's the story of Bonnie and Clyde.
Someday they'll go down together,
and they'll bury them side by side.
To a few it will mean grief
but to the law a relief.
But it's death for Bonnie and Clyde.

About the Author

Mr. Somes is a lifelong resident of the town of Cumberland, Maine, and a graduate of Greely High School. He attended school in the old Greely Institute building. He is also a graduate of the University of Maine and holds an advanced degree in Holistic Theology. He worked for seven years for a bank based in Portland and, during that time, investigated a bank branch after it was robbed. He was a member of the Falmouth, Maine Fire Department and Cumberland Maine Rescue. During that time, he had a gun pointed at him three times. He worked with special ed students at Greely High School. He is a graduate of COPS (Citizens Only Police School). He conducted research for this book at the FBI headquarters in Washington DC. In the last twenty-five years or so, however, he has not stepped foot in a casino. At the age of seven, Barry's father's car was stolen from the parking lot where he worked in Portland and used as a getaway car in a bank robbery at a bank branch at the Falmouth Shopping Center. The robber was never caught, but the car was returned without a scratch just a block from where it was stolen. He is also the creator of the *Mary and Terry* stories and *Webber, the Rain Drop*. This is his first novel and is based largely on his own life experiences.

CPSIA information can be obtained
at www.ICGtesting.com
Printed in the USA
FSHW011857270921
85001FS

9 781645 312352